NEW
DARK
AGES

The X Gang Series

Recipe for Hate
New Dark Ages

WARREN KINSELLA

NEW DARK AGES

THE X GANG

Cover design: Laura Boyle
Cover image: istock.com/kcastagnola
Printer: Webcom

Library and Archives Canada Cataloguing in Publication

Kinsella, Warren, 1960-, author
    New dark ages / Warren Kinsella.

(The X Gang)
Issued in print and electronic formats.
ISBN 978-1-4597-4215-4 (softcover).--ISBN 978-1-4597-4216-1
(PDF).--ISBN 978-1-4597-4217-8 (EPUB)

    I. Title.

PS8621.I59N49 2018   C813'.6   C2018-901779-1
                                                 C2018-901780-5

1   2   3   4   5   22   21   20   19   18

We acknowledge the support of the **Canada Council for the Arts**, which last year invested $153 million to bring the arts to Canadians throughout the country, and the **Ontario Arts Council** for our publishing program. We also acknowledge the financial support of the Government of Ontario, through the **Ontario Book Publishing Tax Credit** and the **Ontario Media Development Corporation**, and the Government of Canada.

Nous remercions le **Conseil des arts du Canada** de son soutien. L'an dernier, le Conseil a investi 153 millions de dollars pour mettre de l'art dans la vie des Canadiennes et des Canadiens de tout le pays.

Care has been taken to trace the ownership of copyright material used in this book. The author and the publisher welcome any information enabling them to rectify any references or credits in subsequent editions.

— *J. Kirk Howard, President*

VISIT US AT

 dundurn.com | @dundurnpress | dundurnpress | dundurnpress

Dundurn
3 Church Street, Suite 500
Toronto, Ontario, Canada
M5E 1M2

To James Muretich, Tom Wolfe, and Barrie Wright

PROLOGUE

Hello, you bastard.

It was hard to believe. Like a bad fucking movie. But it was happening, right there, right then, right in front of our eyes.

It was *that* night. The night before the last day.

I looked over at X, and his eyes — one pupil dilated, one not, as always — were squinting at the TV. His fists were clenched. He looked pissed, as if he was going to punch the screen or something.

The TV cast a bluish glow over my non-family's family room. My mother was standing in the doorway to the kitchen, and she was watching, too. She had her arms crossed, but she seemed to be nodding about some of the things being said. By *him.*

I looked back at the TV, and at Earl Turner, who was still standing behind the podium in downtown Portland. There was an American flag on the front of the podium, and below that, in big block letters, was the word RIGHT. *His* slogan. *His* word.

As usual, Turner was wearing a white button-down shirt with the sleeves rolled up. As usual, his regimental tie was loose at the neck. You could tell he worked out. Behind him, an enthusiastic crowd of supporters were assembled. They were clapping and nodding their heads.

X and I weren't really watching Turner. We were watching one of the people just behind him who was clapping and nodding his head, just like the rest of the assembled crowd.

I could not fucking believe this shit. I hated it.

And hate was what Earl Turner's speech was all about, pretty much. It usually was. Hate for refugees and immigrants and welfare moms and anyone, basically, who didn't look like Earl Turner and his friends. Hate dressed up in fine-sounding words about patriotism and family and country and all that horseshit. Hate was Earl Turner's thing, and it had brought him to this, his big moment. The confetti and the balloons — red, white, and blue — were ready to be dropped from above.

Turner was coming to the big wind-up in his speech. He always ended it the same way. "America," he said, his booming voice sounding tinny on my mother's old RCA. "America is for Americans. America is for the righteous. America is for the bold. America is for those who believe in God, those who love God, those who fear God. America isn't for everyone. America is for normal people like us!" He paused, a big fist hovering above the podium. We couldn't see them, but the crowd at the hotel had started to chant: "RIGHT RIGHT! RIGHT! RIGHT! RIGHT!"

Midway through — and this had happened before — "RIGHT!" changed, and the crowd started to chant a different word: "WHITE! WHITE! WHITE! WHITE! WHITE!"

Earl Turner smiled, that big square-jawed quarter-back all-American douchebag smile of his, and waved for the crowd to settle down. "Right," he said. "Right is …"

The crowd screamed as one, like a beast. "WHITE!"

Earl Turner leaned into the gaggle of network micro-phones. He smiled. *This* was his moment. *This* was it. He had won. He knew it. Everyone knew it.

He started to speak. It was the part of the speech about how God "created" America. At that point, the young guy behind him — the one we'd been watching — stepped forward. He was wearing a white shirt and tie, just like his hero. We could see his broad, freckled face clearly. At that moment, Turner saw him, too, and clapped a big hand on the young man's shoulder.

It was our friend, Danny. When he was drumming in my band, his stage name had been Danny Hate. He looked different now. He *was* different. He and Turner looked at each other and smiled, like father and son, like some fucking Norman Rockwell paint-ing. Behind me and X, my mother whispered just one word: "*Danny.*"

The crowd kept on cheering, calling out RIGHT and WHITE. They were screaming it.

"Enough," said X, and that was all he said.

CHAPTER 1

NO NO NO NO NO.

"What's that mean, Agent Laverty?"

Special Agent Theresa Laverty looked at the NYPD cop who'd let her in, and then she looked at the words again. They were all-capitals, about a foot high, and they had been spray-painted on the wall above the mattress. Laverty shrugged. "Something," she said. "Nothing."

She couldn't tell if the five words had been put up on the wall of the Bowery apartment by the victim, or the killer, or someone else. She couldn't immediately tell if they were new or old, either. She looked at the words for a while longer, and then back at the grubby mattress, where dried blood indicated where the body of the young man — a boy, really — had recently been found. There was blood. A lot of fucking blood.

The body had been removed before she got there. It would have been written up as just another Bowery junkie death, an addict dying at the hands of another in the hot middle of 1980, a squabble over twenty bucks' worth of junk. But the murder of Johnny Raindrops hadn't been routine, which is why someone at NYPD who remembered Laverty from a panel at a conference in Baltimore picked up the phone and called her. "There's some weird symbols and shit in this junkie's place," New York detective Pete Schenk had said to her over the phone. "Maybe you can make some sense of it." So she'd come up.

The victim had copied the style of his junkie hero, New York Dolls' legend Johnny Thunders, and he even cultivated an impressive heroin habit like Johnny Thunders. But he was no Johnny Thunders. He couldn't play guitar very well; he didn't write his own songs. And he had no sense of style beyond what he regularly saw, and copied, on the puny stage up the street at CBGB. So his friends called him Johnny Raindrops.

No thunder, just a bit of rain.

Laverty looked around the apartment, on the Chinatown side of the Bowery, which was noisier and dirtier and more dangerous. Through the open window, she could hear the Chinese merchants selling their fish and vegetables down on the sidewalk off Lafayette. Punk rockers liked the area, she knew, because the rent was cheap, and the Chinese left them alone. And CBGB was their shrine, their Mecca.

On the walls, Johnny Raindrops had tacked up posters and newspaper clippings about his New York heroes —

the Ramones, Television, Richard Hell, the Talking
Heads, Jayne County. And, of course, the New York Dolls.

Over in one corner was a tiny fridge with the door
duct-taped shut. Beside it, there was a sink crowded with
mismatched dishes and, on the streaked countertop, a
filthy hot plate. In the opposite corner sat an ancient-
looking Marshall amp and a black guitar leaning up
against it. Clothes were spilling out of garbage bags, a
battered biker jacket tossed beside them on the hard-
wood floor.

In the middle of the place was the mattress. When a
couple of his friends finally persuaded the super to let
them in, because Johnny Raindrops hadn't been seen
back at CBGB, they found him on the mattress, filleted
like a fish. His throat had been cut, too, in a pattern that
resembled a jagged *W*. Johnny Raindrops's eyes, caked
in mascara and tears, stared up at the wall.

There, above the string of NOs, someone had carefully inscribed a *W* within a circle, with a crown and a
halo floating above it.

The New York cops didn't know what that meant, but
Special Agent Theresa Laverty sure did.

CHAPTER 2

The guys with the big *X*s on the backs of their hands were getting really fucking rough. They were slamming into anyone who came close, hard. All of the girls had moved to the sides, and quite a few of the punk guys, too. The pit was a frenzy of sweat and spit and colliding bodies. And, any minute now, blood, too. It was going to happen.

We were standing on the sidelines at the 9:30 Club in Washington, D.C., with the rest of the X Gang: The Nasties, the Punk Rock Virgins, some of the Non-Conformist News Agency guys who came down. The opening act, the Teen Idles, had brought out a ton of kids from the local punk scene. But they'd attracted a lot of these guys with the *X*s on their hands, too. And these *X* guys were fucking nuts.

The Idles were loud, so we couldn't talk, but when I looked at X, he could tell I wasn't happy. With the situation, or with him. *These are your people, X. See them*? I was thinking. He looked away, toward the pit.

The ones sporting the *X*s were all guys; not one girl among them. They all had short hair or totally shaved heads, too. And they were all buff and tough, like they were in the military or something. Some of them had gotten the *X* on their hand from the 9:30 Club security dude who was wielding a Sharpie, indicating that they were too young to get served booze. But a few of them, I was told, had actually gotten the *X* — or *XXX* or *sXe* — tattooed as a permanent statement. No alcohol, no tobacco, no drugs. For some of them, no meat or dairy or sex, either. Straight edge. Straight edge for life.

As the Teen Idles tore through their one- and two-minute songs, and as the pit got more intense, I saw a couple of the straight edge guys glance our way. They were looking at X. They wanted to see what he was doing, to see if he'd seen them.

Amazing. Even in faraway D.C., they'd heard of him, the Portland, Maine, punk known as X. He wasn't in a band, but he was a fucking punk rock celebrity. And he didn't give a shit, not one. If he was aware of the admiring looks he was getting, he didn't show it.

The Teen Idles finished one song and were getting ready to let another rip. The pit slowed and ground to a halt, like an off-balance washing machine between cycles. I used the lull in the roar to yell in X's ear. My own ears were ringing. "They're pretty good, the Idles," I said, while the band was tuning up. "Better than the Nasties even."

"Not as good as you guys," X said. "But Ian and Jeff are really good."

I waited. Before the band started up again, I figured I'd just say what I was thinking. "Some of these straight edge guys out there are assholes, brother."

X, who'd been straight edge before the term was even invented, looked at me, expressionless. But he couldn't respond because the Idles started playing again, a song called "Fleeting Fury."

"Listen to the words," the lead singer, Ian, yelled as the band launched into the song, like a howling punk rocket. At the foot of the stage, the straight edge types had flipped the switch on their berserk hurricane again. They were going totally psycho, but you could see they weren't listening to any of the words. I was. Later on, I even wrote them down, in the little Hilroy notepad I always have with me. "Tales of youth fighting back," Ian hollered, was "just another load of crap."

The Teen Idles were different from the Hot Nasties. They were younger than us, and their songs were super-fast and super-short. But they obviously shared one thing with us: they were starting to think that the punk scene was becoming just as phony as the rock scene that came before it — more about fashion and fame, less about fury and fun.

Suddenly, X pushed himself away from the wall and un-crossed his arms. His uneven gaze was fixed on the pit now, and he wasn't paying any attention to the Idles. I followed his stare and saw a skinny punk kid, with Day-Glo green spiked hair, torn bondage pants, and a leather biker jacket, in the pit. Whether he'd gone in on his own or had been pushed in, I couldn't tell. Either way, he was at the center of the maelstrom, and a few of the straight edge guys were now hitting him hard and grabbing at his jacket. Then two guys lifted him up and started tossing him around like he was a beach ball or something. You could tell from his face that he was aware that the straight edge guys were not in any way his friends. He looked scared shitless.

As X pushed his way into the pit, with me not far behind, the punk kid was slammed down onto the concrete floor by his attackers. His head bounced off the floor like it was basketball or something. I cringed. He sat up for a second, looking kind of confused, and then fell back, eyes shut, out cold.

Up onstage, Ian MacKaye had seen what had happened. "Stop! Fucking stop!" he yelled at his bandmates. By then X was on his knees beside the kid, trying to wake him up. With all the noise, I couldn't hear what he was saying. Standing around us were all the straight edge guys. They were looking down, but they clearly didn't give a fuck about the kid they'd just about killed. Instead, they all started yelling, "X! X! X! X!"

The kid, as it turned out, ended up being okay.

Me? I wasn't.

Nothing lasts forever, or so the stupid cliché goes; but a part of me actually thought the X Gang might. Our group of misfits had helped us all get through the teen-age wasteland that was 1978–1980. Before the X Gang, there had been the *NCNA* (what we called the Non-Conformist News Agency) and Room 531 (our hangout at Portland Alternative High School, where a bunch of us went), but the X Gang was more of a punk thing, and it was *our thing*. It was who we were. The X Gang was the thing that had kept us whole, and kept us together, through no small amount of shit. It kept us sane last year when two of our friends died.

Who am I kidding? They didn't "die." They were killed, murdered by a psycho Nazi cop. Just for being punks.

It had been in all the papers, what happened to us. We were famous, or at least infamous, for a while. There was X, of course, and the Upchuck sisters, and our various bands — the Hot Nasties, the Social Blemishes, the Punk Rock Virgins. Later on, there was also Mike the bouncer and the others. And then there was me, Kurt Lank, or Kurt Blank, or Point Blank. I played guitar and sang for the Nasties after Jimmy died, and I kept a diary.

The story stayed in the news for a while. There was even a profile of me and X in the *Portland Press Herald*, the local broadsheet rag. We'd refused to speak to the guy who wrote it, Ron McLeod, but he wrote it anyway. He even found a couple of cops to say nice things about us.

We rarely have anything nice to say about cops. Hell, one of them killed our friends Jimmy and Marky, after all. And the bastard tried to kill Danny and Sam and Sister Betty, too. Needless to say, not big cop fans.

The media, who have a shorter attention span than my goldfish, Sid Vicious, eventually moved on to stories about the weather, or the Patriots, or, this year, to the presidential race. We were happy when the media stopped paying attention to us and instead wrote about the soulless creeps who comprised both the Democrats and the Republicans.

The X Gang continued to hang together, and we kept going. We got back to what we wanted to do, which was write songs, play music, and go see bands.

We'd played a couple shows at CBGB, which had been totally epic. But then we were in some bar called Barrymore's way up in Ottawa, Canada, where our record label — bizarrely, inexplicably — wanted us to play before our big tour kicked off. It looked like an old strip club, with faded red velvet on the walls and chipped gilt on the scattering of chairs. It stunk of piss and french fries and gravy. No shower, no sound check, nothing to eat.

No fun. I was in a bad fucking mood.

And then, with only a few hours to go before we were to play to an almost sold-out crowd of locals and music industry people, this hit: Danny Hate, the guy I'd known almost as long as X, the guy who'd drummed for the Social Blemishes since their inception — the guy who almost fucking died because of it — wanted out.

Danny stood there, his big freckled face staring at the floor, and his big freckled arms hanging at his sides. He would occasionally glance at X and me, sideways, gauging our reaction to his statement, which was: "I'm out. I want to go home."

I was shocked and pissed off all at the same time. "Why?" I asked, probably louder than I needed to. "I mean, what the fuck, brother? After everything we've gone through, you want to bail? Why, man?"

X gestured to me to cool it and said, "What's up, brother?"

Danny couldn't look at him. "It sucks, I-I know," Danny stammered. "But I've been thinking about it a long time. I just don't feel the scene is right for me anymore."

I didn't say anything. I waited for X to speak. Danny wouldn't bullshit X.

"So, what do you want to do, brother?" X asked softly, but as if he already knew the answer.

Danny shook his head and went red in the face. "You'll laugh at me," he said, before going quiet.

X crossed his arms. "I'd never laugh at you, Danny." He meant it. Danny could tell. I could tell.

Danny looked up at us. "I'm kind of interested in politics and all that," he said.

"So? That's cool," I said, encouraged. "Almost everyone in the scene is political."

Danny shook his head. "Not that kind of politics," he mumbled, shaking his head. "Conservative sort of politics, I guess. I want to help this new Republican candidate, Earl T—"

I cut him off. "ARE YOU FUCKING KIDDING ME? A FUCKING REPUBLICAN?"

X waved for me to stop. I stopped, but I was beside myself.

"What's wrong, brother?" X said. He didn't seem surprised about what Danny was saying.

"I can't explain," the former Danny Hate said, face red again.

And then he turned around and walked up the stairs and straight out of Barrymore's. Just like that. And I didn't see him again for a long, long time.

X said nothing, as usual. He'd never talked much, but during those days, he talked to me even less than he used to. It sucked. But I knew why. None of us had been on a real tour before, with real promoters and real contracts and all that, so we had nothing we could compare the Hot Nasties' first big tour to. It was a new world for all of us, big-time. But X had days ago concluded that we Nasties were making our upcoming tour of North America way more complicated, and way more stressful, than it needed to be. "They're pissing it away," he'd said.

Because I was *in* the Hot Nasties, and because we weren't talking like we used to, X didn't tell me that, of course. He told Patti Upchuck, who told her sister, Betty, who then told me. The X Gang party line.

He was right, of course. But I didn't tell him that, because of the not-talking-much thing. Instead, I just looked at him as he sat on the stairs to the basement at

Sound Swap, a bit pissed off — pissed off because, just possibly, he was right.

The remaining members of the Hot Nasties were there, in our basement practice space at the used record store in downtown Portland, Maine, in the U.S. of Fucking A., for a big band summit. This gloomy, dirty basement had always been our space, and we were determined to stay there, even after we won the big recording contract and the big tour. But before we hit the road, before the big tour started in earnest, we all had stuff to say.

Being signed to England's Stiff Records had been a huge, huge achievement for a punk rock quartet from a place like Portland, naturally. In all of Maine — in all of New England, pretty much — no other band had been picked up by England's most respected punk and new wave label. The record contract had produced a bit of coverage in the pages of *Creem* and *Bomp!* and even the old-fart tabloid *Rolling Stone.* And there had been a signing bonus, too, all of which went into new Fenders and Gibsons and amps — and leather jackets, of course.

We should have been pleased with ourselves. But we were still bitching and bickering. X sat on the stairs at the used record shop, studying the tops of his black Converse. His long hair covered his face, so it was hard to see that he was unimpressed. But I knew he was.

We had (literally) survived all kinds of shit and turmoil, a fraction of which would have doomed a lesser group. We had been attacked by the tabloids and called big-label sellouts by other bands in the Portland punk scene. We had lost Jimmy. We'd almost packed it in a million times. But we hadn't. Instead, here we were, on the eve of our triumphant first tour as a Stiff act, fighting over the song list.

X sighed quietly. I swore.

Sam Shiller, our other guitarist, didn't want to play any of the songs he had written himself, because he was now worried that all his songs were terrible. Luke Macdonald, our hulking albino bassist, wanted to play some punked-up Mersey Beat numbers, like the band had occasionally done in the old days. Eddie Igglesden, our highly practical drummer, wanted to play whatever Stiff Records wanted us to play, but mainly he just wanted to get laid a lot.

When it came my turn, I mumbled. I said I thought hardcore bands like the Teen Idles were the future and the Nasties — always a pop-punk outfit — probably needed to "play faster and louder."

But I didn't know that for sure, I said, and sniffled. To be honest, I had become disinterested in the endless debate taking place all around me. In recent weeks, I had embraced the oldest rock 'n' roll stereotype: that is, becoming an aloof, moody bastard, interested only in snorting and fucking everything I could get my hands on. I had always been a bit wild, a concerned Sister Betty said to me, but not as wild as this. *True enough*, I thought.

But whatever.

I saw X watching me as I pulled, yet again, on the fifth of vodka in my hand. Sister Betty Upchuck was also looking worriedly at me. I was probably laughing a bit too loudly at whatever it was that she was saying. I'd seen my reflection in the can upstairs, too: my eyes were shiny, my pupils dilated. I was definitely thinner.

The arguing went on. I laughed more. X suddenly stood and went upstairs, where Patti Upchuck had disappeared earlier. They left without a word.

CHAPTER 3

Theresa Laverty was at the center of the subterranean madhouse known as Penn Station, making her way to Newark Airport and then on home to Fort Myers, when she called the field office to see if she had any messages. Pete Schenk, the NYPD cop who had asked her to come and view the Johnny Raindrops crime scene in the Bowery, needed to speak with her again. She was told it was urgent.

So, as tourists noisily milled around the line of pay phones, looking for cabs to their hotels or the Empire State Building or the World Exchange Plaza or wherever, Laverty hung up and called Pete Schenk at the Fifth Precinct.

"We've got another one," Schenk told her. "Another punk kid, same neighborhood, same deal — um, cut from stem to stern, a *W* slashed in his neck, more weird symbols."

"Okay," Laverty said wearily. "I'll head back. What's the address?"

The address, as it turned out, was just off the Bowery, close to CBGB. The victim had been found around the corner, in the filthy, trash-strewn alleyway behind the club. When Laverty arrived in a cab, still pulling a stylish Eastpak wheeled suitcase full of files, notebooks, and a single change of clothes, Schenk was waiting for her.

"Hey, Special Agent," he said. He was big and gruff, with a buzz cut and a nose that looked as if it had been repeatedly broken. He was unhappy, because he clearly now believed there may be a serial killer on the loose. In his jurisdiction. "Sorry to pull you back. But we thought you needed to see this one, too." He led her past the fluttering yellow crime-scene tape toward a battered Guma Dumpster, every inch of which was covered with punk graffiti for bands like the Ramones, Voidoids, and the Dead Boys.

Schenk stepped up on a discarded kitchen chair that had been placed beside the Dumpster. He looked in, confirming the body hadn't gone anywhere since he'd been back at the precinct, then signaled for Laverty to do likewise. She left her suitcase with a uniformed cop, got up on the chair, and winced as she looked in. There wasn't much trash in the Dumpster, so the body was easy to see. Blond wig, pink hot pants, shiny lamé halter, ripped fishnets, cheap pumps. Gutted, hacked up. Dead.

There was blood everywhere. Legs and arms were splayed out at crazy angles, apparently broken. One mascara-smeared eye was open, one swollen shut. And, carefully positioned on the torso, a page from a recent edition of the *New York Post*, with the big *W* written on it in marker. The letter was inside a circle, another crown and another halo floating above. Laverty sighed and stepped down.

Schenk explained to her that a homeless couple had found the body. According to a driver's license that had been found in a bag that lay beside the body, the victim's name was Colleen Tomorrow.

"He was a junkie, a drunk, a punk," he said, "and a fag —" He stopped himself, likely remembering what he had heard at the Fifth about Laverty — that she was gay herself. Some of the cops called her things like "Agent Lipstick Lesbo," but she'd long since stopped caring. She was the FBI's resident weirdo youth subculture expert, and she got a lot of stuff like that.

"Gay," Laverty said, not angry. She was used to it. "And *she*, not *he*."

"Sorry," Schenk said. "*Gay. She* hooked along the Bowery. Been picked up for solicitation and possession a couple of times." He paused. "So, that symbol again. What does it mean?"

Laverty didn't want to share too much, not yet. "It refers to a group," she said carefully. "Extremist."

Schenk scowled. "It'd be news if it *wasn't* extreme, given the crime scenes," he said. He seemed annoyed. Maybe he thought she wasn't telling him everything. He paused, scanning his notepad. "Oh, yeah, there's something else. The two victims," Schenk said, watching her, "they'd both been at this CBGB place pretty recently."

"So?"

"So," Schenk said, "the manager at CBGB said they were both present when this punk band" — he glanced at his pad again — "the Hot Nasties, they're called, played last week. That's the last time anyone remembers seeing either of them."

Hilly Kristal may have been the legendary owner of the legendary CBGB, but there he was, taking stools down off the bar when Laverty and Schenk walked in. He didn't smile.

"Officers," he said. "How can I help you?"

Laverty was impressed. Pete Schenk certainly looked like a typical cop, but she — being shorter, slender, and with a face that was still considered quite lovely — didn't. At least she didn't think she did.

She flashed her FBI badge and Schenk flashed his NYPD detective's shield. Kristal cocked a gray eyebrow. "I've had visits from the Fifth Precinct a few times before," he said, arms now crossed over a sleeveless jean jacket and a Talking Heads T-shirt. "But not the FBI. Did one of my bands violate the *Mann Act*?" He snorted. The *Mann Act* was a seventy-year-old law that prohibited transporting girls over state lines "for immoral purposes."

Laverty laughed despite herself. "Do your bands often kidnap girls and sell them into the white slave trade?" she asked, smiling.

Kristal rolled his eyes. "Wait 'til you meet Dee Dee Ramone and Stiv Bators," he said. "If those two aren't involved in the white slave trade, I'll be amazed."

Even Schenk had a laugh at that one, though he didn't even know who Dee Dee Ramone and Stiv Bators were. Kristal waved in the direction of a dilapidated old couch near the grimy front windows. "Let's sit."

"So," Kristal asked, "what's up?"

Laverty and Schenk looked at each other. They had decided not to tell Kristal about the two murders just yet.

"We'll get to that," Schenk said. "Mind if we take some notes?"

"Knock yourselves out."

Laverty went first. "I guess it makes me sound old," she said, smiling again, pretending to know less than she did. "But what, exactly, is this punk rock stuff? We need to understand it better for a case."

Personally, I thought it was pretty cool: FBI agent Laverty was talking with *The* Hilly Kristal, the guy who gave the Ramones their first opportunity to play in public. *The* Hilly Kristal who can legitimately claim to have created punk, and who helped to completely rewrite rock 'n' roll's script.

Kristal nodded, leaned back, and started talking.

Behind his wispy beard and his big, shaded glasses, Hilly Kristal gazed out onto the noisy intersection of Bowery and Bleecker, just up from SoHo. When the place opened in the early seventies, he said, CBGB wasn't much to look at. The neighborhood was an open sewer, basically. Patrons were charged a buck to get in. The name was an acronym for Country, Blue Grass, and Blues — even though those genres never really showed up on the puny stage. It was always a rock 'n' roll place.

"If I'm going to explain punk to you," Hilly says, "I'm going to have to tell you about the Ramones, who kind of started the whole thing."

Schenk looked unsure, but Laverty was eager to hear more. She'd canceled her flight back to Florida. She had time.

Kristal started talking.

The first time he had heard the Ramones, he could not believe his ears. He could make out, barely, Joey's voice, yelping lyrics that were alternately funny and shocking. Along with that was a barrage of guitars and drums, ripping through three-chord riffs like a chainsaw. As if to drive home the point, Kristal added, "One of their songs was even called 'Chainsaw.'"

"The Ramones were what rock 'n' roll had been meant to be in the first place," Kristal declared. "Simple, fast, loud, and designed to irritate your parents. It was a kick in the ass for the rock business, which had become totally disconnected from the lives of real kids."

Back when it opened up, rent in the Bowery was cheap. So, sort of, was life. "I mean, you were taking your life in your hands if you walked into this neighborhood at night. People were frightened to come here. It had this reputation, you know? There were no other clubs here. So we had a lot of rock bands who nobody had heard of, who had nowhere else to play. And we offered the only place in New York for bands that wanted to play original music."

Laverty stirred. "Have any of your patrons ever gotten badly hurt here? Fights, whatever?"

Kristal shrugged. "Sure," he said. "There's been fights, and we kick them out, or we ban them. But nothing too serious."

"Okay, thanks," Laverty said. Kristal returned to his story.

After word spread about the Ramones' performances, a lot of things started to happen, Kristal recalled. There was a buzz. Who *were* these weird-looking punk freaks?

The Ramones and their fans favored biker jackets, T-shirts, jeans, and tennis shoes. At the start of punk, Kristal explained, Ramones shows attracted people who were anything but typical: Brit-style punks, metalheads, art school types, skateboarders, university students, and even honest-to-goodness bikers.

The band, meanwhile, would always play CBGB shows the same way: heads-down, straight-out rock 'n' roll. No chitchat between songs: just Joey occasionally mumbling "Thank you," and then Dee Dee hollering "One-two-three-four!" before every tune. Sometimes, he'd do the count-ins in German, too. And then another sonic bombardment, washing over the ever-larger crowds like a wave of heat.

"Well," Kristal said, "they were probably the worst band I had ever heard, when I first heard them. I mean, they just weren't together. Their amps were breaking down, and they were yelling at each other onstage. It wasn't a very good beginning." He laughed at the memory.

At this point, Schenk was getting pretty impatient, but Laverty was still enjoying listening to Kristal.

There was a commotion at the door, and an impressively bald, bespectacled man in a biker jacket ambled in, looking for Kristal.

"Let him in. This here is John Holmstrom! He's from *Punk* magazine. Hey, do you guys want to talk to John?"

Schenk frowned. "Not unless he knew Johnny Raindrops or a trans hooker named Colleen Tomorrow, or who might've killed them."

Laverty hadn't wanted that to come out just yet, but it was too late.

There was a pause as Kristal eyed the two cops. "Ah, that's what this is really about," he said, sounding a little less friendly. He told John Holmstrom he'd talk to him shortly. Holmstrom ambled off and grabbed a stool by the bar. "He's the guy who came up with the word *punk*, really," Kristal said of Holmstrom. "That was the name of his magazine." He paused. "He named it, but CBGB started it."

Kristal mused for a moment, now knowing the cops probably didn't much care about punk rock or the Ramones. He started to wrap up. "Anyway, by the end of the summer of '74, all of a sudden, you know, I mean everybody came here. The Ramones turned everybody on, you know? Just high-energy, nonstop, song after song ..." He trailed off. "It was quite a thing."

His punk rock genesis story now complete, Kristal eyed the two cops from behind his shaded glasses. "All right," he said, finally. "What do you want to know about Johnny and Colleen?"

CHAPTER 4

Speed, speed, that's all I needed. Like Johnny Rotten sang on "Seventeen."

It was the punk rock drug, speed was, and it was all we, me specifically, needed. And, sure, many of us would do weed or mushrooms or acid if we could get our hands on some, but speed — amphetamines, or alpha-methylphenethylamine, if you want to get all formal about it — was every punk's drug of choice.

I was introduced to the wonder and beauty of speed at an early Social Blemishes/Hot Nasties gig at Gary's in Portland. There was a British kid in town, and he was a real punk, too. He knew all the latest British bands and read the *New Musical Express* and all that.

I'd caught him giving me a look — *that* look — during the Blemishes set. I ambled over and said hi. We talked music and stuff. Ten minutes later, we were in the filthy, dirty can, doing poppers and grabbing at each other. When we finished, and when the poppers had lost their pop, my new friend was looking unimpressed.

"What?" I asked, pulling up my pants.

"In Britain, this is kids' stuff," he said, indicating the little brown bottle labeled RUSH. "Over there, we prefer speed. It's legal, sort of. Even housewives use 'em. They call 'em diet pills."

I was intrigued. "So, you got any of these diet pills?"

"It's your lucky day," he said, fishing a baggie full of multicolored bite-sized happiness out of the folds of his leather jacket. "It just so happens I do."

And so began my love affair with speed.

I would pop it, of course, when I had pills to pop. But I'd also snort it, and sometimes I'd parachute it — like, wrap it in tissue and swallow it like a pill. I'd never stick it in a vein, of course, because you could never know for sure what it had been cut with, and I didn't want to die just yet.

The first time I really did speed *right*, I was at a big pre-grad party at Sam Shiller's place. Someone I didn't know offered me some, so I took it up my nose. It was the second time, but this time, it hit me like a fucking sledgehammer in the old cerebral cortex. *Bam.*

I knew, then and there, that I had joined speed's captive audience, and I had somehow snagged a seat right there in the front fucking row. And I didn't want to miss a single performance of this glorious, perfect drug. I was buying season's tickets for the entire run!

It made me feel happy. It made me euphoric. It gave me more confidence, and it persuaded me that I was fucking amazing. It also gave me limitless energy and made me as alert as whiskers on a cat. It helped me concentrate. It made me horny. And it wasn't addictive, boys and girls!

It was awe-inspiring and magnificent. Needless to say, I was the life of that party at Sam's that night. And everyone thought I was super funny and engaging.

Except X, naturally.

Eventually, of course, I learned that it wasn't the perfect drug. No drug is. For instance, it made me talk more — and I already talked way too much. And, when I was coming down, it would wipe me out and I'd feel exhausted and out of it. "Grumpy, too," Sister Betty told me.

Also, speed made me skinnier than I already was. Now, when you're in a punk band, as I was, that emaciated and wasted look is much sought-after. But losing too much weight, as I was arguably doing, wasn't a good thing. The shit made my skin pretty itchy, too. And I was … well … a bit *dependent* on it, you might say. In no time at all, it became part of my daily routine, like shaving or going to pee. I wouldn't say I was *addicted*. But I would say that I had become completely and totally *captivated*.

X was not impressed. He was my best friend, my brother of another mother. Since grade seven, he'd been one of the two most important humans in my life. I loved him. I still do.

The other most important human was my dad, but he didn't live with us anymore. My mother had driven him out a couple years earlier. He had a place near the naval base in Kittery, and I didn't see him so much now.

Which may or may not have something to do with my enthusiasm for speed.

But I digress.

X, as noted, was straight edge before there was straight edge. Long before the D.C. punks conceived the straight edge way of life — long before Ian MacKaye started writing songs about it, for the Teen Idles and Minor Threat — X was disavowing drugs and tobacco and booze. In all the time I had known him, I had never seen him partake of any mind-altering substance. Like, *ever*. But me, I popped and snorted and swilled whatever was readily available, and so did some of the others in the X Gang. But X just *didn't*. Good and evil, black and white, cats and dogs, apples and oranges. We shouldn't have been friends at all, but we were.

For the first few years, this didn't create nearly as much tension as you might think. I would imbibe, X would decline, and everything was cool. To his everlasting credit, X didn't go all Woman's Christian Temperance Union on me. When we were drinking beer or vodka or tequila or whatever was at hand, he'd sip his RC Cola. And when someone was doing drugs, he'd just sort of slip away. Speed changed all of that. It turned up the volume, in a bad way. He didn't like it, and I liked it way too much.

So, one night at Gary's, it all kind of spilled out onto the dirty, cracked dance floor. We were there for a Punk Rock Virgins' show, which hadn't quite started yet. I'd excused myself to visit the bathroom for the third time that night, I think. I'd done a line in the can, and I was feeling like the king of the fucking world. I returned to where X was sitting. I was all peppy and upbeat, arms flitting around like a scarecrow in a windstorm. I was chattering away before I even took my seat.

X glared at me, his uneven pupils black. "What the *fuck* are you doing, Kurt?" he said, his voice low, almost menacing.

It wasn't the question that stopped me in my proverbial tracks. It was the use of my *name*. X didn't like using first names: his, mine, anyone's. It's weird, but — as he explained it to me back in junior high — he considered first names way too personal. One day, I asked him why about a million times, and he finally offered up a semblance of an answer. "People use first names to be intimate, at the start," he said. "Later on, they usually use first names to express disapproval. To put you down."

I knew X was expressing disapproval. He was putting me down.

"What?" I said, pretending not to know what he was talking about. I sniffed. I scratched. "I don't know—"

He cut me off. "Don't lie to me," he said, leaning in. "You know what I'm talking about."

I couldn't look at him. Instead, I shrugged and toyed with an empty draft glass on the table between us. "So? I'm not hurting anyone," I said, knowing I probably was. "It's not like I'm doing smack or anything like that."

He stared at me, his uneven eyes flashing, but he was

silent. A few moments slid by, like glaciers. One of the Virgins, Leah Yeomanson, had come up to say hi before the Virgins' set. Relieved, I stood up, hugged Leah, and started chattering away.

When I glanced back at the table, X was gone.

CHAPTER 5

Danny really looked up to X. A lot.

When Danny O'Heran, formerly the Social Blemishes' drummer known as Danny Hate, walked into Earl Turner's campaign headquarters on Congress — the day after he got back to Portland from the bizarro gig at Barrymore's up in Canada — he'd seen his dentist and his doctor and his barber, and he was all shiny and ready. He was nervous, though.

Danny was a big guy, and he didn't actually have any dress clothes. He had slicked back his hair, pulled on some dark thrift-store dress pants, and borrowed one of his dad's white dress shirts and a tie. His parents, who were God-fearing, right-wing nutcases, were mystified but delighted by the change in their son. They'd been worried about him for a long time.

He was wearing a pair of black brothel creepers that first day, although nobody really noticed them. The crepe, thick soles made him even taller as he stepped through the main doors and approached the metal desk where a receptionist sat. She was on the phone and held up a manicured finger, indicating that he should wait.

He looked around. The campaign office was buzzing. Over on one side, in an area without desks, volunteers were putting together campaign signs. Nearby at some folding tables, other volunteers were stuffing envelopes and making calls.

The campaign was headquartered in a former bank lobby, so it was pretty loud and echoey. On the walls, huge posters had been taped up: RIGHT, they said. Below that, in smaller letters: EARL TURNER FOR PRESIDENT. Red, white, and blue, of course.

On the other side of the office, away from clean-cut, WASPy volunteers, were some serious-looking people who seemed to be having serious telephone conversations about serious stuff.

Danny wondered where Earl Turner's office was, but it soon became apparent that he wasn't in it. At that moment, in fact, he was striding across the campaign office floor, smiling broadly at Danny.

Turner was an imposing figure, as journalists would often write, with the physique of a football star — which, naturally, he had been. He still favored the sort of haircut he'd had in the 101st Airborne Division, and not a hair was out of place. He was wearing his patented uniform: a white shirt with a regimental tie carefully loosened at the neck, L.L. Bean chinos, and a big, toothy grin. He extended his hand to Danny.

Turner was also a pretty unlikely candidate for the presidency. He was the junior congressman for Maine's second district, meaning he'd only been in elected office for a short while. His decision to seek the Republican presidential nomination raised a few eyebrows, because freshman congressmen didn't usually run for president. Governors and senators did that.

Turner represented the almost-all-rural part of the state, outside Portland, where the culture was guns and God and America-is-great, and all that fucking bullshit. His constituents were overwhelmingly white, straight, right-wing, and churchgoing Christians, like him. And Earl Turner was their boy, big-time.

They loved his backstory. Decorated war hero in Vietnam, farmer for a while outside Farmington (seriously), then a fisherman in Eastport, where they have a statue erected (seriously) called "Big Fisherman." Grassroots anti-taxation political organizing in the South and the Carolinas. Law degree, then he helped out some similarly racist congressional candidates in other states. Genetically perfect stay-at-home wife, two Hitler Youth–type children.

He decided to run, his campaign propaganda declared, because he was tired of the "out-of-touch elites in Washington" and the "minority special interests" bossing around regular folks "like us." In no time at all, he was mouthing code-words about immigrants and refugees and welfare recipients and demanding "an America for Americans." The backwoods voters were lapping it up.

A big part of his plan for America, as it turned out, was banning all abortions for teenage girls and establishing military-style boot camps for "wayward" boys.

Punk rockers, for Earl Turner, met the dictionary definition of wayward. Turner didn't like this punk movement menace and he occasionally said he wanted to stamp it out. Which, of course, made his fateful encounter with the former Danny Hate all the more significant. It was almost heaven-sent.

Earl Turner grasped Danny's hand in his crushing grip and gave a matinee-idol smile. "Earl Turner," he said. "And you are …?"

"Danny O'Heran," he said, venturing a small smile. "And I'd like to volunteer."

CHAPTER 6

What are we gonna do now?

Almost all of the X Gang had attended Portland Alternative High School, or PAHS. It was where most of the city's freaks, geeks, gays, and artsy types went.

Some of the kids who were part of the local punk scene went to Portland High School, usually referred to as PHS. But when they got tired of getting the shit beaten out of them by the jocks there, they'd usually transfer to PAHS. So there was a pretty big contingent of punks in our graduating class — more than a dozen mohawks in the yearbook and twice as many kids with hair colors not found in nature. And, on a rainy day in June, when a bunch of us assembled to get our pieces of paper and our bit of applause in the PAHS gym, I know I wasn't the only one asking this question: *WHAT ARE WE GONNA DO NOW?*

Not surprisingly, the events of the previous year had really fucked us up. It would've been weird if they hadn't. A cop, a member of a clandestine neo-Nazi group, had come after us, just because we were punks. Before the whole thing was over, he'd killed our friends Jimmy Cleary and Marky Upton, as well as a couple of skinheads, a door guy at Gary's, and three other neo-Nazis. And he had tried to kill Sister Betty, Sam, and Danny, too.

The one he'd really wanted to kill, however, was X. He'd figured X was our leader, and he wasn't entirely wrong about that. Even though X wasn't in a band, even though he didn't look like your average, standard-issue punk rocker, X was the Portland punk messiah. He truly was.

As noted, X didn't have spiked or dyed hair like some of us did. He didn't ever wear British-style punk gear. He didn't pogo or slam dance at shows, and he didn't sing along when a band we liked somehow made it onto a local radio station. He was the guy who was *outside* the *outsiders*. The misfit among misfits, I called him.

His hair, for instance. It was long, Ramones-style. He wore earrings, and he didn't give a fuck what anyone thought about it. His standard uniform was tattered old Converse Chucks on his feet, super-skinny black Levi's, his almost-never-off Schott Perfecto biker jacket, and, usually, one of the T-shirts he designed by hand. Because there was basically nowhere to buy punk gear in Portland in the early days, X had faithfully duplicated the logos of the Clash, Stiff Little Fingers, the Buzzcocks, X-Ray Spex, and Iggy and the Stooges onto various thrift-store T-shirts. Sometimes he gave them to other members of the X Gang as gifts.

I think we all sort of looked up to him because he was our resident philosopher punk: he put on most of the early shows, he nurtured the various bands, he was the guy who knew about punk before anyone else in Portland. It didn't hurt that he wrote these amazing essays in the *NCNA*, that's for sure. All of us looked forward to those. "His 'fuck you' bulletins to the outside world," Sam Shiller called X's essays, and they were. X edited our Non-Conformist News Agency's semi-regular organ, which we distributed semi-regularly at PAHS and PHS. But he'd also write about all kinds of stuff, and what we really liked were his polemics about what it meant to be a punk, and why what we were doing was important, and all that. Those ones gave us a sense of purpose, you might say. Everyone needs a purpose.

But we were all graduating from high school, so what were we gonna do?

For the final issue of the *NCNA*, the one that came out before graduation, he kind of answered that question for some of us. It was his valedictory address. It was actually a bit melodramatic, too, which was unlike him. But it was good. It took up residence in our memories — those of us living verse-chorus, verse-chorus, three-chord lives.

X started by quoting "Clampdown," from the latest Clash album, *London Calling*. A lot of us hadn't liked it when it was released, because the Clash didn't sound as raw and as authentic as they did on their first two records. They were starting to sound like professional musicians now and were experimenting with different sounds and styles. A lot of us were still punk rock purists when *London Calling* came out.

Not X, of course. He liked it.

His *NCNA* essay, titled "What Do We Do Now?" started with Joe Strummer's amazing words from "Clampdown," and then went on:

> High school is over, or it soon will be. Before you know it, you're going to be walking out of the hallways at PAHS or PHS for the last time, and you won't be looking back. You shouldn't.
>
> In our years in these places, we've been taught to conform, and to get along. To believe that we have to fit in if we are going to survive.
>
> Don't believe it. Don't believe it for a moment.
>
> The clichés are true: life goes really, really fast. One minute you're graduating from high school in Portland, Maine, and the next minute you're somewhere in the Midwest, and you've got a mortgage and kids, you've got a job you hate, and you can't escape. You're wearing blue and brown all the time.
>
> If there is one thing that the past terrible year in Portland has taught all of us, it's this: everything you cherish — everyone you love —

can disappear in the blink of an eye. It's here, and then it's gone, just like that.

Hold onto it. Hold onto the ones you met at PAHS or PHS. Don't be what they tell you is normal. Don't just take it. Don't settle. Don't go along to get along. Above all, don't get old.

Which reminds me: one of my friends wrote a great song about immortality.

He wrote that the sky is green, and that the grass is blue, and that they lied to you. What he meant by that is this: Nothing they told you about you, or the future, or anything, was true. NOTHING.

Rage, rage, rage against lies and the liars who tell them. Batter down their walls. If you want to serve the age, someone said, betray it. If you do, I promise you: it will save your teenaged soul.

That song he quoted was by our friend Jimmy Cleary, now gone. And it was a great song.

And that essay was why most of us put off first-year college. We all figured X was right: we didn't want to settle down, and we didn't want to live in suburban slag — and we figured we'd maybe go out in a blaze of punk rock glory instead. Do something amazing and remarkable before we were all forced to start worrying about jobs and mortgages and utility payments, you know?

So we all decided to go on tour.

The big Rastafarian told us his name was Bembe Smith. *Bembe*, he said, meant "prophet."

"I prophesize great success on the Hot Nasties' upcoming tour!" he said, but no one laughed. We just looked at him.

Stiff Records had sent Bembe to manage our first big tour. We didn't think we needed anyone. But the head guy at Stiff, Jake Riviera, explained to a skeptical Sam Shiller that the British label was investing a lot of money in making the tour a success, and they didn't feel we had anyone with the necessary experience. So, they'd send a guy. Bembe was apparently the guy.

X and Mike the bouncer, the only people the Hot Nasties thought had the necessary experience, said we needed someone like Bembe. "I'm a bouncer," Mike said, big tattooed arms crossed over his FUCK THE WORLD T-shirt. "I don't know jack shit about running a fucking tour."

X, sitting on the couch beside Mike, nodded. "Me neither," he said. "I'll sell your merch and roadie for you guys, but that's it. I don't know how to run a tour either."

Bembe Smith was enormous, maybe six foot six. He was in pretty good shape, too; not an ounce of fat on him. He had long dreads that reached to the middle of his broad back and hands the size of dinner plates. He looked like he could break any of us in two.

He was kind of hot, too. But I digress.

Like me and X, Bembe couldn't fully stand up in the basement of Sound Swap because the ceiling was so low. So, he sat on the ratty old couch we'd rescued from a nearby Dumpster, stretched out beside X and Mike. I could see that X liked him already.

Bembe explained that he was from Treasure Beach, which was the actual name of a little place in St. Elizabeth Parish, on the southwest side of Jamaica. His dad had been a fisherman and later the manager of a renowned little hotel called Jake's. But he hadn't lived there since he was a little kid, he told us. He'd spent most of his time in schools in Britain and the States, New York City specifically. I guess that's why he didn't have much of an accent.

Treasure Beach was where Perry Henzell lived, Bembe explained. "You know who Perry Henzell is, don't you? He's the man who created *The Harder They Come*."

We sure did. All of us brightened. *The Harder They Come*, every punk rocker knew, was the film that introduced reggae to pale-skinned people. All of us had the soundtrack, and all of us knew every note. It contained fucking amazing songs by Jimmy Cliff, the Melodians, the Maytals, Desmond Dekker. It was probably my secret favorite record, to tell you the truth.

Bembe, like the characters in *The Harder They Come*, was a real Rasta. He believed in a single God, *Jah*, and he believed that Haile Selassie — the former emperor of Ethiopia, who had died just a few years earlier — was the messiah, the second coming of Christ. Africa was Zion, the Promised Land, and reggae music — and weed — were super important parts of their faith. Cannabis was an actual sacrament to a Rasta like Bembe.

"But don't worry, my religion won't get us arrested on

tour," Bembe said, big hands spread wide, smiling. "I am careful when I am on the road."

"Damn," I said. "I was hoping you'd know where to get some better shit!"

Everyone — the Hot Nasties, some of the Virgins — laughed. X didn't.

The tour was just three weeks away. We had the bands — the Hot Nasties and the Punk Rock Virgins. We had our instruments — Fenders, Marshalls. We finally had a set list, we had a record label (Stiff), we had a roadie (X), we had a driver (Mike), and now we had a tour manager (Bembe). Things were looking up, but there was still a lot to do.

And there was something else to figure out, too. When X got to his place in South Portland, and I got to mine, both of us had worried-looking parents holding message slips from an FBI agent by the name of Theresa Laverty.

Here we go again.

I did most of the talking. X kept quiet.

Theresa Laverty was a special agent with the Federal Bureau of Investigation, yes. She had a badge and the authority to detain us, yes. She had a revolver somewhere beneath her stylish Polo jacket, yes, and could shoot me and X at any time.

Despite all this, I liked her right away. She didn't

sound like a fascist, unlike most of the cops we'd met in Portland. She talked to us like we were actual human beings. And — I'm not sure if X picked up on it, but my gaydar sure had — Theresa Laverty was almost certainly gay, like me. A stunningly beautiful lesbian FBI agent: that's not something you run into every day in Portland, Maine, folks.

We were at Gary's, sitting at one of the battered little, round tables near the stage. The waitress and the cook who had unlocked the bar's heavy reinforced doors off Brown Street had been pretty surprised to find us standing there on the sidewalk when they opened up at 10:00 a.m.

Me and X, not so much. They were used to seeing the two of us around Gary's; we'd been regulars there since the place had become a punk rock venue in late 1977 or so. But the stunningly pretty, well-dressed woman waiting with us? *That* they clearly found weird. They stared at the three of us for a few seconds before letting us in.

On the phone, Theresa Laverty had told me she wanted to meet in the place where the local punk scene was centered.

"The center is my friend X," I'd said. "He *is* the Portland punk scene."

"I had heard that," she said. "But I'd appreciate it if the two of you would meet me just for an hour or so. I've got a case that's quite unusual, and I'd be grateful for your input."

I asked her for more details, but she remained vague. Said she had a general interest in youth subcultures, and a specific interest in the Hot Nasties. She didn't say why. I asked her, half-joking, if we were in trouble.

"No," she said.

Against my better judgment, but intrigued, I suggested we meet at Gary's the next morning. Laverty agreed. I hung up and called X. He, to my surprise, wasn't immediately opposed to meeting with the FBI agent. X didn't like cops either. But he said yes.

Anyway, there we sat, eyeballing each other. Laverty had an RC Cola in front of her, as did X. I had a beer. As Gary's longtime server, Koby, was taking our orders, Theresa had looked right at me when she said "no" to a beer. And she kept looking at me when I said "yes" to one, even though it was before noon. The way she looked at me — it was like she *knew*.

Wow. I didn't know then, but I certainly did later on: not only were we both gay, but we both had a substances problem. *We could practically be a couple. Let's get married!*

She was a knockout, as noted. She could have been a model, I figured, but her diminutive size had probably eliminated that career choice. And the way she dressed, the way she moved — it wasn't like a cop at all. Graceful, elegant, controlled. In person, too, Laverty was very precise with her words, very careful — even more than she had been on the phone.

Methodically, she told us about the murders of Johnny Raindrops and Colleen Tomorrow. She told us about how both were regulars at CBGB. And then she told us about the connection to us. "We've confirmed with the owner that the victims were both at CBGB on the two nights in early summer when the Hot Nasties played there," Laverty said, easing back a bit in her chair. She watched us. "They were both murdered shortly after those shows, we think by the same person or persons."

I slouched in my chair and squinted up at Gary's filthy, prehistoric-looking ceiling. "Fuck," I said. "Not again."

X, meanwhile, hadn't said a word or moved a muscle. He gazed, unblinking, at Theresa Laverty. She gazed right back.

When X finally spoke, he said, "You didn't ask us where we were after the band played."

Laverty wasn't fazed in the slightest. "I know where you all were afterward. You aren't suspects."

"So who is?"

Laverty frowned. She seemed to deliberate whether we could be trusted or not. Finally, she asked, "Are you familiar with the Creators?"

The "Bible" of the Church of the Creator, Theresa Laverty told us, was something called *Nature's Eternal Religion*. It was written a few years earlier, she said, by the COTC's founder and self-described "Pontifex Maximus," Bernhardt Klassen.

Klassen was Dutch-Mennonite, and he'd grown up on a wheat farm in Saskatchewan, up in Canada. He eventually moved to the States, where he worked as a teacher and an engineer, and then as a real estate agent. "For most of his life, he sold real estate, and he became a multimillionaire doing that," Laverty informed us, without consulting any notebooks or anything. "In the late fifties, he settled in Florida and, a few years later, he was elected to the lower house of the Florida state legislature on a platform that was explicitly anti-busing and anti-government. It was around that time that he became extremely concerned with what he called 'the rapid mongrelization of our formerly white America.'"

Shortly after his election to the state legislature, she said, Klassen showed up at a meeting of the racist John Birch Society in New York City, where he was introduced to delegates by the Birchers' leader. After that, he became the Florida chairman of something called the American Independent Party, which was the electoral vehicle for white supremacist presidential candidate George Wallace.

"Later, he had a falling-out with the Birchers, who he said were not radical enough. He looked around for a while for a vehicle for his extreme views," Laverty said. "He couldn't find one. So, in 1973, he founded the Church of the Creator, not too far from the FBI field office where I work in Florida. He started collecting guns and supporters. That's when he came to our attention. And that was the year that he wrote and published his first book, *Nature's Eternal Religion*."

Laverty reached into her purse, also bearing the Polo

trademark, and extracted a few sheets of paper, which she handed to us. They were copies of extracts from Klassen's book, apparently. I scanned through them; X didn't. He just kept looking at Laverty and sipping his soda.

It was the same kind of hateful crap I'd seen before — just as awful as the material produced by the Aryan Nations lunatics we had encountered a year earlier, but with a twist. Where the Aryan Nations fanatics had claimed they were doing God's will, the Church of the Creator seemed to openly mock Christianity.

The COTC was sort of an atheistic neo-Nazi group, apparently. They called Jesus Christ "an imaginary spook," among other things. To Klassen and his followers — he called them "Creators" who followed the rules of "creativity" — Christianity was "a suicidal religion."

"We completely reject the Judeo-democratic-Marxist views of today and supplant them with new and basic values, of which race is the foundation," Klassen wrote. "We mean to cleanse our own territories of all the Jews, niggers, and mud races, and send them back to their original habitat."

Thoroughly disgusted, I handed the sheets back to Laverty.

"Bernhardt Klassen occupied himself with building a neo-Nazi organization that was highly militant and quite violent," she said. "Klassen moved his growing church to a small town called Otto in North Carolina. There, he wrote and published another book, *The White Man's Bible*." She paused and looked directly at X. "That's the book we find most interesting, in the current context."

In it, Laverty said, Klassen called on his fellow Christ-hating Creators to build — and here she could quote from memory — "sound minds in sound bodies in a sound society."

Creators, she said, were urged to eat only fresh, wholesome food, engage in strenuous physical exercise several times a week, fast every once in a while, totally avoid medicines and intoxicants, and participate in what Klassen called the "healthy expression of our sexual instincts."

Holy shit.

Theresa Laverty, who apparently didn't miss much, looked at X: "When your band played at CBGB, were there many so-called straight edge followers there?"

He sipped at his RC Cola, then turned to her and said: "I think you already know the answer to that one, too, Special Agent Laverty."

CHAPTER 7

Click. Ring. Click.

"Hey."

"Hey."

"Is it working?"

"Better than expected."

"No one suspects?"

"No one."

Pause.

"Are they as bad as you said?"

"Worse."

For someone who hadn't ever worked in politics before — for someone who had been a *punk rocker*, no less — Danny's ascent up the political ladder in the Earl Turner campaign was pretty swift. Other people in the campaign noticed, and they didn't all appreciate it.

But Earl Turner liked the former Danny Hate, and — being a candidate for president — he didn't particularly give a shit what anyone else thought. He was indisputably the boss.

Turner was also something else: that year, he was the Republican Party's only true outsider candidate. All the other presidential aspirants were senators and governors and two-term congressmen, and — at the start, at least — none of them paid any attention at all to Earl Turner. "Not a serious candidate," went the Washington wisdom, which is a fucking oxymoron if there ever was one. "A fringe candidate," they called him.

But Earl Turner seemed to love the insults and the put-downs. He loved being the anti-politician politician. Whenever one of the beltway political types said something critical about him, he'd repeat it over and over to the growing crowds who came to hear him, in church basements and veterans' halls all over the early primary states, like Iowa and New Hampshire.

He'd say: "When the backroom boys say I'm not serious, when they go on C-SPAN and say I'm a fringe candidate, well" — and here he'd pause — "well, I say, there sure are a lot of other serious folks out here on the fringe with me! And we want to put America *right*!" They'd always give that a lot of applause. RIGHT! RIGHT! RIGHT! they'd chant.

Earl Turner figured he'd come this far — the come-from-nowhere guy, the one everyone was always underestimating, the one who was now an official Republican presidential candidate — by doing things his way. So, he'd keep doing that. He'd say what he thought, and he'd do what he wanted to do. And, if that meant promoting some weird former punk rock kid he'd taken a shine to, he'd do that, too.

So, within no time at all, Danny went from being a mere volunteer putting together lawn signs, stuffing envelopes, and canvassing door-to-door to being Earl Turner's paid backup personal assistant. Danny had a driver's license, and he was in the campaign office early that morning when Turner's regular personal assistant had a bad bug. Turner asked Danny if he could drive, Danny said yes, and that was that. Turner threw him the keys to his campaign Jeep, and off they went to meet some Republicans in Vermont.

There was plenty of speculation within the campaign as to why Turner so clearly favored Danny over the other ambitious young volunteers and staffers, but most of the speculation was wrong. Danny, Earl Turner quickly decided, was a true convert.

He'd been a *punk*, living an amoral, godless, leftist life. And now — *praise the Lord!* — he had converted to Earl Turner's cause, and he had completely rejected punk rock, atheism, and socialism. Danny had gone over to the right side, and was now like all true converts: he was trying to make up for lost time. Earl Turner realized that, and he knew how to take advantage of it.

Whatever Turner asked Danny to do, he did. If Turner wanted Danny to go and secretly tape record a rally for one of Turner's Republican primary opponents, Danny would do it. If Turner wanted him to poke through the garbage bins behind an opponent's campaign office, Danny would do it. If Turner wanted someone's campaign signs trashed late one night, Danny would do it. If Turner wanted a particularly dirty rumor circulated about a political adversary — an extramarital fling, for example, detailed on some anonymous leaflets and left outside a church gathering — Danny would do it. No hesitation.

On one road trip to New Hampshire, while two press aides napped in the back seat of the campaign Jeep, Earl Turner sat up front with Danny as they made their way west along Interstate 89. They chatted about the weather and the state of the race and the places Turner had worked — in Maine, in the South, in the Carolinas. Conversation turned to Danny O'Heran's past life as drummer Danny Hate.

"So," Turner said. "What was it like, being involved in that godless punk rock stuff, Danny? I'm curious."

Danny glanced at Turner but otherwise kept his eyes on the road. "It's a bit embarrassing, sir," he said. He always addressed Turner as sir.

"Don't be embarrassed!" Turner said, energetically patting Danny on the leg. "You've put all that behind you, and now you're where you belong. I'm just curious about what it was like."

"If I might ask, sir, why?"

"Well," Turner said, folding his big arms behind his head, "I've noticed this punk rock stuff has been getting a lot of media attention lately. So I thought I should start saying some things about it." He paused. "It certainly seems to represent everything that we're against, doesn't it?"

And that is how Earl Turner started his campaign to demonize the godless, perverted, communistic, drug-abusing punk rock subculture.

And his followers loved it.

CHAPTER 8

News of the third murder took a long time to reach Theresa Laverty, mainly because it happened in Canada. And, well, nobody in the U.S. pays much attention to anything that happens in Canada.

The body of the victim had been found quite a few days after we did the Barrymore's gig, the one at which Danny bailed on us for good.

You know: when he stopped being Danny Hate, drummer for the Social Blemishes, and when he became Danny O'Heran, fucking Republican working for the fucking fascist Earl fucking Turner, for fuck's sake.

I was still having a hard time with Danny dropping us like we were a handful of warm dog crap, by the way. X, not at all. He didn't say anything about Danny after that. Not a word.

The only reason anyone eventually noticed that the Ottawa punk was dead — and notified the local cops, who notified the Royal Canadian Mounted Police, who in turn notified Pete Schenk, who then called up Theresa Laverty, still in Portland — was the overwhelming stench. The punk, who called himself Nuclear Age, apparently lived in an apartment above a pizza place on Sunnyside Avenue in Ottawa. The smell of the pizza had been stronger than the smell of Nuclear Age for the first few days, I guess.

His roommate, who had been on a weeks-long trip to gather rock samples in California, was the one who found him. From what I heard, Nuclear Age was all bloated, like a beached punk rock whale.

Person or persons unknown had done to him what had been done to Colleen Tomorrow — sliced him from his balls to his chest, and then hacked what looked like a *W* into his throat. And there on the wall above Nuclear Age's bed was a meticulously rendered letter *W* within a circle, with the crown and the halo up above. No fingerprints anywhere, no other clues.

In his room, Nuclear Age — his real name was Juan Conseco — had posters up of his mainly Canadian punk rock heroes: D.O.A. from Vancouver, the Young Canadians, the Modernettes, and the Viletones from Toronto.

Nuclear Age had been a punk, and from what Laverty told me, the cops and the FBI seemed to agree that he'd been murdered by the same killer or killers. It was the fact that he was Canadian, in particular, that had all the various police agencies freaking out, she told me when we met back at Gary's — this time without X. She wanted to speak with me alone this time, she said.

"Not only are we dealing with a serial killer or kill-ers," she told me, "we're dealing with someone who's prepared to cross international borders to kill." She paused and looked at me, expressionless. "And we're dealing with someone who is very unenthusiastic about Hot Nasties' fans, apparently."

No kidding.

I didn't know what to say that wouldn't sound to-tally insensitive or cynical, so I just shrugged and sipped my ginger ale. Yes, ginger ale. I was queer as a three-dollar bill, and I had, I admit, a bit of a fond-ness for myriad pharmaceuticals, but I actually sort of wanted to impress Theresa Laverty. So I was foregoing the beer and the speed, at least in front of my new gal pal from the FBI.

At that, our second face-to-face encounter, she adopted an almost-maternal tone. I hadn't been a big fan of my mother since she drove out my dad with her ceaseless screaming and abuse, so I didn't immediately object. "You seem to have a case of the sniffles," she said matter-of-factly.

"Yeah, it's a cold that won't go away," I said, obviously lying my face off. "It's a total pain."

"A cold that won't go away in the summertime?" Laverty said, one perfect eyebrow arched. "Really?"

Another pause.

"Kurt," she said, "do you mind if I give you some un-solicited advice?" She didn't wait for me to respond be-fore continuing. "I know what it is like to live in a closet,

in a society as repressive as this one," she said, looking right at and, it seemed, *through* me. "Being gay in
America in 1980 isn't easy. It causes hardships. It sometimes leads to bad choices. And those choices will only
make the hardships much more difficult.… But you're
smart. You already know this."

I looked at her. We were the oddest fucking odd couple ever. Me, a tall, pale punk rocker in a biker jacket
and torn skinny jeans; her, a short, tanned FBI special
agent decked out in high-end designer fashion. But we
both had secrets, and we knew some of each other's.

She waited for me to say something, but I kept quiet.
Whatever I said, I knew it would come out wrong.

Then her expression suddenly changed and she
was all business again. She looked down at her notepad, where she had inscribed some of the details about
Nuclear Age's demise, related to her by Detective Schenk
over the phone. She hadn't been to the crime scene —
getting permission to do so would require the assistance
of the State Department and would take time, she explained — and that meant she didn't know everything
there was to know. She clearly didn't like that. Her pretty
forehead was furrowed. "I need to know more about this
victim, because someone went to quite a lot of effort to
turn him into a victim," she said. "Crossing a border?
It's almost unprecedented. I need to find someone who
remembers him."

I stirred. "Well, actually, I do," I said, confiding in
my unlikely new best friend. "I'm pretty sure I talked

to a guy who called himself Nuclear Age at that show in Ottawa."

Patti Upchuck was unhappy. *Super* unhappy.

Being X's IFOTOS — Important Friend of the Other Sex — was never going to be an easy assignment. I called her that because (of course) X and Patti Upchuck, the Portland Maine Punk Rock Super Couple (PMPRSC), would (of course) object to conventional designations like "boyfriend" or "girlfriend." It wasn't the typical boy-girl, male-female type deal. Not at all. These two floated above the earth and us lesser mortals in an entirely different orbit.

Does that sound bitter and bitchy? Probably. I don't mean to be that way. It's the speed talking, maybe. It's just that the two of them … they were a bit *much*, sometimes. All intrigue wrapped up in mystery and all that. All. The. Time.

Except that X *was* the most mysterious person who ever lived. He didn't gossip, he didn't do small talk, he didn't over-share. Hell, he barely shared at all. And, as a result, being in a relationship with him was capital *D* difficult. Believe me, I know. He's been my best friend since grade seven, but it's been like being best friends with a fucking icicle most of the time.

One night at Sound Swap, when a Punk Rock Virgins practice was wrapping up and a Hot Nasties practice was about to start, Patti and I were away from the others. The tour hadn't started yet, and everyone was finally getting pretty excited. The bickering had stopped, the details were known, and the Virgins were going to open for us at a few of the shows, so we were all practicing our faces off.

Patti's face, I could readily see, was showing signs of X-related frustration. She was packing up her guitar — a one-of-a-kind old Mosrite Ventures copy with a bright green finish and Slits and X-Ray Spex stickers all over it — and she looked pissed.

"Why the funk, punk?" I asked, squeezing her shoulder. "Why so glum, glamorous chum?"

She managed a tight smile. My God, she was a total babe. Big, teased, dyed jet-black spiked hair; lots of black mascara; black-reddish lipstick; dog collar; torn sleeveless T-shirt with I AM A CLICHÉ scrawled across the front. Tight black cargo pants. Cherry-red Docs. She looked fucking fabulous.

"He'll kill me if I tell you," she said, already looking like she had said way too much. "So, don't worry about it."

"Oh, I know who you're talking about, girl," I said, all campy-gay to get her to smile. She did, a bit. "What did he do now? Or, more appropriately, what *didn't* he do?"

Patti gave a little laugh. "Didn't," she said, sitting down on the edge of the landing that separated Sound Swap's cash register from the stacks and stacks of used records. I eased down beside her. "Right. He *didn't* do what he always doesn't do, which is ..." She trailed off, hands in the air, exasperated.

"Let me guess, girlfriend," I said, teasing. "He *didn't* communicate with you. He *didn't* seem to be listening to you. He *didn't* react in the way a regular, normal, garden-variety human being would react."

She looked at me. "Right on all counts," she said. "He didn't do any of those things. Doesn't, either."

I put an arm around her and gave her a little squeeze. "Hate to say I told you so, babe, but I told you so. I seem to recall telling a certain burgeoning punk rock star that she was getting into a relationship with a guy who regards everyday communication as a violation of the Geneva Convention or something. I told you that, didn't I?"

"Yes, you did," she said, sullenly examining her nails. She had recently painted them black, and they looked very cool. "You did."

We kept quiet for a minute, because members of the Hot Nasties had started arriving and were filing down the stairs to the basement. We said hi and waited until they were all out of earshot.

"You warned me," she repeated. "It's just … it's like being in a relationship with the Rock of Gibraltar or something. Sometimes I would even prefer it if he got mad at me, you know? Just fucking yell at me, X, so I have some clue what you're thinking!" She gave a frustrated little scream.

Breeders are super cute.

"He won't ever do that, kiddo," I said. "It's not that he's trying to be cool or something. It's just that it's not in his DNA, you know?" I laughed. "Maybe he's an alien or a robot or something."

She laughed, too, and then she sighed. "But I fucking love that robot," she said, her voice low.

"I love him, too," I said, also quiet. "There's him, there's my dad, there's you and your sister. That is my Pantheon of Besties. Also — and you're not going to believe this — but I think I'm getting a gay man's crush on that FBI agent who has been sniffing around, Theresa Laverty."

"Are you fucking serious?" Patti said, clearly shocked, staring at me. "An FBI agent? An FBI agent is becoming your friend?"

"Nutty, I know. But she's cool. Smart. Gay, too. We've hit it off."

Patti Upchuck eyed me carefully. Now it was her turn to be concerned and give relationship advice. "Be careful, Kurt," Patti said. "She's a cop. I mean, it was a fucking cop who killed Jimmy and Marky, and who tried to kill Sam and my sister, as you may recall."

"I know, I know," I said, looking at her, dead serious. I hesitated. "I know. But crazy shit is happening again. That's why she's been around." I paused, wondering whether to say more. I decided to tell her, lowering my voice to a whisper. "There's been some bad stuff again, Patti."

Her beautiful face dropped. "Oh God, no," she said. "Not again. Kurt ..."

I held up a hand. "Whisper," I said, pointing to the stairs, and the basement, where the Hot Nasties were tuning up. "The guys don't know about it yet. X wants to tell them later."

"Tell them what?" she said, sounding frightened. "What's happened?"

I didn't know how to sugarcoat it, so I just told her straight out. "There've been three murders," I said. She gasped. "Not anyone we know, obviously. But three guys who apparently came to the Nasties' pre-tour shows in Ottawa and New York. A transvestite hooker and a wannabe Johnny Thunders type in New York, and a guy in Ottawa I actually talked to before we played. That's what this FBI agent is investigating. And she has really strong views about our tour."

Patti looked confused. "What do you mean?"

"She doesn't think we should go," I said unhappily. "Someone's gone to our shows, she says, and killed three kids who were there. And she understandably doesn't want anyone else to get killed."

X arrived. So did the recently admitted Bembe Smith, plus Mike the bouncer. X had brought both of them for the pre-tour band summit. The Virgins were there, too.

We were just putting away our guitars and stuff when X addressed us from his spot on the stairs. "So, guys, I've got some bad news."

Sam Shiller, our resident worrier, immediately freaked. "Stiff has canceled the tour! They've canceled the tour, haven't they?"

"No," X said, "the tour's still on."

Luke Macdonald, the Nasties' bassist, asked X what was up.

X looked around the basement. "There have been three murders."

BOOM.

Most of the Nasties and Virgins jumped to their feet, totally fucking freaking out. They yelled and squawked and made unhappy noises. Patti and I watched them. Bembe and Mike, who apparently already knew about the bad news, watched and remained sitting.

X waited before speaking again. "Okay, calm down," he said. "The victims are a guy named Johnny Raindrops in New York, near CBGB, a sex worker named Colleen Tomorrow in the same area, and a kid in Ottawa, Nuclear Age. They—"

Leah Yeomanson, the Punk Rock Virgins' drummer, cut him off: "Wait a second, X. Wait, wait, *wait*. Those were the two places the Nasties played on the pre-tour!"

X nodded. "Yes. All three came to the Nasties' shows in those cities."

At this point, most of the Nasties and the Virgins started freaking out again. X waited for them to stop.

When he continued, he was matter-of-fact: "The FBI agent is concerned that some homicidal maniac is following the Nasties around, obviously. This agent has spoken to me and Kurt, and she doesn't think it is a good idea that we go ahead with the tour."

Sam looked worried. "I don't think Stiff Records would like that. Would they, Bembe?"

Bembe was still sprawled out on the ancient couch beside X and Mike, sounding uncharacteristically somber. "They would be quite unhappy, yes," he said. "They've put a lot of money into promoting this tour. They might drop the band from the label … or worse."

Eddie Igglesden, the Hot Nasties' drummer, suddenly looked stricken at the prospect of missing out on groupies. "Worse?" he said. "What *the fuck* could be worse than getting dropped from Stiff Records?"

Bembe shrugged his exceedingly wide shoulders. "Well, they might demand back the advance they paid you."

BIGGER BOOM.

With the exception of me, the Hot Nasties started freaking out and squawking and screeching and buzzing again. All of them had spent Stiff Records' advance on new guitars, new amps, and shiny new Schott Perfecto biker jackets. The Punk Rock Virgins, meanwhile, merely looked unhappy.

"So," X finally said, sounding impatient, "you guys have a decision to make. Do you go ahead or do you cancel? This FBI agent doesn't have the power to stop us from touring, obviously. But there are risks either way."

Sister Betty spoke up for the first time. "If we go ahead, Mike, are you still coming? Would you still do security and all that?"

"Of course, kid," said Mike, who has the softest of soft spots for Sister Betty, and vice versa. "Of course I'd still go. I'd make the shows as safe as I could for everybody. Bembe told me he'd do the same."

Bembe nodded, all serious. "We'd be making it secure for everyone there. But what happens after the shows, obviously, is something Mike and X and I can't control. And these murders happened after the shows in New York and Ottawa."

I frowned. They did?

There was quiet for a bit as the two bands considered all this.

Sister Betty was clearly torn. "What do you think we should do, X? Should we still go?"

X, who I knew had had time to think about the answer, didn't hesitate: "I think you should go ahead. The FBI agent told us she is worried about more trouble. But, at the same time, she told Kurt and me that the tour gives her what may be her only shot at identifying who's doing this. She told us she intends to be around for some of the gigs." He looked at Bembe and Mike, who both nodded.

Leah was looking even unhappier, if that's possible. "Sounds like we're bait, X."

X shrugged. "Like I said, there are risks either way. Going ahead shows everyone — again — that these two bands will not be intimidated. That is your reputation with a lot of people: that you have guts. And, like I said, it supposedly gives this FBI agent an opportunity to find this bastard. But it's your call, guys."

I waited for someone to say something. No one did. So I said, "Seriously, guys. Our two bands have the worst fucking bad luck in the entire fucking universe."

Sam, morose, gave a dark laugh. "It's the Hot Nasties and Punk Rock Virgins 1980 Doom and Gloom Tour, folks! Buy a ticket, and maybe get killed. Fuck! *Fuck fuck fuck!*"

No one said anything, because everyone seemed to agree. Without taking a vote, I knew that the Hot Nasties and the Punk Rock Virgins were going to go ahead with the tour.

But it still felt like we were standing on the edge of some fucking abyss, ready to fall.

CHAPTER 9

Earl Turner propped his cowboy boots up on a chair and scowled around the room at his senior campaign staff. He made them nervous. He *always* made them nervous.

The campaign staff were seated at the long table in the conference room at the back of the Turner for President headquarters, sleeves rolled up, ties loosened, pens at the ready.

They were all white, Christian, and conservative, just like their man. And they were *mostly* men, too. The only females present were two pretty young women who allegedly worked in the press office, Daisy Something and Stacey Something. It was widely assumed that Earl Turner, God-fearing family man, was fucking both of them.

For reasons Danny O'Heran didn't fully understand, Earl Turner had wanted him present. So Danny stood by the door, saying nothing. Earl Turner preferred people who kept their mouths shut.

By this point in the campaign, Danny had basically become Turner's full-time personal assistant. He was doing everything from driving Turner to private meetings to fetching his dry cleaning — and still occasionally carrying out various low-level dirty tricks at the candidate's insistence. Danny's growing influence continued to cause a lot of resentment within the Turner campaign, but no one had the guts to say anything to the big man himself. So the former punk moved up the organizational flowchart, graduating to his own little box, one directly connected to the candidate by a solid line, not a dotted one.

The senior Turner campaign staffers had been summoned for a compulsory and top-secret Saturday morning meeting to discuss the state of the Republican primary race. The media polls, such as they were, were suggesting that Turner was still somewhat competitive for the party's nomination. But internal surveys — conducted by Derwin Hailey, the ex-lawyer and polling nerd who had been hired by Turner early on — told a different story.

Republicans who knew about Earl Turner liked him, Hailey explained to the group. But too many Republicans still didn't know him, at all. "What they see, they like," he said, "but they're not seeing enough of him to make a difference. We're losing, gang."

The room was silent. Earl Turner let Hailey's words sink in for a minute, and then he swung his cowboy boots off the chair. He leaned forward, big hands clasped in front of him, and faced his advisors. "We're losing," he said, quietly. And then, at the top of his voice: "WE. ARE. LOSING." He slammed a fist onto the table to punctuate each word: *bang bang bang.*

The staffers jumped. Even Daisy Something and Stacey Something appeared worried at that point. The men looked terrified. Danny, having seen Earl Turner practice for this performance, wasn't. He knew what was coming next.

Turner turned his gaze on Derwin Hailey, who seemed about to have a stroke. Immediately, his face softened and he gave Hailey a thousand-watt smile. "But," he said, "there's something else you found out, isn't there, Derwin?"

"Yes! Yes, sir, there is," Hailey said, visibly relieved, leaping up and pulling a stack of stapled sheets of paper out of a file folder. He passed them around the room, including one to Danny. Once back in his seat, Hailey started talking about his graphs.

"Chart one," Hailey announced. "As I said, we found that too many registered Republicans in the early primary states don't know who we are. When they find out, they like the candidate's backstory, a lot. They become open to switching. But they know the establishment candidates way better."

Everyone flipped to the next page.

"Chart two," he said, clearly loving that the senior campaign staff were listening to him. "We get better known by ramping up our ad buy, and by changing the creative we are doing. We need to get a lot more aggressive in our messaging, and we need to have our spots seen by a lot more people." Hailey paused, sounding uncertain. "This will be, um, costly."

Earl Turner waved a dismissive hand, but kept his eyes on chart two. "Don't worry about it," he said. "Danny and I are going to see someone about that right after this meeting. Keep going."

"Yes, sir," Hailey said, practically saluting. "Chart three, everyone ... well, it's actually a few charts on one sheet."

There was the sound of pages being turned, and then silence. Shocked silence. Hailey continued.

"These charts and data represent a summary of everything we've been able to find out about the core attitudes of the available vote," he said. "That is, the significant number of Republican swing voters who haven't really committed to a candidate. They're the ones who are nominally Republicans but are very dissatisfied with the establishment candidates. There are also some independents in there. All of this gettable vote wants one thing, above all else."

For drama, Hailey paused. But he didn't need to. What the senior campaign staff saw before them already *was* dramatic. Basically, it was a bunch of pie charts legitimizing appealing to people's worst instincts: even Danny could see that. It was a strategic map that said Earl Turner could win if he started pushing white supremacy.

"They want someone to speak for them," Hailey said, triumphant. "And what they want that candidate to say is something that no other candidate will, in either party."

He paused again.

"They want—"

Earl Turner cut him off, held up a beefy hand, and slowly stood up. "They want a candidate who will not be afraid to tell it like it is," he said, quieter, starting to pace around the table.

Danny watched him. Turner was mesmerizing when he got like this. Scary, but mesmerizing.

"They want a candidate who will say *no* to the immigrants. *No* to the refugees. *No* to the illegals. *No* to the parasites, the ones who come here to rape and impregnate white women. *No* to the white punks and the black thugs and the brown perverts and the yellow thieves and the hook-nosed international bankers. *No*. No more. We will round them up, and we will ship them back to whatever rock they crawled out from under."

The senior campaign team was staring at Earl Turner, stunned. Some would tender their resignations shortly after this meeting. Earl Turner, anticipating this, had told Danny he would be delighted to shed "the cowards" who had been dragging down his campaign.

Turner stopped and suddenly pointed at one of the big red, white, and blue posters with RIGHT on it. "Right," he said. "*Right* means *white*, from this point on in this campaign."

There were a few audible gasps. Earl Turner was going where no previous Republican presidential candidate had gone before. If he couldn't win the country, he was essentially going to set the countryside on fire.

Earl Turner watched them, then nodded for Derwin Hailey to continue.

"It's time to go big or go home, folks," the spidery pollster said, spinning his web. "This strategy will get us noticed, hugely, and it will get us support. It's going to be bumpy, and the special interests and the minorities and their fake media will go nuts, but that'll help us in the long run. Our voters *like it* when the liberal media and minorities get upset. So, with the right execution, with the right discipline and resources, we think this strategy will work."

Earl Turner was still standing. He crossed his big arms and looked around the room. "We need a candidate who will speak for white, small-town America," he said. "And that candidate is me."

CHAPTER 10

It was a few days until the tour began, so I decided to go see X at his family's place. His mom let me in. He was packing when I stepped into his bedroom.

X pointed at the old hockey bag, previously used by his little brother when he played junior A. "Couple pairs of jeans, underwear, lots of T-shirts, extra pair of Converse, some books and toiletries," he said. "Also bringing my jacket, my sweater if it gets cooler somewhere, and that's about it. You?"

"Same kind of stuff," I said, sitting on the end of his bed, back against the wall. I didn't tell him about the little baggie full of white power I'd also stuck in my own hockey bag, hidden away inside a sock and then stuffed into the toe of a Doc Martens boot. He didn't want to hear about that, I figured.

I sniffed. I scratched. I looked around. It had been quite a while since I had been in X's spartan bedroom.

Nothing much had changed: on one wall, an early framed picture of the Hot Nasties in front of Gary's, with Jimmy Cleary between me and X. We were all smiling and laughing — happier, better times. On the other wall, a super-rare poster of an October 1968 Iggy and the Stooges show in Ann Arbor. And on the middle wall, above his typewriter, a Polaroid of Patti onstage with the Punk Rock Virgins. A bit blurred, but looking cool.

When he saw me come in, X wasn't surprised. But he never really looked surprised about anything, like, *ever*. We hadn't really been hanging out as much as we used to. Since he had quietly started seeing Patti Upchuck — and since I had even more quietly started making speed a staple of my diet — we'd undeniably drifted apart. He disapproved of what I was doing, and I disapproved of the fact that he disapproved.

However, given that we were going on the road together with five other guys, crisscrossing the hinterland in Eddie's 1977 Ford Econoline E150 van, things were going to get pretty crowded pretty fast. We'd be towing all the Hot Nasties' equipment in a U-Haul cargo trailer, but it was still going to be cramped and smelly in the van. Our short pre-tour trips to Ottawa and New York City certainly had been.

The Punk Rock Virgins, meanwhile, were going to be exclusively opening for us at some of our gigs, but not all of them. So the three of them were going to be using the Upchuck family's station wagon for Patti and Betty's guitars and amps and Leah was going to be sharing Eddie's drum kit.

Anyway, I was mainly at X's to see if we could get things back on track a bit. Anyone who has ever been on tour will tell you that things can get tense in close quarters, even with the best of friends.

X kept folding and packing shit, and I kept looking around his room, and occasionally at him. Even when he was folding underwear, the fucking guy was charismatic. Silent, stoic, slender: he was a teenager like no other.

X, as I always told everyone, had been the one who introduced me to punk rock, way back when. But not the Clash or the Pistols — those bands came later. Before I even knew him, X was listening to the early, early stuff: MC5, the Dictators, the aforementioned Iggy and the Stooges. X had been into the punk scene before there *was* a scene.

How a seventh-grader in Portland, Maine, could know about MC5's "Kick Out the Jams" — let alone own a copy of that record — was totally fucking amazing, in retrospect. I couldn't even picture him, all of thirteen years, sitting on the floor of his room beside his tinny record player, listening to Rob Tyner, the MC5 front man, shouting: "Kick out the jams, motherfuckers!"

Thirteen years old! I mean, I was barely out of G.I. Joe at that age, and here X was listening to these banned

Michigan punk rock communist revolutionaries!
Amazing.

Anyway. X was silent, now almost oblivious to
my presence. I examined his profile. He was, as Patti
Upchuck had said before, "More than handsome." His
face was *intriguing*. Unusual. Was he hot? Speaking as
the resident gay guy in the X Gang, yes, X was decidedly
hot. But there was something else about him, too — not
bad on the eyes, but also fucking scary sometimes. In a
fight he was like an animal.

One time I saw him hit a big biker type so hard in
the side of his head, the guy's eye sort of half popped
out. Seriously. It was fucking insane. The biker didn't
get up again.

Beneath his long, dark hair, X's face was a bit broad,
with these killer cheekbones, dark eyebrows, and "those
eyes," as Patti put it. His pupils were different sizes, the
infamous outcome of a fight at a community hall gig,
when a couple guys jumped him, and one of them hit
him hard in the face. I was elsewhere, at the same gig,
having a scrap of my own with a couple other assholes.
The uneven pupils made him look like Bowie, which is
never a bad thing. But he'd refused to get it fixed. "Don't
care," he said, and he didn't.

He had scars, too, most of them from other fights
at other gigs. A half-moon-shaped one above an eyebrow, and a couple smaller ones on his chin. But it
was when he pushed his hair back that people would
get a bit of a surprise: they could see, right away, that

some of X's left ear was missing. It kind of looked like it had been chewed off by a hungry dog, and there was this triangular chunk of skin just *gone* from his earlobe.

It had happened when one of the small hoop earrings X wore had been ripped out by a big biker in a fight. X then proceeded to beat the biker until he was hustled off to the Mercy, the Portland hospital where members of the X Gang had been patched up at various times over the years. It was a bit gross, that ear, but it also sent a message: *Do not fuck with me.*

Nobody fucked with X. Or, if they did, they regretted it.

The upcoming tour, however, presented a unique dilemma, even for a guy as intimidating as X could be. By going ahead — as Theresa Laverty had warned us — we were potentially putting some Hot Nasties' fans at risk. Us, too, I suppose.

But by canceling the tour, we might also be ensuring that the FBI would take a lot longer to find the bad guy. Or maybe making it *impossible* to find the bad guy, who might then, you know, go on to kill yet more punks.

All of which reminded me of a question that had been nagging at me: Why had we only heard from Theresa Laverty? Why hadn't we seen any *other* FBI agents around?

I asked X what he thought about that, and he paused in his packing. "Wondered the same thing," he said, one eyebrow up.

"I mean, she's obviously intelligent and capable. But dealing with a serial killer all alone? I'm no expert on police procedure, but that seems really fucking strange, to me," I said. "Doesn't she have a partner or something?"

X shrugged.

"And what about this Church of the Creator shit?" I asked, warming up. "If another fucked-up neo-Nazi group is killing off punk rockers, yet again, shouldn't that involve *multiple* police agencies?"

X paused. "The cops weren't much help last time," he said, then gave another small shrug. "We were the ones who solved it."

"Yeah, I know," I said. "But this cop, I think I trust her." I paused. "We share … *a point of view*."

X looked at me but said nothing. He kept packing.

"Anyway," I said, deciding to change the subject, "I still wonder if we're gonna be able to handle it, if there is trouble at a show, you know?"

X shrugged. "Mike and Bembe and I have gone over it. There'll be no violence at any of the shows," he said. "That's our objective."

I squinted at him. "Even with the straight edge guys?" I asked, trying not to sound like I was accusing him of something, but knowing that I kind of was. "A lot of them seem to only go to shows to cause trouble."

"Yeah," X said, eventually. "But they'll regret it if they do."

Ring ring ring.

We could hear the phone going somewhere in the X family house. His mom, Mrs. Bridget X, yelled down to us. "Boys, it's a Ron McLeod from Associated Press. He says he wants to talk to you about your tour."

"Great," I whispered. "Fucking great."

X frowned and walked out of the room to take the call. I followed.

McLeod had wanted to meet us downtown at Matthew's, the chicken and chips place the X Gang frequented on Saturdays. I was surprised he knew about it, actually.

McLeod had been a reporter at the boring old fart's newspaper of choice, the *Portland Press Herald*, for a really long time. It was there that X and I had gotten to know him. And while we didn't trust him — we didn't trust any reporters, basically — we also didn't *distrust* Ron McLeod. He hadn't ever broken his word to us to keep stuff off the record. And he had been a pretty reliable source of information for us — me, for my writing, and X for finding out what the cops had been up to. So, we agreed to meet.

He was a little guy, balding, with a ginger mustache and John Denver–style glasses. When we walked into Matthew's, McLeod was sitting alone at a table near the can, gnawing on a piece of chicken. He half-stood when he saw us. "Fellas," he said, waving a chicken bone in our direction. "I'd shake your hands, but …"

"Don't worry about it," I said, as we pulled up seats and sat across from him. "You're looking prosperous, Ron."

He was, a bit. After he'd written all of his stories about the clash between the X Gang and the neo-Nazi killer who'd been stalking us, McLeod had won a bunch of regional media awards and had even been put up for a Pulitzer Prize by the *Press Herald*. He didn't win, but the nomination had made him a bit of a local star.

So, he'd taken a better-paying job with Associated Press. He was still based in Portland, but he wasn't just on the police beat anymore. Now, McLeod was writing about the presidential race as it played out across New England. Reporters love to write about political strategy, and Ron McLeod was no exception. He was really enjoying his new job, he told us, between mouthfuls of chicken and chips.

"Glad to hear it," I said, as X stepped away to get food for the two of us. "So, what do you want from us?"

McLeod wiped his mouth on a greasy napkin and looked at X's receding back. He seemed to want to wait for him to return, but didn't. He frowned. "So," he said, "this is off the record."

"If it wasn't, we wouldn't have come," I said. "What's up?

McLeod looked around to see if anyone was listening. No one was. No one had even noticed we were there, in fact. Matthew's regulars were old army veterans, retirees, and some characters who looked like they bunked on the sidewalk. None of them cared what we were talking about. "I've been writing about the presidential primaries and both parties for a month," he said. "And it's been bizarre on the Republican side. I mean, really strange."

"All Republicans are strange. All of them are closet Nazis, if you ask me." Like most punks, I despised conservatives in general, and Republicans in particular.

McLeod laughed. "Yeah, well, I can't call them that," he said. "But strange things certainly are happening in the Republican race."

"Such as?"

"Such as Maine's own favorite son, Earl Turner, has turned into a full-fledged Klansman, minus the white robes," he said. "He's taken to peddling racism, big time, and it's paying off for him. Big time."

"See? All Republicans are racists. No news there."

"Well, not all of them," McLeod said, waggling an index finger at me. "They are the party of Abe Lincoln, after all. But Turner's racism stuff has shaken up the race. He's slowly gaining on the more establishment Washington candidates, to everyone's amazement. He's bringing in people who have never really been involved in politics before …"

"Because they've all been too busy attending cross burnings," I scoffed.

"Yeah, well, maybe," he said, chortling again. "But his

polling numbers are freaking out the establishment. So, instead of condemning him — like many of them are telling me they want to, off the record — they're keeping quiet.... Some of them are even saying that Turner could actually win this thing."

"So? Doesn't affect me or my friends."

"I'd have to disagree with that," McLeod said. "He'd wreck this country if he got a chance."

Then I noticed that X was standing behind me with a tray of chicken and chips, along with a couple RC Colas and a couple draft beers. He sat down and looked at me. "I agree with Ron," he said quietly. "It matters."

There was no point in debating X. He'd forgotten more about politics than I would ever know. For my entire life, I hadn't spent five minutes thinking about the presidential primaries or the Republican Party. I mean, who fucking cares about those douchebags? That is, I guess, until our friend Danny Hate joined them. Which — surprise, surprise — was really what Ron McLeod wanted to talk about. He cleared his throat, waiting for X and me to start eating. We ate and listened.

"So, fellas," he said. "I've been spending a lot of time paying attention to the Turner campaign, just like a lot of other reporters have been doing. Everyone is trying to figure out how he has turned into a contender. Lots of come-from-behind stories being written about him."

We waited, listening.

"But I'm really the only local guy writing about the background of our, um, illustrious local political star," he said. "I'm the only one who really knows the local angle, I guess."

"So?" I said, mouth full of chicken.

Say it, Ron, you chickenshit.

"So," he said, finally, "I would like to know a bit more about your friend — and Earl Turner's right-hand man — Danny O'Heran."

CHAPTER 11

Danny sat in the campaign Jeep. Waiting, watching.

The Jeep had the Turner campaign's RIGHT logo affixed to the sides. But now, below that, it also said: AMERICA FOR AMERICANS. Nobody needed to ask Danny what the new slogan meant. They all knew. Everyone knew.

Danny had parked the Jeep on Commercial Street on Portland's waterfront, at Earl Turner's direction. Turner was going to meet some rich donor at the Hilton, which overlooked Casco Bay. As always, Turner told Danny to position the Jeep in a prominent spot beside the hotel, so it would be seen. "I want everyone to know we're here."

It's unlikely anyone would have missed him, anyway. With his quarterback's physique and his telegenic looks, Earl Turner was a bona fide local celebrity. And he was always pretty easy to spot in and around Portland.

For those few who weren't sure who he was, however, a recent addition to his entourage resolved any doubt: now that he was edging toward front-runner status in the Republican primary race, Earl Turner had been provided with his very own Secret Service detail. Secret Service agents read the polls, too, Danny figured. So, now, two burly dark-suited guys wearing sunglasses followed Earl Turner as he strolled near the hotel.

It was sunny, and nice out, so Turner and his rich friend had decided to take a walk. Danny was instructed to wait in the Jeep. Occasionally, Turner would stop to shake the extended hand of a well-wisher or give a friendly wave to gawkers driving by. But, mostly, his focus was on the diminutive man walking beside him. The man looked to be in his sixties, maybe his seventies. He was wearing a black suit, black tie, and black wingtips. His hair was short and slicked back on top. On his nondescript face, the only thing that distinguished him was a small, neatly-trimmed mustache.

As they walked, Secret Service in tow, Earl Turner was smiling and gesturing. The anonymous little man had his hands clasped behind his back. He was nodding at whatever Earl Turner was saying.

When Danny had pulled up to the Portland Waterfront Hilton, Turner said. "My friend Ben is up from the Blue Ridge Mountains, visiting. He's an important man. He's going to help us out with the new ad campaign." Turner paused. "Ever been to the Blue Ridge Mountains, Danny?"

Danny said no. He'd never even heard of the Blue Ridge Mountains.

"Beautiful part of America," Turner said, opening the door of the Jeep. "And not a nigger or a kike to be seen anywhere. Back shortly."

Danny O'Heran had winced at Earl Turner's racist language, but he said nothing. Since the campaign's pollster had laid out the radical new strategy, Earl Turner had embraced it with a vengeance. Any pretense of moderation had been abandoned.

To Danny's surprise, very few of the Republican faithful objected to the now openly racist tone of the campaign. At rallies and debates and meet-and-greets around New England, Republicans would nod whenever Turner denigrated blacks or homosexuals or other minorities. Occasionally, they'd let out a whoop of support.

Sometimes, when he figured his audience knew what he was talking about, Earl Turner would go on about how America's youth were drifting away from "traditional values," and getting into drugs and radicalism and awful stuff like punk rock. "Punk rockers, calling themselves the Antichrist and celebrating hard drugs in their disgusting lyrics!" Turner would say, referring to the Sex Pistols. And then Turner would steal a glance at Danny, and Danny would always give him an encouraging nod or a thumbs-up. "These punks deserve a beating!" Turner would say, and everyone would cheer.

A few times, protestors got into the rallies and started yelling at Turner. They'd shout that he was a racist and a bigot, or say his race-baiting was un-American. But they'd always be quickly hustled out by volunteers or local cops or the Secret Service. Once the protestors were gone, Turner would say something like: "You see that? See that? That's what we are up against, my friends. I support free speech so those nobodies can use their speech to say whatever they want. Let them holler." Then he'd pause. "But let them do their hollering when they're repatriated back to their own countries!"

And the crowd would cheer some more.

Sometimes, Danny would sit at the door when Turner was meeting with a reporter or a newspaper editorial board. Every single time, the reporters or editorial writers would challenge Turner about what they called his "racist rhetoric." Every single time, Turner would give them his local football hero smile and spread his big arms wide. "If I'm wrong to say what I'm saying, then why are so many people coming out to support me?" he'd ask. "Are *they* all wrong, too?" And then he'd recite some distorted statistics about the percentage of minorities and immigrants who commit crimes. He'd quote George Washington, who had said that the Indians were "beasts." Or Woodrow Wilson, who had backed what he called "the great Ku Klux Klan." Or he'd quote Thomas Jefferson, who had said Indian tribes needed to be "exterminated" — and that "blacks are inferior to the whites."

Or he'd just point out that his new slogan was actually borrowed from one successfully used by President Calvin Coolidge a half-century before: "America must be kept American."

If the reporter said something like "That was then, this is now" — and that Earl Turner now had a responsibility to reject the racism of the past and represent all Americans, not just the white ones — well, Turner would always have a quick answer for that, too. "Let the other Republican candidates say what the media and the special interest groups and minorities want to hear," he'd say. "I'm saying what normal Americans think."

That was another of Earl Turner's favorite language tricks, Danny knew. He'd call his campaign, and the growing number of people who supported it, "normal." That way, he didn't even have to say that anyone who opposed him was "abnormal." They already knew it. They felt it, too — Danny observed that the Turner campaign rallies had started to acquire a Klansmen's night-rally feel to them. All that was missing were torches, pitchforks, and nooses.

Danny slouched in his seat in the Jeep, watching Turner and his mysterious friend Ben stroll along the sidewalk, the two Secret Service agents not far behind. Turner looked to be in full flight now, gesturing energetically. His dark-suited friend was nodding away. Danny wondered how much this Ben was worth. If the shiny new limo parked in front of the Hilton was his, Danny figured Ben was rich as hell.

The two stopped on the sidewalk. They had apparently reached an agreement, judging by the nodding and gesturing. Then they shook hands and Earl Turner happily patted Ben on the shoulder with his other hand. Turner looked ecstatic.

After a bit more talk, they shook hands again and parted ways. Earl Turner started walking to the Jeep while the Secret Service guys moved toward their black Chevrolet Suburban with the tinted windows. They didn't like Earl Turner wheeling about in a Jeep, Danny knew, with just a kid behind the wheel. But Turner refused their requests to change his ways.

"I'm the people's candidate," he had said to Danny. "I need to be seen *by* the people. I need to be accessible to the people. They don't want to see me cowering behind bulletproof glass."

Turner opened the door to the Jeep and jumped in. He was clearly very happy. "Danny, my boy, let's go get some lobster rolls at the Old Port Tavern!" he said, pulling the door shut. "We need to celebrate! The big buy for the America for Americans campaign is a go!"

Danny nodded and pointed the Jeep toward Moulton Street in the Old Port.

CHAPTER 12

They had been talking for a while.

"Fuck, man, it's bad. It's so bad."

"I'm sorry."

"It's okay. It's just … fuck, they are so fucking evil."

"That bad? They're not faking it?"

"Some of them, maybe. But not all of them. Not the ones at the top."

"I'm sorry, man. You know …"

"I know, I know. Gotta go."

Click.

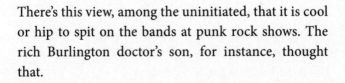

There's this view, among the uninitiated, that it is cool or hip to spit on the bands at punk rock shows. The rich Burlington doctor's son, for instance, thought that.

But I'm in a punk band, and I'm telling you: if you fucking spit on me, I'm going to beat the shit out of you.

The historical origins of the gobbing-at-punk-shows phenomenon are unclear. I read somewhere that the Damned's drummer, Rat Scabies, started it. He claimed that the Sex Pistols' guitarist, Steve Jones, spat on him at a show, so he spat back. Floods of phlegm ensued. Another article said that the Pistols' Johnny Rotten was the first — he had sinus issues, he claimed, and he needed to spit onstage a lot. His fans copied him, goes the tale.

Anyway, soon enough, gobbing at punk shows was all the rage. In no time at all, bands like the Pistols and the Damned were on the receiving end of steaming geysers of warm spit at punk shows all over the U.K., all the time.

None of the bands liked it, however. Someone spat right into the open mouth of Clash front man Joe Strummer one night, for example, and he got hepatitis. Another punk, Adam Ant, started wearing an eye patch — which actually became part of his ridiculous pirate-punk look — because someone horked a loogie in his eye and he got a nasty case of conjunctivitis. The Banshees' Siouxsie Sioux got both: conjunctivitis and hepatitis.

Anyway, here's a pro tip, punk rockers: It's fucking disgusting.

But still, some people — usually people who aren't punks but who think it's a punk thing to do — spit at the bands and each other.

So there we were, on the first night of the tour. We were playing a close-to-sold-out show at Higher Ground, the best place in Burlington, Vermont, to see a real band. It was near the end of the set, and we were ripping through one of the Hot Nasties' noisier, faster numbers, "I Am a Confused Teenager." That's when the rich doctor's son crawled up onto the stage. We'd been warned about him. He'd sneak into the venue and try and start trouble.

I was singing at that moment and playing my guitar, but I could see he was getting ready to spit on me, point-blank. Before he could, I kicked him in the face.

Naturally.

I didn't do it hard, but hard enough, I guess. The doctor's son flew back into the slam-dancing crowd at the foot of the stage, then he crashed into the concert floor at Burlington's premier rock 'n' roll venue. The security guys, in yellow shirts, looked down at the inert form of the doctor's son — clad in black leather, from head to foot — and then up at me. And then things got *really* crazy.

Cops, punks, yellow-shirted security guys, a dozen straight edge types, a couple skinheads — along with one huge Rasta guy (Bembe), one huge ex-biker (Mike), and one sort-of huge punk rocker (X) — started to mix it up in the middle of Higher Ground's ballroom bar. Never being one to miss out on some good-natured fun, and feeling some speed-induced super-duper powers, I stripped off my Fender Strat and jumped into the melee. The Nasties kept playing, except they switched to an impromptu version of "Gloria," with Sam Shiller adopting the lyrics to suit the occasion:

> *Lemme tell ya about Kurt a bit*
> *He don't take no shit*
> *He don't like your spit*
> *He's six feet and a bit*

Burlington had been the first stop on the Nasties/ Virgins tour and — until the rich doctor's son decided to gob on Yours Truly — everything had been going unusually well. We'd left Portland without incident, we'd done the four-hour drive to Burlington without incident, we'd checked into the Holiday Inn without incident, and the sound check at Higher Ground had gone off without incident, too. For the Hot Nasties and the Punk Rock Virgins, the first day of the tour — which had been dubbed the "Better Off Stiff Tour" by Bembe Smith — had started remarkably well. It was unprecedented, for us.

Higher Ground was this cool venue inside a former movie theater on Williston Road in South Burlington, close to I-89. When we'd pulled in off the Interstate, the club manager had been effusively cheerful and helpful. He got a couple of his staff to help us load in, introduced us to his sound guy, and was about to leave when he stopped.

"Oh, one thing," he said. "There's one guy you need to watch out for. He sometimes sneaks in and gets past the guys at the door and causes some trouble. He's a rich doctor's son."

Right.

At the moment, however, the rich doctor's son was out cold in the middle of the dance floor while a massive brawl raged above and around him. It was hard to tell who was on whose side, or who was winning. I was near X, Bembe, and Mike, naturally, trying to keep troublemakers — the straight edge crew, mostly — from getting near any of the Punk Rock Virgins or the remaining Hot Nasties, still playing their epic-length version of "Gloria." Some of the security guys were battling with some drunk punks, and some drunk punks were fighting with the skinheads. And the cops, about four of them, were standing at the doors to Higher Ground, unsure who was a good guy and who was a bad guy.

Eventually, the Nasties stopped playing "Gloria," and the various combatants stopped fighting. The security guards hauled a couple skinheads toward the cops, who then hauled the skinheads outside.

As all this was going on, the rich doctor's son stirred and got onto his feet. Unsteadily, he made his way toward me. Sensing more trouble, X stepped closer, as did Mike.

The rich doctor's son, blood still flowing from his nose, looked at me, bleary-eyed, then twisted his mouth into what might have been a smile.

"That was fucking awesome, man," he said. "You guys kick ass. Thanks."

And then he turned and walked away.

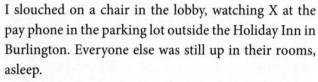

I slouched on a chair in the lobby, watching X at the pay phone in the parking lot outside the Holiday Inn in Burlington. Everyone else was still up in their rooms, asleep.

Speed, however, conspired against getting much shut-eye. So I was up. I sniffed. I scratched.

I wondered why he wasn't using one of the pay phones in the hotel. Weird. Maybe he didn't want to wake up Patti.

Last night, after we loaded up our equipment at Higher Ground, I had taken X aside and asked if we could talk about what had happened at the show. We agreed to meet in the lobby in the morning, before everyone else came downstairs.

His call finished, I watched X lope across the parking lot and into the lobby. He saw me and walked over.

"Hey," I said.

"Hey."

"So, what happened to the solemn promise that there would be no violence at any of the shows?" I asked him, as he sat down across from me. "I thought you said you and Mike and Bembe had it handled?"

X frowned, looking away. I knew I was sounding a bit like a rock 'n' roll diva, but I knew I was also right. Stiff would not hesitate to end the tour if it turned into a circus. And last night was a fucking circus.

"You're right," he said. "Although it probably didn't help that the Hot Nasties' lead singer stripped off his guitar and jumped into the crowd when the fight started."

I couldn't help myself and laughed out loud. Point made. "Okay, okay," I said, hands raised in protest. "Guilty as charged. I shouldn't have done that. And I probably shouldn't have kicked that douchebag in the face. But I don't like to get spit on."

X nodded. "Anyway, you're right. We lost control. I apologize."

I had heard X apologize for stuff before, but it was a pretty rare fucking occurrence, believe me. So I let his words hang in the lobby air for a minute, savoring them. That done, I suggested we go get some of the "food" that was found at the free continental breakfast.

We lined up for Raisin Bran while various suburban moms and dads and kids stared up at the big, scary-looking punk rock guys. They looked at us like we were escaped convicts. As we waited, I made small talk: "So, brother, what was the mystery call you were making out in the parking lot? Didn't want to get overheard, hmmm?"

I was joking, but X looked at me with a flash of ... *something* on his face. It disappeared as quickly as it came. "Patti was asleep, and I didn't want to wake her up," he said after a moment. "Figured I'd take a walk and make some calls."

"Uh-huh," I said, vaguely aware that he seemed to be fibbing. "You like taking walks along the Interstate?"

He didn't answer.

After we finished our cereal and several thimble-sized glasses of orange juice, I looked down at my Mickey Mouse watch. "Shit! Now I'm the one who has to make a call. Be right back, brother."

I headed out to the pay phone X had used and dialed the toll-free, long-distance number I'd memorized. They patched me through to Special Agent Laverty. "Good morning, Kurt," Laverty said. "Quite the night last night. I hope no one got hurt."

"How do you know about that?" I asked, frankly amazed that she was aware of the brawl at Higher Ground. "Were you there?"

"Yes, I was," she said, "but I kept out of sight." She paused. "I had bureau business here, so I decided to come by."

Wow.

"So, are you still here in Burlington?"

"Yes, but I'm leaving soon," she said. "I'm nearby. Do you and your friend have time to meet me?" She meant X.

We agreed to meet at a Denny's just down from the Holiday Inn. Fifteen minutes later, X and I slid into a booth where Special Agent Laverty was already sitting, stirring a cup of coffee. She didn't have a hair out of place. She looked amazing, as usual.

"Good morning," she said, indicating to a Denny's menu. "Can I get you something to eat?"

We declined, saying that we had already eaten. I ordered a coffee, X got a tea. We waited for the waitress to move away.

"What's up?" I asked Laverty, half-expecting to hear that another gay kid or punk kid was murdered for wanting to see the Hot Nasties. "Any … trouble?"

"No reports of anything bad," Laverty said. "And we are certainly paying attention."

"That's good," I said, and X nodded. "So you think the killer wasn't there last night?"

"We don't know," Laverty said, her pretty face impassive. I got the sense that she wasn't being totally candid about something. "Obviously, we're happy that nothing serious happened." She paused. "Except for the brawl, that is."

X looked away and I blushed. Laverty was already one of the few people who could actually leave me a bit tongue-tied.

I stammered a bit. "Yes, well, I probably shouldn't have, uh—"

"Kicked that fellow in the face?" Laverty said, smiling.

"Um, yeah."

"I agree," she said, looking at us like a disapproving parent. "Given what took place in Ottawa and New York, I would suggest, gentlemen, that every effort be made to keep your performances violence free. Obviously."

We finished our drinks and discussed the next stop in the tour, which would be in Montreal. Laverty said it was unlikely that she'd be there. It was Canada, and it would require too much paperwork.

We crossed the border at this little town called Beebe Plain, in Vermont. The main drag was called Canusa Street, and half of it was in America and the other half in Stanstead, Quebec, Canada. Super weird.

Anyway. Our arrival there — the Hot Nasties in the Econoline, the Punk Rock Virgins following in their station wagon — caused no shortage of confusion for the French-speaking Canadian border guards. When we pulled up and stepped out of our vehicles, the border cops acted like some biker-jacket-wearing space aliens had landed on Canusa Street. I heard what sounded like a lot of French swear words: *Câlisse! Sacrament! Tabarnak!*

Admittedly, we were probably not the kind of folks they were used to seeing at their sleepy little border crossing. Decked out in black leather, the X Gang probably looked like we'd kill someone for spare change. Adding to their consternation was Bembe Smith, this giant, dreadlocked Rasta, wearing white shorts and a bright green Burning Spear T-shirt. And the Punk Rock Virgins, too, all in matching army jackets with "PRV" spray-painted across the back, and with wild, spiked, jet-black hair. Leah Yeomanson, meanwhile, was also wearing a T-shirt that read SMASH THE STATE.

"Bonjour, messieurs," Bembe said, switching to what sounded to us like perfect French. "Devons-nous commencer?"

Wow. Bembe spoke French. Who knew?

The border guys stared up at Bembe, mouths agape, and then nodded. "*Oui*," one finally said, pointing to the door to their little office building.

Off they went with Bembe, who had everyone's passports, as well as the other paperwork: contracts with venues in Montreal, Ottawa, and Toronto, addresses for the places where we'd be crashing, a list of all our instruments and gear, and a breakdown of all the merch X sold at the shows — mainly Hot Nasties and Punk Rock Virgins T-shirts, the Nasties' first extended-play single on Stiff Records, and the Virgins' homemade cassette collection, *Feminist as Fuck*.

We waited outside for Bembe, where we got a lot of stares from the locals. Now, when you're on the road with a band, you quickly learn things about yourself and the people you're traveling with. Weird alliances get formed, health inevitably deteriorates, friendships get strained, romances begin and end. And sometimes, bands break up.

None of that stuff had happened yet, but there was no shortage of tension, that's for sure. The knowledge that our pre-tour had maybe resulted in the deaths of three people — Johnny Raindrops, Colleen Tomorrow, and the kid in Ottawa, Nuclear Age — had left us all with no shortage of guilt. It was hard to enjoy ourselves when people who had come to see us were getting, you know, killed.

I needed some speed.

So, as we waited for Bembe, I thought about how the Nasties-Virgins caravan had already formed little groups. There was X and Patti, off in their own ultracool, stoic Punk Rock Super Couple world. There was Mike and Bembe and Sister Betty and Leah Yeomanson, improbably, having a grand old time, despite how totally different they all were — the biker, the Rastafarian, the skinny white punk rock girl, and the skinny Native-American punk rock girl. There was Sam, Eddie, and Luke, of course, sticking as closely together as they had done since Jimmy Cleary had been killed. And then there was me, with my new best friend, Baggie.

I know, I know. I shouldn't have been treating speed like it's a food group. But, when you're on tour like we were, speed was kind of indispensable, you know?

The problem was (a) sleep and (b) the weird hours. On tour, you don't get nearly enough of (a) because of (b). But you need to maintain (b), because the shows are usually pretty late at night, and so (a) suffers. Sleeping in a Ford Econoline — or on the floor of a Holiday Inn, because you don't want to crash in the same bed as Eddie Igglesden, and Sam Shiller and Luke Macdonald had decided to share the other queen-size bed — doesn't work too well.

So, you start looking for a bit of pharmaceutical as-sistance. Some guys do smack, some do coke. Being in a penniless punk rock band, all I could presently afford was speed. It did the trick.

My consumption accordingly started to go up. My weight and mood started to go down. The others started to notice.

While Bembe was still inside talking to the border guards, Sister Betty strolled over to the patch of grass where I was sitting. I'd been watching sedans full of regular folks — Mom, Dad, and 2.5 white kids — get waved through the border crossing without being asked anything. They would stare at me; I would stare back.

Sister Betty sat down beside me.

"Hey, big brother. How's it hangin'?"

"Hangin' long and low, little sister," I said. "Hangin' low."

She laughed, which made me laugh. I looked at her. She wasn't as drop-dead gorgeous as Patti, but she was still lovely. Thousand-watt smile, green eyes, dimpled cheeks.

Betty Kowalchuk, Sister Betty Upchuck, was the Punk Rock Virgins' bassist, Patti's little sister, and probably the glue that held us all together. Patti was like X, sort of: quiet, a bit moody, intense. Betty was like the pre-speed me: louder, upbeat, easygoing. But Betty, I liked to say, was also sort of the patron saint of the lost and the lonely. She took in strays, of all human and animal varieties. She volunteered for stuff, helping out little old ladies at bake sales and veterans in fundraising drives. And she was the one who could always keep the X Gang's factions in a state of balance and harmony.

I thought she probably had a promising career ahead of her in the U.S. diplomatic corps.

Like everyone else, Betty had been observing me with growing concern — and maybe even alarm. With the exception of X, most of us had always done the same drugs everyone else did — weed, mushrooms, the occasional tab of acid. But the speed thing was new, and Sister Betty was concerned. Unlike X, however, she had a way of talking to me about it that didn't make me feel defensive and angry.

"So," she said, trying to sound casual, and not entirely succeeding. "You look like you've lost some more weight, there, big brother."

I shrugged. "Corporate Deathburger," I said, meaning McDonald's. "Junk food doesn't agree with my constitution. I'm a delicate punk rock flower, remember?"

Sister Betty didn't smile. "It's not McDonald's that's making you lose weight, baby," she said, serious. "It's something else."

I winced. "Oh, you're not going to give me a lecture like *him*, are you?" I said, gesturing in the direction of Patti and X, both of whom were leaning against the Punk Rock Virgins' station wagon, talking in low tones. We watched them. X said something to Patti that we couldn't hear, and then he disappeared into the Canadian border guard hut.

"No," Betty said, shrugging. "No, I'm not going to lecture you. It wouldn't work, anyway." She paused. "I'd just like you to cool it a bit, you know?"

She didn't want to annoy me, but she was annoying me, a bit. The speed — a line or two of which I'd done before we left Burlington — did sometimes give me a less-sunny-than-usual disposition, I admit.

"Look, I'm fine," I said. "There's no fucking problem.

Everything's fine, okay? Besides, from what I've seen, the only people causing us trouble on this tour are those fucking straight edge fanatics, you know? The ones who, like X, have sworn *off* drugs …"

I stopped. X was walking straight toward the patch of grass where Sister Betty and me were sitting. Quickly.

"Uh-oh," Sister Betty said, watching X.

Uh-oh is right.

He stopped and stood over us, his face dark. "Bembe is doing his best to delay them, but the customs guys are demanding a search of all of our bags. They are going to be coming outside any minute."

"Fuck," I said.

"Betty, you need to go inside and help Bembe delay them," X said, glaring at me. "Kurt, there is a men's bathroom out back. You need to get to your bag, right now, get whatever is in there, and flush it down the fucking toilet. Do you understand me?"

"X, look—"

"Shut up, Kurt." His eyes were black. "Just do it."

I blinked. It felt like he had slapped my face.

My eyes stinging, I scrambled to my feet and quickly went over to the Econoline. I could feel everyone watching me as I went. Reaching for the door handle, I saw that my hands were shaking.

CHAPTER 13

The strategy, if that is what it could be called, was working. Card-carrying Republicans were flocking to his campaign. Soon enough, so was a senator from Kentucky, then some congressmen from Florida and Michigan and Wisconsin.

Earl Turner was winning.

He wasn't burning any crosses at his well-attended campaign rallies, but he could have, and no Republicans would have cared. The junior representative from Maine had gone full-bore racist, and the Grand Old Party of Abe Lincoln was eating it up. "America for Americans! America for Americans!" the mob chanted at his rallies. Turner would stalk the stage, urging them on, big fist pumping the venomous air.

The media, and official Washington, were flummoxed. They didn't get it. No mainstream party candidate had openly peddled prejudice like this for generations. How could it possibly be working? On the day in New Hampshire when Turner declared that he would hold refugees at detention centers — so they could be vetted and checked for "communicable diseases and links to terrorist groups," he told the cheering crowd in Concord — the media went bananas.

"Earl Turner has gone too far this time," the serious-sounding pundits said on PBS political panels. "With his promise to place refugees in Nazi-style concentration camps, Turner has dealt a death blow to his presidential hopes," they'd say.

"This is a nation built by refugees and immigrants," the New York Times editorialized. "Mr. Turner himself is the descendant of immigrants from Great Britain. Under his announced policy, Mr. Turner's great-great-grandparents would have been barred entry into the very country he seeks to lead. Shame on him."

And so on and so on. The press called Turner a bigot and a white supremacist and everything in between. But to most Republicans, it didn't matter. The media didn't understand that the Republican faithful weren't gravitating toward the Earl Turner campaign despite his racism — they were supporting him because of it.

In the days after the Concord rally, Danny O'Heran would carry around a copy of the New York Times in an oversized manila envelope. At the appropriate moment in Turner's speech, Danny would extract the newspaper from the envelope and walk across the stage to hand it to him.

Turner would hold up the paper and his faithful would boo. Then he'd say: "Thank you, Danny. I want you to stay and listen to this." And Danny — along with the crowd, wherever it was they were that day — would stand there and listen, fulfilling his assigned role in Turner's little stage play.

Turner would quote the editorial, pausing to let the mob boo and call out. When he'd get to the end, to the part about shame, he'd hand the paper back to Danny, who would quickly move offstage.

"Shame?" Earl Turner would say, big hands up in the air, as if in surrender. "Shame? SHAME?"

The crowd would go wild.

"Shame? I don't care what the pointy-headed intellectuals and elites at the *New York Times* have to say about me," he'd say, voice booming. "But they're talking about *you*, too, my friends. They're talking about you — they're saying you should be ashamed!"

Boos, catcalls. Chanting.

"Do you feel ashamed?" Turner would holler, and the crowd would start yelling, "NO! NO! NO!"

"Should you feel shame for wanting to take back America?"

"NO! NO! NO! NO!"

"Should anyone feel shame for wanting to get rid of a gangster from Jamaica, or a heroin dealer from Vietnam, or some God-hating punk, or some pervert from Pakistan?" he'd say. "I don't feel shame for wanting that! Do you feel shame for wanting that?"

"NO! NO! NO! NO! NO!"

And Earl Turner would smile, fist pumping in the air. Danny O'Heran, meanwhile, would watch from the sidelines. The crowds were getting bigger, and they were getting a lot angrier, too.

Earl Turner was winning.

CHAPTER 14

Eager to change the subject from the baggie incident — and not super enthusiastic about what X was going to say to me when he got me alone — I'd picked up a day-old copy of the *New York Times* at the little convenience store in this tiny placed called Georgeville, Quebec. After getting across the border, we'd stopped there to get some lunch.

"Holy shit," I said to no one in particular, staring at the newspaper's front page. "Holy fuck."

We'd made it across the border, yes. As X had directed, I'd gotten my Doc Martens out of my bag and hustled to the washroom, located at the back of the customs checkpoint. Door locked behind me, I fished the sock out of the boot, extracted the baggie full of speed, and quickly flushed the white powder down the toilet. I had to flush a couple times. There was a lot of it.

I was rinsing out the baggie with water at the sink when one of the Canadian border guys started knocking on the door. "*Monsieur*?" I could hear him say. "*Est-ce que ça vas?*"

I think he was asking if I was okay. All traces of the speed now flushed away, I stepped out of the can, holding the Docs in one hand, and giving the French-speaking border cop a friendly wave with the other. "*Bonjour!*" I said, then hustled back to the rest of the X Gang.

Knowing the journey with the guys in the Econoline would now be a bit frosty, I hitched a ride with the Punk Rock Virgins in their cramped station wagon. Half an hour down the road in rural Quebec, both ve-hicles pulled over in Georgeville, which looked like a quaint New England hamlet, except all the signs were in French.

The locals, who all resembled extras in a Ralph Lauren Polo photo shoot, all stared at us like we were circus freaks.

Just like home!

Anyway. I was getting a submarine sandwich — the boy wearing the Metro Prep T-shirt at the cash had called it a *baguette*, I think — when I spotted the *New York Times*. I quickly forgot about the sandwich, bought the newspaper, and walked out front, where Patti and X were talking with Sister Betty. Without saying anything, I handed them the newspaper.

"Holy shit," Sister Betty said.

"Oh my God." Patti looked stunned.

X said nothing, inscrutable as always. The Hot Nasties and Leah walked over to see what the fuss was about.

There, on the front page of the fucking *New York Times*, was a photo of Earl Turner at a podium in Upstate New York, holding up a copy of what looked like *another* edition of the *New York Times*. He seemed to be reading from it.

And there, just a few feet away, in a dark suit and tie, hands in pockets, was a young man.

Danny O'Heran.

CHAPTER 15

The New York Police Department's Fifth Precinct was on Elizabeth Street, just off Canal and a few blocks south of CBGB. The precinct was housed in a four-story old brownstone, wedged between a bunch of bodegas and dry cleaners run by Chinese families. It was crowded, dirty, and run-down, just like the neighborhood it served. In 1980, the Fifth Precinct was no dream assignment for any New York City cop.

Detective Pete Schenk's office basically wasn't one. It was a banged-up metal desk in the middle of Homicide's space, up on the fourth floor. When FBI special agent Theresa Laverty asked Schenk where they could talk in private, Schenk grunted and pointed at an old wooden chair beside his desk.

"Let's go somewhere a bit quieter," she said. "It's lunchtime, and I know a place not too far from here … and it's actually relevant to what we're gonna discuss."

Schenk shrugged and followed her out.

To Laverty, it took what seemed forever to find a parking spot for Schenk's rusty old Buick Skylark. But, spot secured, they finally stepped into Fanelli's, just before the lunchtime rush.

The bartender, an old guy who was weary and wary all at once, squinted at them. "Want food or drink?"

"Both," Laverty said.

"Then over there." The bartender indicated a row of small tables covered by red-and-white checkered cloths.

Fanelli's had been at the corner of Prince and Mercer in SoHo for more than a century, Laverty told Schenk. It was a bar, first and foremost, but it also served food. Their burgers, she said, were considered the best — and most affordable — in the upscale fashion district west of Broadway.

Schenk looked around. "This isn't the kind of place I figured you'd know about, Laverty," he said, sounding amused. "This looks like the kind of place *I'd* know!"

They sat at one of the tiny tables, one that looked out onto the cobblestone on Mercer. Schenk grinned. "I'm impressed. I've worked a few blocks away from here for years, and I didn't even know this place existed. You work way down in Fort Myers, and you do?"

Laverty smiled and waved a hand at what she was wearing — at the moment, a linen jacket and a silk blouse. "I don't have a dog, I don't have a cat, and you know I certainly don't have a husband," Laverty said to Schenk. "My weakness is fashion. I know all the best places to get Roger Vivier stilettos, anywhere in North America. This neighborhood has haute couture."

Schenk didn't know what or who Roger Vivier or haute couture was, so he shrugged and started examining Fanelli's menu. "So, why talk here, Laverty?" he said. "I know my office ain't grand, but this place ain't much better."

"Maybe," Laverty said, scanning Fanelli's menu for a salad, or salad equivalent. "But this place is actually kind of relevant. Look around, but try not to be too obvious about it. There will be a test."

Fanelli's main door was at the corner of the bar, opening onto where Prince and Mercer Streets meet. Eight tiny tables were positioned parallel to the bar, at which two regulars were presently nursing beers. There was dark wood everywhere. Tin roof, painted yellow. Cracked, octagonal tiles on the floor in a *fleur-de-lis* pattern. The can was beside where the bar ended, under an old sign that said LADIES AND GENTS FITTING ROOM. Beyond that, there was a room of some sort, with a dark curtain drawn across the opening.

On the wall behind Laverty, the main feature of the place: dozens and dozens of framed photographs of boxers. Many of the photos were faded now, and the glass was cracked and dirty. But they were of some of the greatest boxers to ever live — and some he hadn't even heard of. Muhammad Ali, Paul Berlenbach, Mickey Walker, Mike McTigue, Stanley Ketchel, and more. Knowing a bit about what old guys like to call the sweet science, Schenk looked at the boxers' faces admiringly. "Jesus, there are some great ones up there," he said, big arms crossed. "Did fighters use to hang out here or something?"

"Not really," Laverty said, not looking up. "Tommy used to box. He put them up."

"Who's Tommy?"

Laverty jerked a manicured thumb at the hulking figure of the bartender, who was doing his best to ignore them. "The guy behind the bar," she said. "He's got an interesting story to tell."

CHAPTER 16

Earl Turner's ad campaign hit with the force of a hurricane. It pulverized the Republican competition. It reduced them to red, white, and blue confetti.

In the primary states where they were competitive, Turner's staid establishment opponents had been putting the usual stuff on air: images of amber waves of grain and purple mountain majesties, and the candidate riding a horse and wearing a cowboy hat. Or grainy images of America at war — the Second World War, Korea, Vietnam — and the candidate modestly recounting how he got his Purple Heart. Or the candidate at home, at church, on Capitol Hill, fighting for Middle America and all that was right and good. Squared jaw, clenched fist, stirring musical track. The usual conservative bullshit, in other words.

Earl Turner, being a junior congressman from a state many Americans wouldn't be able to locate on a map, couldn't compete with all of that. He didn't have a long

CV like his opponents did. So, aided and abetted by his pollster, Derwin Hailey, Turner crafted thirty- and sixty-second spots, as they are called, that had all the subtlety of a hand grenade in a bowl of porridge. They were racist rockets, aimed right at Middle America's middle.

In one ad, the camera surveyed a dirty, garbage-strewn city street. Broken-down cars were seen here and there and burned-out homes loomed in the background like ominous apparitions recalling better times. On the sidewalk, slightly out of focus, a group of young black men smoked cigarettes and conspicuously passed little bags — presumably filled with drugs — back and forth. They glared at the camera. Doom-and-gloom music played.

Then Earl Turner's voice: "America is broken. America is lost. America, once the greatest nation on earth, is no longer. Its streets are filled with drug dealers and pimps and thieves and killers from other cultures, from other countries. They are destroying our way of life."

Pause.

The screen then cut away to Turner's handsome face, looking earnest, looking concerned. "My name is Earl Turner. I say we need to take back our country. Take back our streets. Take back our culture. We need to do what's *right* — we need an America for Americans. I hope you'll join me in our crusade."

It wasn't a "campaign" anymore. It was a "crusade." Every one of Turner's ads ended that way — with him facing the camera, shirt open a bit, tie loosened, his features radiating an earnest, pained look. There was one targeting blacks, one targeting Hispanics and Latinos, one that went after Asians, and one that slimed gays, implying that we carried communicable diseases and molested children. For certain media markets, there was even one about capital punishment for drug dealers, all of whom looked like they were members of punk rock bands.

Danny O'Heran had helped Turner and Hailey put that one together.

One particularly controversial ad showed a bunch of fat, balding men with big noses sitting around a boardroom table that had been stacked high with money. The men were all dripping with jewelry, smoking fat cigars, and laughing uproariously. A couple of them seemed to be wearing yarmulkes.

That one was called the "international bankers" ad, and it ended with Earl Turner pledging to imprison the "foreign bankers who have stolen away the livelihoods of God-fearing Christians whose hard work has made America great, from the family farms to the factories."

That ad, which caused a firestorm of controversy, didn't use the word *Jew*, but it didn't need to. Everyone knew who Earl Turner was talking about. Derwin Hailey's polls had found that a surprising number of Republicans believed that Jews were behind the twin evils of godless satanic communism and unsupervised Wall Street capitalism, and that they had killed Jesus to boot. So the Turner campaign put together their commercial targeting Jews, and it caused no end of outrage at the *New York Times* and in Hollywood, just as Earl Turner had hoped.

Some TV channels, in some urban media markets, refused to run Turner's ads, correctly noting that the Earl Turner ads were openly racist and anti-Semitic. This, too, was what Earl Turner and Derwin Hailey had predicted would happen, and they were ready for it when it did.

The Turner campaign immediately published ads in right-wing newspapers — and they held raucous press conferences, with Earl Turner front and center — denouncing the owners of the TV channels as censorious "elites, atheists, and foreigners" who were trampling on the First Amendment to the U.S. Constitution, the part that guaranteed freedom of speech.

In his ads and in his press conferences, Turner would call for boycotts of the stations and their advertisers — and his legions of followers would comply. In a day or two, then, most of the TV channels would capitulate. They'd start running the Turner campaign's "America for Americans" ads.

No one could mistake "the message" — as Derwin Hailey put it — that wound through any of the Turner ads like a big slippery snake. They were a naked appeal to bigotry and hate. They were disgusting and horrible and wrong. And they were *highly effective.*

Turner's "America for Americans" ads worked for two reasons. One, they had "given voice to what white

Americans felt but were afraid to say," Derwin Hailey told a rapt senior campaign staff at the Turner campaign's Portland headquarters one night, as they pored through the latest internal polls. In other words, quite a few older, white men with high school educations — "the white working class," Hailey called them — had found a champion in Earl Turner.

"Two," Hailey continued, "they want their old lives back. They want things like they used to be. They don't like technological change, they don't like cultural change, they don't like all of the stuff that they feel has been imposed on them — civil rights, feminism, pacifism, being careful about saying the correct thing, all of that crap. They are nostalgic for the good old days, when they felt they still ran America. And Earl Turner is the only guy who wants to give it to them."

But there was probably another reason why the ads were working, Hailey said, as the senior staff listened, bewitched — and as Danny O'Heran stood again by the conference room door, looking bored.

"And that reason can be summed up in one word: *repetition*," he said. "Our fucking ads are fucking everywhere."

And they were. Every channel, at every hour, on just about every network. Hailey bragged that Earl Turner's little campaign had embarked on "one of the biggest media buys in the history of the Republican primaries." Turner's ads were on everyone's mind, because everyone had seen them, multiple times. Repetition, simplicity, and volume work, Hailey said.

Hailey went on about "gross-rating points" and "cost per point" and "designated market area" and something he called "dayparts," but Danny — and not a few of the others — found it all confusing. The bottom line was that the budget for Turner's "America for Americans" spots was essentially *bottomless*. That was something Danny, and everyone at the meeting, understood quite well. Money bought exposure, and the Turner campaign suddenly and inexplicably had more money than it could spend.

"Our ads are winning us support because Republicans like our message," Hailey concluded. "That's obvious. But they are working because they have been seen so many times, the message has literally embedded itself in the minds of millions of angry, isolated, white American guys who yearn for yesterday." He paused, then ended with a flourish: "And those angry, isolated white Americans are helping us win this thing, folks."

There was silence, and then there was a knock on the conference room door. A volunteer timidly stuck her head inside and signaled to the two press assistants, Daisy Something and Stacey Something — the ones that Danny now knew Earl Turner was fucking, sometimes simultaneously.

"Um, Stacey or Daisy," said the volunteer, looking at a pink message slip with URGENT written on it, "there's a Ron McLeod from Associated Press on the line, and he says he has urgent questions about the ad campaign budget, and about someone called Ben."

Derwin Hailey turned white — as white as a Klansman's sheet — and he dashed out of the conference room.

CHAPTER 17

When I came downstairs at the McGill University student residence on Sherbrooke Street, I found X on a pay phone. Again. He hung up when he saw me.

Now we stood in the lobby, staring up at the black-and-white TV they had hung above the registration desk.

The Canadian TV network was doing a story about Earl Turner's campaign ads, and broadcasting bits and pieces from them. They showed a clip from the one about the drug trade. All of the actors in it were dressed up like cartoon punk rockers, slouching near an elementary school playground, openly passing drugs to kids who looked to be ten or eleven. Earl Turner's voice came on, steeped with worry: "These punks and drug pushers are preying on our kids. They are getting them hooked on drugs and anti-Christian lifestyles."

The ad cut to a brief shot of the drug dealers now in a bar somewhere, a really bad punk-like band playing onstage, and people shooting up right beside it.

*Because, you know, all of us always mainline drugs
right out in the open, when our bands are playing onstage.*

Earl Turner continued: "These punks and thugs hate
God, hate America, and hate normal people like you and
me. When I become president, I will send these punks
and creeps to jail, and, when deserved, the electric chair."

*Well, there you go. He's going to kill us. Full points for
clarity, Earl.*

The screen cut away to the surprised-looking
Canadian news reporter, standing near the White
House. She concluded by saying that Earl Turner's ads
have become the talk of the Republican primary race.
"They may be controversial," she said in her Canadian
accent, "but the ads are reaching the Republican faithful. Earl Turner is surging toward the front of the pack
in the race to become his party's presidential nominee."
She signed off.

"Jesus fucking Christ!" I said to X, my voice low.
"How could Danny have anything to do with such a pile
of racist fucking lies?" I sniffed.

X just shrugged.

"Anyone from Maine knows what Earl Turner is," he
said, unfazed. "He's always been a racist liar."

"Yeah, but …" I was, uncharacteristically, at a loss for
words. "I just can't believe Danny would have anything
to do with that piece of shit! Doesn't this *bug* you, man?"

X shrugged again. "Sure."

I felt a flash of irritation. "Well," I said, "you don't
seem like it does."

X said nothing.

We were staying in a student residence building because — as Bembe had explained to us when we pulled up out front — rooms were more readily available during the summer months, and the place was cheaper than staying at a hotel. Among the Hot Nasties and the Punk Rock Virgins, there was some skepticism about that, but we all agreed that the student residence was a step up from sharing a floor at a youth hostel — which is how we used to do things, before the Nasties got signed to Stiff Records. My room, as it turned out, even had a nice view of the big cross that had been planted on Mount Royal, the mountain at the center of Montreal.

I was mad. Not so much about the secretive pay phone calls: X is *always* secretive. I was pissed off about Danny getting involved with a fucking fascist's political campaign — and I was a bit pissed off that my best friend, the anti-racist fighter X, wasn't as pissed off as I was.

But I said nothing. We waited in silence.

The elevator door slid open, and Patti and Sister Betty Upchuck stepped out. "Who's hungry?" Betty said. "I heard there's this great deli a five-minute walk away — Ben's or something like that."

We had a few hours until load-in at Les Foufounes Électriques, the punk club where we'd be playing. Having given up on getting X to be as outraged as me, I agreed, and the four of us set off for Ben's. We walked along Sherbrooke Street toward Peel Street, drawing zero attention as we went. This, I found highly unusual.

Here's why. My hair was spiked and dyed blond; Patti
and Betty had jet-black hair, also spiked, and were wearing ripped white T-shirts (Slits and X-Ray Spex, respec-
tively), skin-tight jeans, and bondage pants. Meanwhile,
X and I were in our biker jackets, over suitably edgy
T-shirts (mine was bright yellow and the cover of the
Buzzcock's "Orgasm Addict" single, which featured a
naked woman with an iron where her head should be,
while X's was homemade and featured Joe Strummer's
immortal words, I'M SO BORED WITH THE USA, in
big block letters).

We kind of stood out in the crowd.

Patti noticed it, too. She said, "Hey guys, no one is
staring at us."

"They don't give a rat's ass, unlike American subur-
banites slowing down to gawk at us," I said.

"I *like* Montreal." Sister Betty beamed. "It's laid-back.
It's *nice* to punks."

Ben's was as good as Betty had heard. After we'd finished these mile-high smoked meat sandwiches — along
with potato latkes and coleslaw — we settled back. Patti,
Sister Betty, and me had beers, something called Labatt
50, and X was drinking a Cherry Coke.

"That was fucking awesome," I said. "Why don't we
have a Jewish deli like this in Portland?"

"Well, Earl Turner isn't making Portland very hospit-
able for Jews these days," Patti said.

"Or Maine. Or the U.S. Or for blacks or Hispanics or
any other minority, basically," I said.

There was quiet. We drank our drinks and watched the white-shirted Ben's waiters ferrying food around. I simmered.

"This Danny shit," I said, finally. "I just can't deal with it. I just don't understand it. Front page of the fucking *New York Times* — our friend!"

"Yeah," Patti said, sullen. "Our friend, the actual right-hand man to a fucking Nazi."

Sister Betty looked around. "Have any of you guys tried to talk to Danny? Have you tried calling him?"

"I called his folks' place, but they're ultra-religious nutcases, as you guys know," Patti said. "They wouldn't let me talk to him and hung up on me."

"Same thing happened to me," I said. "Although Danny picked up once. I'd barely gotten six words out, and then he mumbled that he couldn't talk to me and hung up."

Sister Betty looked at X. "Have you talked to him, X?"

X kind of shrugged, but said nothing.

Weird. Fucking weird.

X looked up at the clock on Ben's wall, over by the cash register. "It's getting late," he said. "We need to get to the gig."

Les Foufounes Électriques was on the Eastern part of St. Catherine Street, which is the main drag in downtown Montreal. Les Foufounes Électriques was a bar, basically, with red lights reflecting off everything, weirdo art hanging on the brick walls, some standard-issue bar tables and chairs, a patio up on the roof, and a can that rivaled CBGB for graffiti and grime.

The owners hadn't turned on the air conditioning yet to save money. So the place was as hot as the Ninth Circle of Punk Hell when we got there.

Ten minutes after we arrived, however, Bembe and Mike discovered that various things we'd need for the gig — Sam's two guitars, Eddie's snare drum, and a milk carton full of the Shure microphones shared by the Hot Nasties and the Punk Rock Virgins — had somehow been left back at McGill's student residence. So X and Mike asked me to watch their biker jackets, and they left with Bembe to go get our stuff. I said I'd stay put and watch over the equipment that was there and the merch.

The Virgins, meanwhile, took off to explore the vintage shops on St. Catherine Street, and the rest of the Nasties went backstage to work on a new tune Luke had written called "Fashion Show":

> *Hey all you punks, come on down*
> *To the biggest joke in town*
> *The Nasties are playing somewhere tonight*
> *Maybe if you're lucky, you can start a fight*

> *Narrow ties, bottles to throw*
> *Welcome to the fashion show*

Lots of fights, whaddya know?
Welcome to the fashion show

It was an ironic song, I guess, because it had this pop-punky feel to it, with Sam doing a little reggae riff thing while I spit the words out, sounding as sarcastic and as caustic as I possibly could. But the words, written by Luke and me, reflected our growing disenchantment with what was happening to our beloved punk scene. The straight edge bastards, in particular, had made shows a lot more violent and more dangerous than ever before.

And were we getting a little cynical about the whole punk thing? Yes, you could say that. To Luke and me — not so much to Sam and Eddie — punk was, in fact, perilously close to getting swallowed up by the corporate rock 'n' roll machine monster. This was a problem, 'cause we had gotten into punk rock to *destroy* the corporate rock 'n' roll machine monster, you know?

We wanted to see Fleetwood Mac and the Eagles and Rod Stewart beheaded in the public square. We wanted the Strolling Bones and Dead Zeppelin to be exiled to an old folks' home. And we liked the fact that punk rock had started out as this private little club for freaks and geeks, you know?

For punk purists — and X and me, in particular, were the resident punk purists — popularity was a curse. It was an indication you were doing something *wrong*, in fact. But, more and more, punk combos that nobody had ever heard of were getting signed to major labels for tons of dough. Hollywood stars were spiking their hair and wearing safety pins on their designer clothes. And the kinds of jocks who used to beat us up at PAHS and PHS were coming to our shows and pretending they loved punk rock. And us.

It was enough to make you puke.

Admittedly, being as, um, reliant on diet pills as I was, my perspective could have been a bit off. If I wasn't wired, I was cranky. And, at that moment, I wasn't wired. Ipso facto, I was cranky.

I looked around. I sniffed. I itched. In no time at all, I was also fucking bored. After sorting through our merch, and checking and rechecking our equipment, I had absolutely nothing to do. So I sat down on the stage, beside X's and Mike's jackets. And then I saw a bit of white in the pocket of X's Schott Perfecto, the one he'd taken off because it was too fucking hot at Les Foufounes Électriques.

I looked around. No one was there. Just me. So I reached into X's pocket and plucked out the sheet of paper, which turned out to be two pieces of paper.

They contained his distinctive script: half printing, half writing, double-spaced. At the top, he had written: IS THERE A FUTURE PUNK CAN CHANGE?

I read on:

> Yes. Yes yes yes!
>
> In my case — in the case of my friends and in the case of punks everywhere — punk is not merely music. It is a way of thinking, one

that urged us to take action (like Joe Strummer does) and not just give up on the future (like Sid Vicious did). By demonstrating that anger is energy and that we have the power to do just about anything ourselves, punk is like a cosmic collision that creates a noisy, colorful, alternative universe crammed with new bands, new politics, new art, new poetry, new ways of being oneself. It's stupid to regard punk as just a genre of rock 'n' roll, or some peculiar new approach to fashion.

It has always been more than that. How so?

Okay, listen: Imagine that you're sixteen again (just like the Buzzcocks' song), and you're getting beaten up by jocks at school because you look a little different, or you talk different, or you're gay, or you wear funny clothes, or you aren't very athletic. Or you're being hassled by your teachers because you're not like the other kids and you've got a bit of a rebellious streak. Or you're being pushed around by some kids because you don't want to try drugs or because you like to read books.

Or imagine that your dad left you all a long time ago or that someone at home is pushing you around when they get drunk, or — in the night, when they think no one is looking — someone who is supposed to love you is running their hands all over you. And that you are only sixteen years old.

Or imagine that, like a lot of sixteen-year-olds, you have yet to develop the capacity to be unaffected, or uncaring, about television footage of thousands of children literally starving to death. Or that you still pay attention, and you still cry, when you hear about someone who is weak and alone being hurt by someone who is rich and powerful. Or that you have a rage — a wordless, black rage — building up inside of you about all of this and none of this, and that you cannot imagine that life could ever have any meaning, anywhere, anytime. Or imagine that you cannot conceive that God can exist in a world that is so fucking cruel and bleak and evil.

Just listen and just imagine living through any of that. Because, for a lot of sixteen year olds, they don't have to bother imagining a life like that. It's their life already. That's why punk was invented, and why it will never die.

Punk takes a young person's anger and makes them do something, and feel something, and be someone. It makes a kid feel that he or she actually can shape the future — and, sometimes, it helps them to actually do it. It makes those unlivable parts livable again. It gives hope. It sings.

Close your eyes and slip into that dark, crowded, sweaty, noisy little nightclub and listen to the punk sound, the three-chord sound of fury's hour. And, as you stand against the wall at the

back — or as you dance the bad stuff away, right
down in the front — know that this is the sound
that punk makes, now and tomorrow and forever:
YES.

I blinked I reread it. I marveled. X has *defined* punk
rock. I paused and thought to myself: *How do I get back
to that world?*

YES.

I could hear the Nasties coming back toward the
stage, so I quickly folded up X's essay and tucked it back
in his jacket pocket. I nodded to the guys, who were
chattering about the new song. I didn't tell them what
I'd read, naturally.

But X's words pinballed through my head all night,
even after the Hot Nasties had played to a wild, sellout
crowd. I couldn't stop thinking about what he had written.

And these questions, too: *Why don't I feel that way
anymore? In fact, why don't I feel anything at all?*

CHAPTER 18

They were all in the boardroom at the Turner campaign headquarters in Portland. Present were Earl Turner, a bored Danny O'Heran, one of the press secretaries — Daisy Something or Stacey Something, Danny could never be bothered to remember who was who — and a serious-looking reporter from the *New York Times*. Turner had been trying to charm the reporter, but she refused to be charmed. She did not like Earl Turner, and it showed. She'd come to Portland to destroy Turner's campaign, having told her colleagues back in New York that she was the Nazi hunter, and Earl Turner was the Nazi.

The reporter frowned. "So, Mr. Turner, you do not dispute that you personally approved your anti-Semitic and racist campaign ads?"

Turner beamed at her beatifically. "You shouldn't call them anti-Semitic or racist," he said. "But you should call me Earl." He flashed a radiant smile.

The reporter pressed on: "Mr. Turner, your ads have been characterized as anti-Semitic by the Anti-Defamation League of B'nai B'rith and racist by the NAACP. There is no dispute that your ads are—"

Interrupting her, Turner pointed at the full cup of coffee that had earlier been offered to the reporter. "Would you like my girls to refresh that for you? I think it's getting cold," he said, smiling.

The reporter was irritated. "No, thank you," she said. "It's fine. I'd like you to answer my question, please, Mr. Turner. The *Times* is publishing a major profile on you and your campaign, whether you participate or not."

Earl Turner shrugged. "Well, as I told you, I don't really understand why the big old *New York Times* would be interested in us, way up in the little state of Maine," he paused and grinned. "I mean, your readers aren't going to vote for me, and my voters don't read your newspaper, so I don't really understand the attraction, Miss …"

The reporter clicked her ballpoint pen repeatedly. She was pissed. "*Ms.*," she snarled. "Ms. Goldberg. *M.-S.* And, as I explained to you at the outset, your campaign has propelled you to the front of the Republican pack because of, not despite, your obvious racism and anti-Semitism and misogyny. That is why I am here."

Turner eased back in his chair and linked his big hands behind his big head. "Well, sure," he said. "And we are delighted that you are here, aren't we, Danny?"

Danny nodded, mute.

Turner continued. "But I have to say, Mizz *Gold*berg …" He emphasized to deliberately annoy the reporter. It was working.

"We aren't racist or any other 'ist' at all. We are just regular, normal white folks, and we are proud Americans. Black folks have black pride, and homosexuals have *homo*-pride, so why can't we have white pride out here in the countryside?"

Looking triumphant, the reporter was now scribbling furiously in her official *New York Times* notepad. "White pride," she snapped. "Isn't that a phrase first popularized by the Ku Klux Klan and neo-Nazi groups? Aren't you just appropriating their lexicon to get their support?"

Turner was completely unfazed. "I don't know anything about the Klan or any of those groups," he said. "But if they want to vote for me, I'll take their vote. I need every vote I can get."

The reporter kept up her note-taking, apparently convinced that she was still the Nazi hunter, and the Nazi was now in her sights. "So you won't denounce the Klan or the neo-Nazis, Mr. Turner?" she asked. "You'll take their support?"

Earl Turner waved his hands like he was conducting an invisible symphony. "Oh, I think there has been way too much denouncing in this country already," he said cheerfully. "Way too much denouncing and demeaning and defaming … of the people who built this country into the greatest country in the world."

"You mean white people, don't you?"

Turner, Danny could see, was still conducting the invisible symphony. He also could see that the reporter was unaware that she was being played like a fiddle. "Well, of course," he said. "When the pilgrims arrived at Plymouth Rock, the Indians were living in caves and cannibalizing each other and shooting bows and arrows. It was our European Christian ancestors who created modern America."

And here, he smiled, looking straight at Ms. Goldberg of the *New York Times*. "Well, *my* ancestors, anyway," he said, his eyes like ice. "Perhaps there weren't any Goldbergs on those pilgrim ships."

She looked completely shocked. "Mr. Turner! Are you actually saying Jewish Americans and Native Americans didn't help to build America …?" Her voice trailed off. She looked like she might cry.

Turner continued, as if instructing a misguided pupil. "Mizz *Gold*berg, I'm not putting anyone down," he drawled. "I'm just saying everyone knows who built America. It was God, and it was us."

"By *us*, you mean white Christian people," she protested, sounding defeated. She looked like she was going to be sick.

Turner came back to life. "That's right! Now you've got it." He beamed.

"And you don't see that as the purest expression of bigotry?" she asked, quieter, now.

Earl Turner smiled broadly. "Well, up here in Maine,

we don't think it's bigoted to tell the truth. It's just telling the truth."

The reporter looked stunned. She was speechless. "I don't know ..."

Earl Turner's smile disappeared. He leaned in close, so that she could feel his minty breath on her face. "Mizz *Gold*berg, there are two Americas," he said, almost hissing. "You live in one down there in New York City, which has the highest rates of crime and poverty and drug addiction in the nation. You've got race riots and drug deals out in the open on the street, and you've got corrupt politicians and minority lobbyists demanding payoffs. You've got garbage on every street. You've got perversity and destruction. That's what you've got, in your America. And you've been running things for a while."

He paused, then looked back at her. "But up here, in the other America, we don't have any of those things. So we think it's fair that we get to run things for a while, you know? We think we'd do a better job than, say, the *Gold*bergs have done."

The reporter was slumped forward a bit, now. She didn't say anything.

Turner, meanwhile, leaned back, smiling again. He pointed at the reporter's coffee cup.

"Danny, could you get Mizz *Gold*berg a fresh cup?" he said. "I think she takes it black."

He paused. He grinned.

"I'll *bet* she likes it *black*."

CHAPTER 19

We were in the lobby of the McGill University residence, the morning after the gig — a successful one because no one in attendance had been murdered, at least as far as those of us in the Hot Nasties and the Punk Rock Virgins knew.

Present were all of the Virgins, Sam Shiller of the Hot Nasties, Bembe Smith, and X. And me.

Also present, perched on the arm of a ratty old couch, was Danny Lett, a writer with the *Charlatan*, the student paper at Carleton University in Ottawa. Lett had convinced Bembe Smith to let him interview us by suggesting he hoped to peddle the resulting profile to the Canadian Press. Bembe agreed.

It was morning. All of us were exhausted from being up too late. We were pretty enthusiastic, however, about the first real media interview of the Nasties-Virgins tour. So we were all sprawled out around Lett, trying to appear and sound blasé.

Lett was friendly and enthusiastic. "Thanks for agreeing to the interview, guys!" he said. "You were great last night. And I've loved your stuff for quite a while …"

I immediately started doing my best to emulate John Lennon's comedic approach to band interviews. "You wouldn't love us when we've been worshipping Satan and dropping acid," I said. "We're not very lovable then."

Sam, laughing, joined in. "Or when we have been wrestling midgets in a Jell-O tank. Also, not so lovable."

"Got it," Lett said, laughing. "Satan and midgets, band not lovable. So, it's a cliché, but I have to ask: Where did the Hot Nasties' name come from?"

"A pornographic movie," Sam said. "Seriously."

Danny Lett kept writing in a big notepad. "And the Punk Rock Virgins' name?"

"Irony," Patti said, and she and Sister Betty laughed.

"Got it," Lett said. "Okay, then, how is the tour going?" He paused and got a bit serious. "You guys all had a rough year last year. Is this tour your first … since all that stuff happened?"

Danny Lett was referring to the murders of Jimmy Cleary and Marky Upton — and the attempted murders of Danny Hate, Sister Betty, Sam Shiller, and X. Everybody's jocular mood vanished.

I offered up the answer we'd all agreed to in advance and which had been suggested by X: "We don't really talk about that stuff so much," I said. "But we just want to say we miss our friends a lot."

Danny Lett sounded genuinely remorseful. "Yeah, I'm really sorry about what happened to all of you. I can't imagine what you went through," he said, then speedily changed the subject. "What's it like for the Nasties being signed to Stiff Records?"

"It's fucking awesome," Sam said. "They're great. They don't tell us what to do, and they've paid us millions for our first full-length album ..."

Everyone laughed. "It's a double concept album, about the meaning of life," I said. "We're calling it *We Are Shit from Hell*."

Danny Lett was clearly enjoying himself. "Nice title," he said. "Subtle. Seriously, though, no complaints?"

"Nada. All good."

"What about some of your fans — I've seen what they've written in punk fanzines — who say signing to Stiff was a bit of a sellout?" Lett asked. "Not as much as the Clash signing to CBS, but a bit ... unpunk, just the same?"

I shrugged. "It's a fair criticism, actually. Should a punk band sign to a corporate label? Other bands have to decide what they should do, but we felt pretty comfortable signing to Stiff ..."

"Stiff isn't CBS," Sam said. "They were the ones who discovered Costello, Wreckless Eric, Ian Dury, Devo ..."

"Lene Lovich," Sister Betty added.

"The Damned's first single," Leah said.

"Agreed," Danny Lett said, nodding. "They aren't a traditional corporate record label. So, who writes most of the band's songs?"

"All of us," Sam said. "Luke or me will write a tune, Kurt will write the words. Or the reverse. And Eddie participates in writing all the songs, too."

"Where are Luke and Eddie, by the way?"

"They're upstairs, out cold," Leah said, giggling.

"The Satan worship thing," I joked. "We were up late making sacrifices to Lucifer."

"Gotcha," Lett said, scribbling away. "Now, what about what's going on in the U.S. these days? Us Canadians always have politics that is more progressive than what you have down there. But some of the stuff I've seen … *wow*. It's pretty out there."

I immediately thought about Earl Turner and Danny. "Yeah, it's fucking awful," I said. "We've got actual fascism happening back home."

"That Earl Turner guy?" Lett asked.

Sam frowned. "Yeah, him. The Klansman from our home state of Maine. And you can quote me on that: he's a fucking Klansman."

"A sexist, racist, anti-Semitic pig," Patti said.

"What about the theory that punk rock flourishes when right-wing politicians are in power?" Lett asked. "That punk needs something to oppose?"

"That's like saying everyone who has a cold should use heroin, because it's an analgesic," I said. The others looked at me.

Danny Lett looked surprised. "It is?"

I glanced at X, who was looking unimpressed. "Yeah, it is," I said, then loudly sniffed, deliberately, to piss him off. "*Anyway*, we are hopeful that Earl Turner isn't going to win, and that the U.S. will go back soon to something resembling sanity."

Danny Lett was wrapping up. "And what does the future hold for the Hot Nasties and the Punk Rock Virgins on their first big tour?"

"Satan worship, midgets, and untold millions for our *Shit from Hell* concept album!" I said, to general laughter.

X stood and headed upstairs to get Luke and Eddie.

CHAPTER 20

Detective Pete Schenk looked at FBI special agent Theresa Laverty intently. "You were right," he said, deadpan. "This place has the best fucking burger in SoHo."

They both laughed.

"Told you so," Laverty said, pleased that she knew something about Schenk's neighborhood that he didn't. "Now, a bit of business."

Fanelli's had almost filled up with the lunch crowd — a weird mélange of fashion models, retail clerks, photographers, construction workers, and New York City transit workers — and the place was hopping. Laverty looked in the direction of the bartender, Tommy, and when she caught his eye, gave a discreet nod. If he noticed it, he gave no sign.

Thirty seconds later, Tommy was at their table, clearing their plates and utensils. "In the back," he said quietly, not looking either of them in the eye.

Ten minutes later, they were in Fanelli's back room,

behind the thick black curtain. Schenk looked around. All but a couple of the overhead lights were off, but he could see it was an overflow area for the restaurant. Tiny rectangular tables were up against one wall, covered by the same checkered tablecloths; along the other wall, stacks of chairs. Laverty took down three of the chairs and placed them by a window spanning Mercer Street. She sat down and indicated that Schenk should do likewise.

After a few minutes, Tommy slipped into the room. The bartender looked to be in his sixties, with a receding gray hairline, high cheekbones, inexpressive mouth, and downcast eyes. He was a big guy. Not an ounce of fat on him, well over six feet. His gait and posture suggested military or police service. He wasn't young anymore, but something about Tommy suggested that he was … *tough*.

It was his hands that gave him away. On both, some of the knuckles — the metacarpals — were simply missing: boxer's fractures, caused when a clenched fist hits an immovable object. The knuckles had been pushed back into the tops of Tommy's hands. Tommy had been a fighter in the past. And, on Tommy's face, around the eyes and the mouth, tiny scarring could be seen.

"So," Laverty said. "This is my friend Tommy. That's what everyone calls him, but it probably isn't his real name."

His real name wasn't going to be forthcoming, either. He shook hands with Schenk and the two big men sat, knees almost touching, as Laverty quietly told Schenk

Tommy's story. Tommy's expression did not change through any of it.

Tommy, she explained, was from Bosnia, a Serb. His family had been monarchs, but had lost everything to war and the Nazis. His mother fled to the United States after his father was assassinated by an Ustaše death squad. They arrived in New York City penniless and unable to speak any English. Tommy's mother started to clean the houses of rich New Yorkers, and — when things were very tight — toilets at bars in and around the Houston. She cleaned the toilets at Fanelli's, too, Laverty said. She would bring Tommy, from the time he was a toddler, with her, because she had no relatives in New York and a babysitter was out of the question.

The boy was getting big, like his father had been, and he was also getting into fights at school. He was a poor student, although he excelled at languages and writing short stories. He was also good with his fists.

Exasperated, his mother took Tommy to a place on Bleecker Street where she thought he would learn to put his hands to better use.

He did; he learned to box. Though wiry and lanky, he soon gained a reputation for viciousness in the ring. He was faster than anyone his age and he had an ability to identify an opponent's weaknesses in seconds. He started to win titles around the city and seemed destined for great things — until he was seventeen, that is, when his mother was murdered in a mugging that went wrong.

The day after her funeral — attended by Tommy, a Serbian Orthodox priest, and two dozen other cleaning ladies of all faiths and ethnic backgrounds — Tommy walked into the FBI field office in Federal Plaza and said he wanted to be recruited. The two agents at reception looked at the wiry boy with a black eye and laughed. "What can you do?" they asked him. "How old are you?"

"I can fight," Tommy told them, and then proceeded to relate his age and a list of his boxing titles in a dozen different languages. The agents stopped laughing.

Eventually, Tommy's language skills, and his quickness — on his feet and with his mind — propelled him toward counterintelligence at the bureau. There, he excelled and was posted to U.S. embassies and consulates across Eastern Europe, Asia, and South America. His particular area of expertise, Laverty said, was embedding and extracting "assets." He was the best at whisking defectors to safety in the U.S. or placing agents in the institutions of foreign governments. No one ever got killed in any of Tommy's operations.

He'd kept boxing, too, and taught hundreds of agents how to do so over the years. "I'm one of them," Laverty said, smiling for the first time. "Tommy said I'm mean in the ring." Tommy, big arms folded, grunted but said nothing.

The post–World War era presented a new kind of threat, Laverty continued. Extremist groups in the United States were proliferating — groups that wanted to import Europe's conflicts into North America. These groups were prepared to take up arms and commit acts of treason against their own country. They were found on the Far Right and the Far Left, and they reminded Tommy of what his mother had said about the fascists in the Ustaše death squad who had killed his father. Tommy was reassigned.

"We know many of these groups are no real threat," Laverty said. "They talk tough, but they don't ever do much. They're a pain in the ass, but that's about it — the price of having a free society, and all that. But a few groups, mainly on the right, are now well funded, well trained, and deadly serious. And they have big, big plans." She paused. "And the Church of the Creator is at the top of that list."

CHAPTER 21

We were up in Canada again. Our lodgings in Ottawa were officially called the Beacon Arms. In the local punk scene, however, the hotel — a dump of biblical proportions — was referred to as "the Broken Arms." It was on a busy street in downtown Ottawa, not far from the hangout for all of the Canadian congressmen or senators or whatever they're called.

It was at a pay phone near their Parliament Hill that I finally reached FBI special agent Theresa Laverty. She was back in New York City and I had been patched through to her by the FBI field office in Fort Myers.

"Special Agent Kurt Blank reporting for duty," I said, once Laverty was on the line. "No bodies to report, ma'am."

Laverty laughed a bit. "That is correct," she said. "I can confirm that the RCMP and Canadian police agencies are saying the same thing."

"Glad to hear it," I said. "But are you any closer to figuring out who killed Johnny Raindrops and the tranny in New York, or … uh … the guy from here?"

Shit, I thought. I'd forgotten the Ottawa guy's name. I'd talked to him at the Barrymore's gig and I'd already forgotten his fucking name.

That was speed for you.

"Nuclear Age …"

"That's it," I said, remembering. "Nuclear Age. Nothing new in his case?"

"Nothing," Laverty said. I thought I could hear an announcer's voice in the background.

"He was a nice guy," I told her. "We talked about the Ottawa scene and politics in Canada. He was really interested in politics, I remember. I think politics are super boring, but he actually made it sound interesting."

"Politics is certainly interesting *here* this year," Laverty said.

"Yeah. How is that fascist fucker Earl Turner doing, anyway?"

"Officially, I'm not permitted to have political views," Laverty said dryly. "But unofficially, I can say that he is doing quite well, unfortunately. He was at the bottom of the primary pack, and now he's near the front. His ads are working, apparently."

"I guess you know about our former friend Danny."

"Yes, I know about him," she said. "His transformation has been pretty … surprising. I understand that a reporter from Portland has been asking questions about his involvement. Also about how Turner is raising funds."

I didn't ask Laverty how she knew about all that. Were the feds tapping reporters' phones? Was the FBI spying on Earl Turner?

Working for him, more likely.

"Yeah, that's this guy named Ron McLeod," I said. "We know him."

"He was the one who did that profile of you and your friend X last year, wasn't he?"

"That's him," I said. "It was stupid. We didn't want him to write about us, but he did anyway. Reporters suck."

"No argument here," Laverty said, then paused a long time. "How are you doing, Kurt?"

I knew what she was talking about, but I pretended I didn't. "I'm fine, thanks."

"You sure?"

"Yes, I'm sure, thanks."

There was another long pause. The phone line crackled. Behind me, a bus full of Japanese tourists had pulled up onto Parliament Hill. I heard a second muffled announcement over the phone line.

"Kurt, I don't want to pry," she said cautiously. "But as someone who has struggled in the past with those same demons — and always will — I am simply concerned."

"I appreciate the concern," I said, trying not to sound impatient. "I really do, Agent Laverty. But it's under control. I'm not a speed freak, and I'm still happily in the closet, and everything is fine. Really."

This was total bullshit, of course. I was doing way too much of the stuff, and I had started to wonder if I was going to crash and burn. And I was very pissed about being in the closet to all but a few people.

But I didn't feel like acknowledging that Theresa Laverty was right. So I tried to steer the conversation to another subject.

"You had mentioned that fucked-up Nazi church group to X and me, when we met at Gary's," I said. "Are they still part of your investigation?"

"I can't say."

"Why not?"

"Because the First Amendment to the U.S. Constitution permits freedom of speech, and freedom of religious expression in particular," she said, unen-thusiastically. "The FBI is not permitted to investigate a group or individual simply because they use extreme or offensive language."

"With great respect, Agent Laverty," I said, "I think we both know that is total bullshit. I even remember from history class at Portland Alternative High School that your boss, that Hoover asshole, wiretapped minor-ities and communists and gays all the time, so he could blackmail them and destroy them."

"Hoover is dead. He hasn't been our director for years, since 1972," Laverty said. I suspected she was re-calling her own efforts to keep her sexual orientation a secret while working at the gay-hating FBI. "And, in fact, some of us wonder whether Hoover was gay himself."

"Yeah? Well, if that's true, he was a self-hating sick fuck," I said. "And it's that kind of shit that makes it hard for most of us to trust cops." I paused. "And it makes it easier for sick bastards to get away with killing the three kids who came to our shows in New York and here in Ottawa—"

"I know, Kurt," she said, cutting me off. "I agree, believe me. I have a very progressive boss in Fort Myers, and I believe that is why I was assigned to this case."

I didn't say anything. Had I made a mistake in trusting this FBI agent? Maybe she had just hinted to me she was gay and a former substance abuser to get my trust and suck me in, you know? X and Patti Upchuck had been worried when I befriended Laverty, and maybe they were right. I waited.

Theresa Laverty seemed to sense all this. "Kurt," she finally said, "I have taken a considerable risk in speaking to you as I am. I think we have some things in common. I want to help. And I, and all of the FBI, want to solve these murders."

"Fine," I said, not totally convinced. "So, what happens next? Ottawa is where one of the murders happened. Should we be concerned?"

"We don't think so," she said, and I could now make out a flight being called in the background. She was at the airport. "But I am at JFK, waiting for a flight to Ottawa. I will be there tonight, along with quite a few undercover RCMP officers."

I was surprised. "Is there something we should be concerned about?" I asked her.

"Until we catch the killer or killers, vigilance is advised," she said. "I'm sorry, Kurt, I have to go. My flight is boarding."

Not helpful.

The Ron McLeod story about the former punk rocker known as Danny Hate becoming the right-hand guy to Republican primary candidate Earl Turner, that is. Not fucking helpful at all, particularly in the middle of our first big tour as a Stiff Records band.

"From punk rocker to political shocker: the bizarre story of how one outsider became an insider," read the headline, taken from the morning's edition of the *Portland Press Herald*.

And then the lede paragraph: "Danny Hate used to keep the beat for Portland punk rockers the Social Blemishes. Now he's known as Danny O'Heran, and he keeps the trains running on time for a Republican presidential candidate. And that ultra-conservative candidate is everything the ultra-leftist punk movement despises."

X's mom was reading the story to X and me as we gathered around the receiver in my shitty room at the Broken Arms in Ottawa. She'd called us right away, unsure whether the story was a good thing or a bad thing.

It was a bad thing.

It went on:

Danny O'Heran is someone you've seen on TV many times, but you probably don't know his name. O'Heran would probably prefer it that way — his punk rock past is something he'd rather everyone forget. But O'Heran's presence on the surging Earl Turner campaign is one of the most bizarre political pairings in a season of many bizarre political happenings.

O'Heran, at just 19, is the personal assistant to Republican presidential candidate Earl Turner. He's the gatekeeper, the one with the coveted role of who gets to decide who gets to get near Turner on the campaign trail. Everyone interviewed for this story sang his praises, but very few of them knew about his punk rock past. Many were shocked to hear Danny O'Heran used to go by the name Danny Hate.

Earl Turner isn't one of them. "Everyone makes mistakes, and the Lord says everyone should be allowed to atone for their sins," Turner said in an exclusive interview with Associated Press. "Jesus taught us that. Danny started as a volunteer after he had repudiated his godless, leftist punk rock past. And he's shown us that he's hardworking, discreet, and smart. He's left behind all that punk rock insanity, and he's become an important part of our crusade," Turner said in an interview at his bustling Portland campaign headquarters....

X's mom asked us if we wanted her to keep reading. We didn't, but we also did. She kept reading.

> Turner's deeply religious parents could not be more proud of their son, who is the oldest of six children. Reached at their modest Portland home, the O'Herans were delighted that Danny had joined the Turner campaign and proud that he had been named the GOP candidate's full-time personal assistant.
>
> "We are so happy," said O'Heran's beaming mother, Edith. "We prayed that he would leave behind all that radical punk nonsense, and God answered our prayers. And Mr. Turner is a great man who wants America to be great."

I felt like I was going to puke.

> The O'Herans attend Mass at Portland's Cathedral of the Immaculate Conception, overlooking Casco Bay. During his rebellious punk rock years, the O'Herans said, their son stopped going to church and started wearing what they called the "weird clothes" favored by nihilistic punk rockers. He'd given up on God, they said. He fell under the sway of a pair of influential punk rockers who attended Portland Alternative High School with him.

X's mom stopped reading. "Are the 'influential punk rockers' you and Kurt?" she asked, sounding something between bemused and bothered. "Is that good?"

X asked her to keep reading.

> Earl Turner changed Danny O'Heran. "Mr. Turner put Danny back on the right path," Edith O'Heran said. "He saved our boy. God bless him."
>
> Danny O'Heran refused multiple requests by AP to comment on this bizarre tale. Like most Turner campaign senior staff — the ones who wear the distinctive triangular Secret Service lapel pin that identify them as individuals who are allowed to get close to the presidential aspirant — O'Heran resisted all attempts to seek on-the-record comment.
>
> It's that discretion that persuaded Earl Turner to promote O'Heran, Republican insiders say. And it's his willingness to do any job — from picking up Turner's trademark button-down shirts from the dry cleaners, to ferrying Turner to campaign events all over the primary states — that has put O'Heran's political career on the fast-track, they say.
>
> "He does whatever Turner tells him to do and he keeps his mouth shut, and that's why Turner likes him," said one senior Republican in a rival's camp. "No one really knew who this kid was,

or where he came from. This punk rock thing probably won't be helpful to Turner. His voters won't like it."

But some observers aren't so sure. One Republican operative, presently undeclared, notes that Turner has drawn significant support from the evangelical community, who like his attacks on minorities and his willingness to invoke God's name in every campaign event. Said this senior Republican: "Turner's base is ultra-religious, and they love a good redemption story. You might say Danny O'Heran got struck by the Turner lightning bolt on the road to political Damascus," said the Republican, who spoke to AP anonymously. "It's a great little morality tale, even if it's bogus. It shows Earl Turner can bring just about anyone over to his side. That's what Republicans want to hear if they are to retake the White House."

The story went on like that for a while. Wildly inaccurate stuff about the punk movement, Republicans talking about how we were all practically Satanists or Stalinists, sensationalized accounts of what happens at punk gigs in Portland, and — of course — a few paragraphs about how Danny "heroically" survived a possible murder attempt the previous year. The punk rocker had been found barely alive beside the cold waters of Casco Bay, Ron McLeod wrote.

"After that traumatic event, some said Danny Hate changed. He rejected punk rock and became Danny O'Heran."

We thanked X's Mom and signed off. We both sat on the creaky old bed in my room at the Broken Arms.

I spoke first. "That isn't helpful," I said. "Stiff won't like it. It makes us look like a joke."

"Maybe, maybe not," X said, toying with the zipper on his biker jacket. "It's worse for Danny."

I thought about that, then another thought occurred to me.

"What about that shit that McLeod wrote, about how the murder attempt changed Danny?" I asked him. "Do you think there's anything to that?"

X looked right at me with those uneven pupils, his expression blank. "Last year changed all of us, brother. All of us."

CHAPTER 22

Click. Click. Ring.

"Hey."

"Hey, man. How are you?"

"Good. You?"

"Well, I could live without some things, but otherwise, okay."

"Yeah, sorry about that."

"Whatever. Doesn't matter. You predicted it."

"Doesn't make it any easier, though."

"No, it doesn't. But it's necessary, like you said."

"Yep."

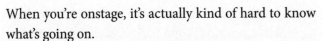

When you're onstage, it's actually kind of hard to know what's going on.

Behind me was Eddie Igglesden, sitting behind his battered, sticker-covered Tama drum kit. He was banging the shit out of his snare and floor tom, sweating so much that he'd taken off his T-shirt between the last couple songs.

To my left, as always, was our albino maniac, Luke Macdonald, twitching around the stage like someone had attached jumper cables to his balls. He was wearing cargo shorts, a Red Brigades T-shirt, his Schott biker jacket, and black Converse. He was going at his bass so hard I could see a bit of blood on his Fender Bullet's pick guard. A madman in a punk rock–induced delirium.

To my right, Sam Shiller, also bathed in sweat, was lost in the moment. He was wearing skin-tight black Levi's, cherry-red Docs, his black Perfecto biker jacket, and a T-shirt X had made for him with JEW PUNK emblazoned across the front. His guitar — his only guitar — was a black Les Paul Custom. He had covered it with Democratic Party stickers. Sam was sort-of screaming, sort-of singing backup as we played "Fashion Show" for the fashionable, almost-sold-out Ottawa crowd.

I, meanwhile, was at the center of the Barrymore's stage, wearing neon-green bondage pants, yellow Converse, and another T-shirt X had made: EARL TURNER IS A COCKSUCKER, it said, in orange and red spray paint. I also had a porkpie hat on my head, mainly to keep the sweat out of my eyes. At the moment, I was wearing (but not really playing) my hacked-up and much-beloved Fender Stratocaster, covered with Rock Against Racism stickers and Pollock-style paint dribbles.

Off to the right side of the stage, just behind Barrymore's curtains, were the Punk Rock Virgins, dancing away. Beside them, carefully eyeing the crowd, was Bembe Smith. Down on Barrymore's sticky floor, just outside the slam-dancing Ottawa punks, was Mike the bouncer, arms crossed, intently watching for any trouble, too.

And, behind all of that, beyond the reach of the stage lights, I knew X was at our merch table, likely standing on a chair, watching us and watching for something, anything, to happen.

Also out there in the dark, I figured, was Theresa Laverty, in designer jeans and a designer jacket, looking like a fashion model who had stepped into Barrymore's by mistake.

All around Barrymore's — by the bar's sound board guy up on the second level, at the bar on the top level, and scattered here and there throughout the place, leaning up against the faded red velvet and gilt on the walls — were maybe a dozen undercover cops, totally looking like cops who were undercover.

The Hot Nasties gigs, when they go great, are better than sex. When you're up there, and playing your songs, there is nothing more epic than pausing during a chorus and hearing a hundred kids you don't know singing along. That wasn't happening at the moment, because "Fashion Show" was a new song they hadn't heard before. But the Canadian kids had shouted back the words on "Secret of Immortality" and "I Am a Confused Teenager," and it made me feel like I was ten fucking feet tall.

Hey everyone, would you look at me
Or at least at what I'm supposed to be
Anything this, is it anything new?
Frustrated, confused, and acne, too ...

I didn't have acne so much anymore. One helpful side effect of speed, for me at least, was it cleared up unsightly acne blemishes. But frustrated I was, aplenty.

We were halfway through the song when I spotted some unusual movement to the left of the stage, at the perimeter of the pit of swirling, surging punks. A flash of fabric and limbs and, in seconds, X was at the center of it, with Mike and Bembe not far behind.

We kept playing, but we could sort of see a trio of three mesomorphs with close-cropped blond hair, tight white shirts, and hairless faces twisted into sneers. They had attacked two guys who had been holding hands near the front and singing along to the older songs. The two were now cowering and trying to shield their faces from their attackers' blows.

X was on the three guys instantly. They were bigger than him and he was outnumbered, but X was undeterred. He was hitting them, hard.

At this point, most of the crowd was watching the fight. The Barrymore's security and the various undercover cops were pushing through the punks at the foot of the stage. We stopped playing.

I was about to take off my guitar when X whirled around and caught my eye. He shook his head and held up his hand. *Stay where you are*, he was saying. *We've got this.*

And they did. In less than a minute, X and Mike had the three big bastards on the ground, and the undercover cops were whipping out handcuffs.

The three weren't Nazi skinheads. They were straight edge guys, I learned later. They apparently "disapproved of the gay lifestyle," some Ottawa guy told me backstage after the gig.

"It's not a fucking lifestyle," I replied. "It's our fucking *life*."

CHAPTER 23

Tommy walked with his old Labrador, Sloane. Pete Schenk walked beside him.

"That's it," Tommy quietly said, nodding in the direction of the nondescript, low-slung building on Kenmare Street, at the point where Center and Lafayette Streets met. "Don't stare at it."

Tommy and Sloane and Schenk were at the tiny triangular parkette. The NYPD detective, who looked too much like an NYPD detective for Tommy's liking, glanced across at 114 Kenmare Street. There was no sign of life. The dry-cleaning business — Lighthouse Cleaners — was at street level, with a couple signs in the tinted windows: WE GET YOUR SHIRTS WHITE and WE CAN CLEAN ANYTHING.

"Cute suboptimal messages there," Schenk said.

Schenk meant to say "subliminal," but Tommy didn't correct him. "Yeah," he said, as Sloane sniffed the overflowing trash cans, filled by the previous night's revelers.

"They think they're clever."

And they were, at least compared to other hate groups. The others drew too much attention with their cross burnings and their ridiculous homemade Nazi and Klan uniforms. The Creators were more careful. They blended in.

Their New York City meeting place was for "the faithful" — that's what the area's Church of the Creator hardcore called themselves, Laverty had said. Its mission was as ironic as the signs in the windows at Lighthouse Cleaners. The Church of the Creator, Laverty had explained to Schenk as Tommy listened, didn't believe in God or Christ.

In fact, she had said, the Creators dismissed Jesus Christ as a loser, a failure. "A Jewish homo nailed to a tree," is what the Church of the Creator called him. "A made-up ghost story." If Jesus had really been the messiah, the Creators believed, he'd never have surrendered and allowed himself to be executed. "They think only losers get captured in war," Laverty had said. "They don't ever surrender."

To the Creators, she explained, race is their religion. Their founder, Bernhardt Klassen, had written up sixteen "commandments," all of which asserted that whites are nature's finest — and that their enemies are what Klassen called "Jews, niggers, and mud races." Mud races, Laverty explained, are also non-whites. They are called that because they are literally dirt to Klassen and his followers.

As far as the FBI knew, Klassen had never traveled to 114 Kenmare Street. It was too risky — and, besides, he generally preferred to stay in Otto, North Carolina, where the population was overwhelmingly white.

Schenk and Tommy followed Sloane around Cleveland Place, looking like just any other older gay couple out walking their dog through SoHo. Schenk continued to assess the dry-cleaning place without being too obvious about it.

"What's with the name Lighthouse? That mean anything?" Schenk asked.

"Yeah," Tommy grunted. "Lighthouse, Florida, is where Klassen founded the Church of the Creator." He paused. "They also see themselves as the light in the darkness. Shit like that."

Schenk shook his head. "So, they don't ever meet upstairs?" he asked, voice low.

"Never," Tommy said, his eyes on Sloane. "Too risky. They're paranoid. Like I told you, they have a lot more room downstairs. No possibility of being seen. And only the ordained ministers and the security legion get to go down there. The ones trained and approved by Klassen personally."

Tommy had told Schenk that at the back of the tiny dry-cleaning business, there was a metal door painted the same drab color as the walls. The door had no handle. When a Creator "minister" came into the dry cleaner carrying a set number of shirts, the burly young man behind the counter would press a buzzer under the counter to open the door. The visitor would slip downstairs and the metal door would clang shut behind him, Tommy had said. Blueprints attached to old New York City building permits described a long flight of stairs into what was effectively a sprawling dungeon beneath Kenmare Street.

Still watching Sloane, Tommy continued, "It used to be a wine cellar during Prohibition times. They have room down there to accommodate dozens of Creators for days at a time. We think they've stored lots of food and water down there, and we think they've got enough guns to outfit an army."

"How do they get out without being seen?"

"Klassen basically owns the entire block through a Delaware numbered company. And there's hidden exits onto Broome, Lafayette, and Center Streets," Tommy said. "But sometimes, they just walk through the front door of the cleaners in broad daylight." He grunted again. "Always carrying five white shirts."

"Why five?"

"Klassen makes them adopt five fundamental beliefs, as he calls them. They're all about the supremacy of the white race."

They stopped as Tommy paused to pick up after Sloane.

"So, you think our guy was there that night?" Schenk asked.

"Yeah, for sure," Tommy said, heading toward one of the overflowing trash bins. "Not much doubt. That's headquarters. Slip in, slip out. He wouldn't have to go far."

"And no one can get a fucking search warrant?" Schenk looked bewildered. "Don't we have probable cause?"

"No," Tommy said, as Sloane led them back toward Fanelli's. "The Church of the Creator has been certified as an actual church by the Internal Revenue Service, believe it or not. We can't touch them — not yet, anyway."

CHAPTER 24

Theresa Laverty was angry with us. We were kind of angry with Theresa Laverty.

"You need to seriously consider rescheduling this tour," she said. "The level of violence at these things is appalling."

"And the police need to be the police," X said. "Policing is your job, not ours."

We were in the ridiculously tiny band room at Barrymore's, off to the side of the stage. The walls were covered with graffiti and band stickers, and there was a single broken-down couch to one side. All of the Nasties' and Virgins' guitars were stacked in front of it, like a coffee table. The door was closed.

X and I were there, along with Sam Shiller and Patti Upchuck, and Mike and Bembe. Standing uneasily beside Laverty was a local Ottawa Police Service cop named Racicot or something. Like Laverty, she was wearing jeans and a blouse and jacket. She didn't say a word.

Mostly, the debate and/or argument was between X and Laverty, with the rest of us watching. X, as usual, wasn't intimidated in the slightest. Laverty, meanwhile, was one of the few people who clearly didn't find X intimidating, either. She gave as good as she got.

Even though X didn't like cops much, I think he sort of respected Laverty. He liked women who were, in Patti's immortal phrase, "feminist as fuck."

"As you know, I don't have jurisdiction here to do anything," Laverty said. "This is Canada. Officer Racicot is in charge, not me."

"Canada. Right. Thanks," X said, not giving an inch and frankly sounding like a bit of a dick. "We don't care. We care about the kids who pay to come see these shows."

"Everyone does," Laverty said.

"And we want those kids to be safe, and not end up dead," X said. "That's your job."

"Security at your shows is entirely the responsibility of you and your friends," Laverty said, pointing a manicured finger at Bembe and Mike. "Not us."

X wasn't backing down. "We are not going to cancel this tour," he said. "And if another kid dies, it's on the head of the police."

Laverty glared at X.

The brawl in the middle of the Hot Nasties' set hadn't been all that bad, frankly. X and I had been in plenty of worse ones, to tell you the truth. No one got seriously hurt, mainly because X and Mike had moved so fast to take down the three straight edge bastards.

Except it turned out that they weren't straight edge after all; they were "Creators" from that fucked-up church. And two of these bastards were carrying big Buck knives under their pant legs, down by their ankles. One of them had a card in his wallet that indicated he was a "minister" in the Church of the Creator. This "minister" was American; the other two guys were Canadian.

The knives were kind of a big deal. At the punk shows we went to, there were always lots of fights and crap. But nobody ever, ever, ever brought a knife. And a gun was just totally beyond the realm of the possible. I had never seen that happen.

The X vs. Laverty staring contest was continuing, with neither side giving an inch. Finally, X spoke. "Were these the guys who killed that kid?"

"We don't know yet," Laverty said. "It's possible."

After a pause that felt longer than a Hot Nasties' sound check, X spoke. "Don't you have a partner, Agent Laverty?"

Laverty didn't blink. "I work alone," she said. "Why?"

X ignored her question. "Not that I'd ever tell the police how to do their job," he said, his voice low. "But you guys should *do your job*."

Hoo-boy. Toronto, here we come.

The Republican Party, being made up of lying fucking douchebag motherfuckers, planned to hold lots of "debates" between the lying fucking douchebag motherfuckers who wanted to be their presidential nominee. But they weren't debates at all.

They were just big Ku Klux Klan rallies with the cross burnings and lynchings artfully edited out, and with dark suits and ties and pearls substituting for the Klansmen's white sheets, all helpfully broadcast in prime time by every single U.S. network, which I guess believed that providing an uncritical platform for white supremacy was good for American democracy.

Do you sense that I'm not a card-carrying member of the GOP?

Anyway, the Canadians, who I had thought were less insane than us Americans, also insisted on broadcasting the first official Republican presidential nominee debate from start to finish on one of their three available TV channels.

They, too, apparently thought that they had an obligation to give free airtime to crypto-Nazis. It was totally bizarre.

Sitting on the bed in a room at the Rex Hotel on Queen Street West, I said as much to X and Patti and Sister Betty, who were also hanging out before sound check. There'd been nothing else on Canadian TV, apart from a kid's show about a giant who was talking to a puppet, and some weirdos on boats in a logging town out west. So we flipped to the Republican's klavern gathering.

"Why the fuck do the Canadians think they should put this shit on TV? I thought they were saner than us," I said.

X, sitting on the floor and leaning against the bed, shrugged.

Patti had a theory. "Everyone in politics is a liar," she said. "Maybe Canadians are governed by liars, too."

"Sure, but they're all socialists up here, with free health care and no guns and an obviously gay-friendly prime minister," I said. "I mean, why the hell would they broadcast this orgy of white supremacy?"

X shrugged again. "Makes them feel better about themselves," he said, which seemed as good an explanation as any. We settled in to watch.

It started with the usual bullshit with supposedly smart journalists murmuring about the cosmic significance of the debate, then moved on to the requisite playing of the "Star Spangled Banner," with the dozen neo-Nazi motherfuckers all clutching the spot on their chests where their hearts were supposed to be. When it was over, the moderator solemnly reminded all of the assembled candidates about the rules, which nobody intended to observe for the next ninety minutes.

But we weren't interested in the other candidates. We were only interested in one: Earl Turner. You might say we had a personal connection to the racist bastard cock-sucker shithead.

The stage had been decked out in garish red and white and blue, of course. But in the preshow crap, they'd shown all of the candidates arriving at the Capitol Center in Concord, New Hampshire. And that's when we'd caught the first glimpse of our former friend.

The rest of the candidates had arrived in limousines and were greeted by all-white throngs of frat boys and sorority sisters, clothed in the finest Brooks Brothers casual wear. A phalanx of Secret Service dudes surrounded them all.

But not Earl Turner. No, he pulled up at the debate in his modest campaign Jeep with the stickers on the sides — the same one we'd all seen plenty of times in and around Portland. He was alone, with no visible security. He was wearing his usual uniform, too: white button-down shirt, L.L. Bean chinos, regimental tie loosened at the neck, and a big aw-shucks grin that made me want to punch him in the face.

The crowd that had assembled to await his arrival were completely different from the storm troopers who had greeted his opponents, the ones who were senators and senior congressmen and satanic Washington insiders. Turner's crowd was made up of farmers and truck drivers and waitresses and construction guys — all of them white, of course.

The objective had clearly been to leave the visual impression that Earl Turner was of, by, and for regular,

everyday Americans. The people's candidate. The populist guy. And it worked. Without even saying the word,
the bastard had already made every other candidate
look like an out-of-touch rich prick.

As Turner leapt athletically out of the Jeep, his telegenic all-American crowd cheering him and swarming
him, the TV camera briefly settled on the young guy behind the wheel of the Jeep. He was dressed exactly like
Earl Turner, except he was wearing a navy Polo blazer.
There was a triangular pin on his lapel.

We could see a flash of Danny's freckled face and blue
eyes. He seemed to be holding some sort of a file folder.

All of us stared at the screen, speechless. It was surreal.

Punk rock was always overwhelmingly progressive,
you see. Almost every punk placed himself or herself on
the left side of the spectrum. We were the kids in every
high school who were feminist or gay or socialist or artsy
or overweight or lonely or unathletic or homely or geeky
or lost. We were not on the football team or the cheerlead-
ing squad or student council. We were the rejected and the
outcasts. And we were, almost to a one, political lefties.

Conservative punks weren't unheard of, I suppose.
Johnny Ramone was known to be a Republican, and
Johnny Rotten had railed against abortion in "Bodies."
Others, like Agnostic Front or Fear or Exene of the L.A.
band X or (astonishingly, sadly) Iggy Pop — who even
had a song about being a conservative! — were also
right wing, but not necessarily racist pieces of shit. But
they, the right-wing punks, were in the minority.

When I thought back to the earliest days of the Social Blemishes, when Danny and I were the only permanent members, I recalled that my big drummer friend had never been all that political or progressive. He didn't ever object to any of my onstage rants about Nixon, but he didn't ever join in, either. He didn't dye his hair like I did, and he never wore super-strange clothes. And he rarely, if ever, voiced an opinion about politics, left or right, like I did.

X and me and the Upchucks knew his family were ultra-conservative Catholic psychos, of course, but we didn't tease him about it. Lots of punk kids had conservative families. In fact, lots of them got into punk to *escape* their conservative families.

But Danny had now taken being a conservative to an entirely different level, you know? As we sat there watching the unfolding fascist rally, we were all thinking the same thing: *What the hell happened to our friend?*

After the other candidates gave their opening statements, it was Earl Turner's turn. He had changed out of his usual outfit into a dark suit, and thereby looked way younger and way better than any other candidate onstage. He waited until the applause died down. It was louder for him than for any other candidate.

"My friends," he said, "America is in bad, bad shape. America is in trouble. America — our home, our homeland — has been lost. For too long, America has been run by men like my opponents." Here, Turner paused and pointed at the unhappy-looking men to his left and right. "And they have run America into the ground. They have done the bidding of international bankers and let in dark hordes no other nation wants. They have let in scum and garbage who have stolen from us, and leeched off us, and defiled our homeland with their foul presence. They have let in the worst of the worst."

Some in the crowd were cheering, of course, but some were now booing, too. Turner gave no indication he had noticed.

"Our Western European brothers and sisters have a wonderful phrase: political correctness. My opponents say I'm not politically correct, because I say what I think. I'm politically incorrect." He paused. "Are you politically incorrect, too?"

There were some boos, but most in the crowd were lustily cheering him on.

"I thought so," Earl Turner said as the moderator vainly tried to tell Turner that his time was up. Turner started shouting over him. "Well, if you're like me, you want to make America right again! You want to make an America for Americans again! You to make America … what, again?"

The crowd screamed as one, like a mob at a lynching: "WHITE! WHITE! WHITE! WHITE!"

Earl Turner didn't need to say anything else. He just grinned, basking in the heat and the hate.

His opponents looked shocked, now having seen up close what they had previously only seen on TV or read about. The media's talking heads were expressing how shocked and appalled they were, too. Some of them pointed out that this kind of racism, this kind of hate, would never "sell" in modern America. It would not fly, they said. It was a huge political mistake on Earl Turner's part.

But the crowd didn't care. They belonged to Earl Turner. "WHITE! WHITE! WHITE!" they kept shouting.

"I'm not going to watch this," X said, and he got up and walked out.

CHAPTER 25

Earl Turner was agitated. Derwin Hailey and Danny O'Heran watched as he paced back and forth in the campaign headquarters conference room. Hailey was there because he was the one who had devised the "America for Americans" campaign. Danny was there because Danny went everywhere that the candidate did.

Danny watched Turner out of the corner of his eye. He knew to keep quiet at times like these. Turner was one of those political candidates who would occasionally lash out at whoever caught his attention. So, the longest-serving Turner campaign staff members had long ago learned to blend into the background, like chameleons. Danny sometimes thought that Turner's senior staff were actually *worse* than lizards.

Derwin Hailey, however, was the lizard who was the focus of Turner's attention at that moment. The candidate was seriously pissed off, although probably not at Hailey personally. But Hailey was there, so he was taking the brunt of it.

"What the fuck?" Turner said, not expecting an answer, and not getting one. "What the fuck? How the fuck am I supposed to dial up the racism stuff? I mean, we're practically the Ku Klux Klan campaign already, but he wants more? What the fuck can I say that I haven't already?"

Hailey undoubtedly thought he should maintain his courageous silence, but the curiosity was probably killing him. "What does he want?"

Turner glared at him, and Hailey immediately looked as if he regretted opening his mouth. "He wants more attacks on niggers! More attacks on Pakis and slopes and kikes! That's what he wants, Derwin!" Turner glared even more, fuming. "What the fuck for? It's not like anyone else is competing for the Hitler Youth vote! I'm out here all on my own!"

Danny kept his eyes on the floor. He, like everyone else on the campaign, knew Turner enjoyed saying these horrible things. He hadn't been forced into it.

Danny glanced up at Earl Turner and marveled. Turner had gone from nobody congressman from a nowhere state, a place with as few Electoral College votes as Idaho or Rhode Island, to what he was today: the guy who came from behind to shake up one of the most powerful political machines in the history of the world, the guy who was in the top tier of Republican Party candidates for president of the United States. Or, as Turner's friend Ben called the country, "The Jewnited States."

If Turner wasn't in second place, he was definitely in close third, now. He had blazed past candidates with ten times as much experience and a hundred times the money. In the past few weeks, Turner had been on the cover of *Time* and *Newsweek* and had been profiled on the front pages of every major newspaper. None of the press — or "Jewsmedia" as his pal Ben called them, to Turner's amusement — liked him, but it didn't matter. The more the media hated him, the more the pointy-headed intellectuals dismissed him and said, for the millionth time, that he had gone too far this time, that his campaign was never going to recover, *blah blah blah*, the stronger Earl Turner got.

Danny had a ringside seat at Turner's circus, and he figured he had seen everything there was to see. Along the way, he'd formed two conclusions: one, calling Earl Turner a racist and a bigot wasn't ever going to work, because a lot of Americans were racists and bigots, too. They *liked* what he had to say about the minorities who they believed had taken away their jobs and their culture and their country. And they *didn't* like elites who called Earl Turner a racist and a bigot, either, because those elites were basically also calling *them* racists and bigots.

The second reason the mainly rural, high-school-educated, angry old white guys loved Earl Turner, Danny knew, wasn't just because of what he said. They worshipped him because of *how* he said it — the *way* he said it. They loved him because he talked like they did when they were in the privacy of their homes. They loved that he didn't use twenty-dollar words when two-dollar words would suffice. They loved that he said outrageous, offensive things, and that the TV commentators couldn't resist reporting what he said, and then analyzing it over and over and over. They loved that he stirred up the elites and the intellectuals.

And when they did that, Danny also knew they were letting Earl Turner control the agenda. They were letting him "dominate the dialogue," as Derwin Hailey had put it. Turner was getting a thousand times the coverage his more experienced rivals were getting. "They hate him, but they can't stop talking about him," Hailey said. "It's fucking hilarious. They chase every shiny silver ball he rolls past them."

The political correctness thing had been a stroke of evil genius, Danny acknowledged. Turner had gotten one of the pencil-necks in the campaign policy shop to analyze the phrase. "Political correctness" first showed up in a 1793 U.S. Supreme Court decision, apparently, and then occasionally appeared in other "white, Anglo-Saxon Protestant" countries after that. Ironically, the memo noted, the phrase was used in a 1970 book called *The Black Woman*.

But no one had ever used the phrase as effectively as Earl Turner. For him, it paid dividends for a couple of reasons. For one, it gave a patina of respectability to Turner's racism.

"This may not be politically correct," Turner would say, "but I think all refugees should be thrown in detention when they arrive in America!" And, sometimes,

Turner would whip out the "political correctness" club to beat down legitimate criticism of his views on issues like abortion (against it, even in cases of rape and incest), or gay rights (against them, even when gays were being strung up for "choosing" to be gay), or refugees and immigrants (against them, even when Turner himself was the third-generation descendant of Turners from England, who came to the U.S. in search of work).

In Earl Turner's hands, "political correctness" was both a shield and a sword. It allowed him to get away with political murder. And it made his critics worry that they were being too "politically correct." It was a bullshit phrase, Danny knew, but it had helped make Turner a front-runner.

At the moment, however, Earl Turner was still pissed off. He glared at Hailey, who blinked behind his thick, horn-rimmed glasses. Danny continued to examine the tops of his L.L. Bean penny loafers. "He's hinting," Turner said. "He's hinting he'll stop donating if we don't start escalating."

"M-meaning?" Hailey stammered.

"Meaning the ad buy ends, Derwin, and I start laying off my well-paid campaign staff!" Turner said, pointing at Hailey. "Meaning the fucking party is fucking over!"

"We are doing great with earned media," Hailey said, using the fancy phrase that campaign lizards use to describe what is just plain old news coverage. "If our buy drops off, earned could fill the void—"

Turner cut him off. "That's fucking retarded, and you know it, Derwin," he said. "The only media we ever get is negative. That ad campaign gives us the only positive exposure we ever get."

"Right," Hailey said.

"Right," Turner said, glaring at him.

There was a knock at the door. Danny opened it a crack. Daisy Something whispered a few words to him before beating a hasty retreat.

Danny looked at Turner and Hailey. "It's Ben," he said. "He has something he wants to feed to Ron McLeod. He says it's good."

CHAPTER 26

Pete Schenk didn't know much about Tommy beyond what FBI special agent Theresa Laverty had told him that day at Fanelli's. But, more than once, Schenk found himself wondering who the old bartender really was — and how he knew as much as he did. *CIA? NSA? Mossad?*

They'd met again, early one morning, to walk to Tommy's Lab, Sloane. Tommy had told Schenk to meet him near the Bowery in the East Village, near CBGB.

As they strolled past, Schenk looked up at the club's tattered sign. He squinted. "What's that mean again?" he asked.

"Country, Blue Grass, and Blues," Tommy said, without looking up.

"No, the other word, what does that mean … OMFUG?"

"Other Music for Uplifting Gormandizers," Tommy said, stooping to pick up Sloane's crap. "Don't ask me what that means. But the only kids who hang out here are punk rockers. No country or blues or anything else. Place is a shit hole."

Having seen CBGB's infamous toilet when he and Laverty had met Hilly Kristal, Schenk wasn't about to argue. "Gotcha."

Schenk and Tommy walked around to Second Street, to the alleyway that ran behind CBGB. It was a minefield of broken glass and discarded used syringes. Sloane would not be walked through there today. Instead, the two men stood and looked south, in the direction of First Street and Houston — and the Dumpster where Colleen Tomorrow had been found.

"So," Tommy finally said, as they continued walking. "Klassen has a son."

Schenk looked at Tommy, surprised. "I didn't know that."

"Yeah," Tommy said, heading toward Houston. "In his twenties. Was off the radar for a while, now he's back. Klassen is the Pontifex Maximus, as he calls himself — the high priest, basically. The son is just under that, a senior minister type. His name is William. Billy."

"What do we know about him?"

"He's a sociopath. Big boy. Does steroids and works out all the time, like a lot of the Creators. Pursues what he calls 'salubrious living' — no alcohol, no meat. He does a bunch of martial arts and is known for his rages, probably caused by the fistful of steroids he does every day. He's feared within the Church, and not just because he's the son of the Pontifex Maximus. The other

Creators are all homicidal nutjobs, too, but Billy takes it
to a different level."

"In what way?"

"He was in the Marine Corps, got discharged dishonorably. Got kicked out for refusing to eat or bunk with
the black marines. Called them niggers to their faces.
Stabbed one black marine for looking at him sideways.
Spent six months in the stockade before they kicked
him out."

"Sounds like a nice guy."

"Yeah. And now he's back with the old man."

They kept walking toward the blare of traffic on
Houston. Tommy was heading to Fanelli's to open up
and Schenk was going to the precinct to learn more
about the Klassens.

"You figure the son for the murders?" Schenk asked,
as they got to the corner of the Bowery and Houston.

"One hundred percent," Tommy said, reaching down
to pat Sloane. "He did 'em all. Even the kid up in Canada."

"So why don't we take him in?"

Tommy looked at Schenk. "Because the bureau
doesn't know exactly where he is." He looked disgusted.
"He may be in the bunker under the dry-cleaning place,
but no one's sure."

"And we still can't get a search warrant?"

"Not yet, I'm told," Tommy said. "Friends in high
places."

"Okay," Schenk said, filing that away for a later discussion with Laverty. "Do we at least know why Billy

Klassen killed these kids? Because they were punks or gay or whatever?"

"That was part of it, but it wasn't the main reason," he said.

"What was?"

"You wouldn't believe me if I told you."

CHAPTER 27

When we got back to the Rex, we saw that X's mom had been urgently trying to reach us, again, about yet another Ron McLeod story. But we had already seen the Associated Press story in one of the local rags, the *Toronto Star*. The headline read: "PUNK BAND'S FANS SLAIN IN OTTAWA, NYC."

The subtitle read: "Police fear serial killer crossing borders."

And the story was just as shitty. X and the Upchucks and I huddled over the paper at a restaurant along Queen West called Shanghai Cowgirl. We'd gone there for lunch when X spotted the story. We read it more than once.

"Fuck," I said, sitting back in the booth. "Fuck fuck fuck."

PORTLAND (AP) — Police fear a sadistic killer
is stalking followers of a bizarre youth subculture

following a trio of bloody murders in New York
City and Ottawa earlier this spring.

Two young men were slain in New York's
gritty Bowery and another not far from Ottawa's
picturesque Parliament Hill, following gatherings
of area punk rockers, police confirm. And all three
victims had attended performances by a Portland,
Maine, punk rock quartet, the Hot Nasties.

The same band was in the headlines a year
ago, when a member of a hate group killed its
lead singer.

"These punk rockers are into shocking
people," said one Portland police detective, who
spoke on the condition of anonymity. "But it now
appears that they're into murder, too."

The detective added, "If your kid is involved
in this punk stuff, get them out, now. They could
get killed."

After I read this enough times to memorize it, I looked
at X. "I guess we know why Ron McLeod was trying to
reach us last week," I said. "What a fucking asshole."

X shrugged. "It wouldn't have done any good to talk
to him," he said. "He was taking dictation. He wasn't
being a journalist. Someone talked him into this."

"But we could have given him our side of the story.
We could have reminded everyone that punks are the
victims, not the fucking perpetrators," I said to him,
exasperated.

"Journalists aren't interested in that. They're interested in what sells papers."

The AP story went on with some stuff about the three victims.

> The first victim, known as Johnny Raindrops, was an aspiring musician and a regular at a New York punk rock bar called CBGB. He was butchered at his apartment in nearby Chinatown. The body of the second victim, a transvestite and prostitute known as Colleen Tomorrow, was found in a Dumpster in an alleyway near the punk rock mecca.
>
> Both victims had been gruesomely mutilated, a detective close to the investigation said. And both had been in attendance at one of two performances by the Hot Nasties group at CBGB. Police estimate the pair were murdered a day apart. The third victim, a student at Ottawa's Carleton University named Juan Conseco, was known in that city's punk scene as Nuclear Age. Conseco was in his first year at Carleton's journalism program and had also attended a Hot Nasties' show at Barrymore's, a popular local rock 'n' roll venue. Conseco had been mutilated in the same manner as the two New York City victims, Ottawa Police Service spokesman Ian MacLeod said. MacLeod echoed the call for young people to stay away from punk rock shows. "We don't

know who the killer is, yet. But we are working
on the theory that this boy and the others were
murdered by someone who knows this youth
subculture, likely by another punk rocker."

MacLeod and New York City police would not
comment on suggestions that the Federal Bureau
of Investigation is involved in the cross-border
probe of the killings. However, Canadian and
American police confirmed that a joint police task
force had been established to solve the vicious
murders.

"What a load of fucking bullshit," I said. "Punks killing punks? Never. And a 'joint police task force' has
been set up? Also bullshit. No cop, anywhere, gives a
shit when a punk is killed."

"They will now," Patti said, poking at her burger, appe-
tite gone. "This is going to stir up a ton of hysteria. Again."

"Yes," X said, looking out on Queen Street West. "But
that's not why this thing was written now. The murders
happened months ago."

"Why now, X?"

"This story was leaked to McLeod for a specific reason.
It came out now because it pushes someone's agenda."

"Who, X?" Sister Betty said.

X, gazing through the Shanghai Cowgirl's window,
didn't say anything. But I figured I knew who he was
talking about.

I need some speed, I thought.

Tit Sweat.

That's what the local opening act was called: Tit Sweat. It was the most epic, awesome, fucking kick-ass punk band name we'd heard yet.

On our tour, you see, the opening act that traveled with us was — as you already know, *duh* — the Punk Rock Virgins. They'd get a percentage of the door plus all of whatever merch they sold, and we shared the minuscule per diem we got from Stiff Records with them — twenty bucks a day, mostly just for food and hotel stuff. X and Patti would have a room, of course, and then Eddie would crash with me, or Sam, or whoever. That way Leah and Sister Betty would have their own room.

Mike and Bembe, meanwhile, would usually get a room with a couple beds in it. I personally found that hilarious: Mike (from the all-white biker culture) and Bembe (from the all-black Rasta culture). They had become pretty good pals, despite the wildly different lives they led.

In any of the places we'd played so far — Burlington, Montreal, Ottawa, and now Toronto — the bill had only included us and the Virgins. But in Toronto — where the likes of the Viletones and the Diodes and Crash Kills Five and the Demics and the fucking amazing Teenage Head were located — the scene was huge, bigger than any place outside of New York or London or L.A. It was one of the best cities to see punk bands in North America. Those bands were legends to us, so we were pretty humbled to be playing at the Horseshoe Tavern, on their turf.

Tit Sweat, meanwhile, were an all-girl outfit, like the Punk Rock Virgins. And they were all members of a couple of the local Native tribes — the Mississauga somethings, I think. And these chicks were fucking hard core. We walked into the Horseshoe when they were doing a sound check, and they were on the Horseshoe's postage-stamp-sized stage and — holy fuck almighty — they were totally ripping it up.

The bassist and guitarist had these super-cool neon mohawks and tons of piercings, and they were wearing hacked-up biker jackets over homemade T-shirts. One said: AMERICAN INDIAN MOVEMENT. The other said: WE WERE HERE FIRST, MOTHERFUCKER.

Like I said, hard core.

The drummer was just a kid, skinny and tall, and maybe a hundred pounds soaking wet. She beat on her drum kit like a guy twice her size would, like her life depended on it. She was wearing all black, and she didn't smile once. Totally in the zone.

Meanwhile, none of us could take our eyes off Tit Sweat's lead singer. She was wearing the standard Ramones-issue uniform: a biker jacket, skin-tight jeans torn out at the knees, white Vans on her feet, and a T-shirt with KILL THE INDIAN ACT written on the front.

And she was stunningly, drop-dead gorgeous. She had the face of a model and this killer, killer body. I'm as queer as a three-dollar bill, boys and girls, but if I ever have sex with a female human, I'd want it to be with her. She was just fucking amazing.

She had charisma like you wouldn't believe, too. All of us — the Nasties, the Virgins — couldn't stop watching her. When we walked in, she was howling on this hardcore-ish number, like she was making the last radio transmission from the end of the world.

Her name was Nagamo, which Leah Yeomanson said meant "she sings" in Ojibway.

The song came to a stop, and we were stunned. Tit Sweat were *incredible*. We all clapped. The band waved and bowed and said thanks. But Nagamo didn't say anything. She just stared at us, still holding onto the mic stand.

Scratch that. She wasn't staring at us. She was staring at X. Like, right at him.

I had seen this sort of thing happen before, with both males and females. X is a pretty good-looking guy, and he often attracts lots of approving glances. Occasionally, he'd get propositioned. I'd seen it happen at Gary's a few times — some girl (or guy) would walk up to him and just hand him their phone number scribbled on a napkin or whatever.

Before Patti, and after, he always just politely declined, or said nothing at all.

But — even as we all stood there, Patti Upchuck included — this chick was just staring at X. And her look left no doubt about why.

Patti noticed — I mean, it was hard not to — and she reached over and touched X's arm, and said something to him, something I couldn't hear. But out of the corner of my eye, I could see X was still looking in the direction of Tit Sweat (generally) and Nagamo (specifically).

It was wild. It was also getting super uncomfortable. So, Kurt Blank to the rescue!

I clapped my hands again, loudly, and yelled: "Tit Sweat kicks ass! Who wants a drink on me?"

Eddie and Mike and Luke are always up for a drink, day or night, and indicated their support. So we all headed over to one of the Horseshoe's two bars, the one near the front door where a woman in an Eddie and the Hot Rods T-shirt was serving.

Tit Sweat followed us over to the bar. There was lots of musician talk, lots of sharing of notes about the scenes in our respective hometowns. Suddenly, I noticed some movement farther down the bar and raised voices. Patti Upchuck was storming out of the Horseshoe, with Sister Betty not far behind.

A minute later, Sam Shiller came over and stood between me and Eddie.

"Whoa, brother," he said, voice low. "Whoa."

"What, man? What happened?"

Sam looked down the bar, to ensure that no one other than Eddie and me could hear him. Motörhead was playing over the sound system, which helped.

"That chick from Tit Sweat walked right up to the bar, between X and Patti, and just looked at him and said, 'I'm going to fuck you,' just like that. And Patti heard it!"

"What did X say?" Eddie asked, always interested in someone talking about fucking, or actually fucking someone.

Sam shook his head. "That's the thing — he didn't say anything! He just kept looking at this gorgeous chick, like he wanted to or something!"

I sighed. Toronto was going to be memorable for more than the gig, apparently.

CHAPTER 28

Earl Turner wanted Danny O'Heran to understand exactly what he was saying. Typically, this involved speaking to Danny like he was a fucking moron.

"Danny, no one else on the campaign can know about my friend Ben, do you understand me?" he said, emphasizing just about every word, as if Danny no longer understood the English language. "Not my so-called campaign management team, not the press secretaries, not anyone, do you understand?"

Danny nodded. Derwin Hailey knew Ben the Billionaire existed, and quite a few others on the campaign did, too, but he decided against reminding Turner. Some political candidates, he had learned, live in a separate reality. So, he kept quiet. "Yes. I understand."

They were sitting in the Jeep, parked on Commercial Street and near the Hilton on the Portland waterfront. Turner looked at Danny. He was squinting a bit. Danny tried to return his gaze, but couldn't.

"Danny," Turner finally said. "You know how much I trust you, right?"

"Yes, sir."

"Good. And you know how well things are going, right?"

"Yes, sir."

"Things are going well because of the efforts of guys like you, and the people on the campaign I trust and who I am close to."

Danny suspected this included Daisy Something and Stacey Something, whom Earl Turner had taken to fucking on a regular basis at a motel near Mother's Beach in Kennebunkport, across from a submarine sandwich place. After he'd finished banging their brains out — almost always accompanied by lots of screeching and moaning by Daisy Something and Stacey Something — Turner would then open the door a crack and ask Danny to go across the street to get them submarine sandwiches. Sometimes, Danny would pick up a couple sandwiches for the Secret Service guys, too. They liked Danny, but they didn't like Earl Turner very much.

"So," Turner said, looking up and down Commercial Street. The only people around were tourists, and none of them seemed particularly interested in the campaign Jeep at the moment. "So, we need to keep my relationship with Ben totally off the books, do you understand? No mention of it to anyone."

"Yes, sir," Danny said. He figured Turner wanted to hide his relationship with the mysterious Ben — or, more specifically, the millions Ben was wiring to one of Turner's personal accounts at the Bank of Credit and Commerce, for use in the ad campaign — because it could get him in a lot of trouble. Danny correctly suspected that Ben's millions were being donated illegally. But he also sensed that something else had Earl Turner nervous. He suspected, but didn't know, that this other Ben-related secret had something to do with the two or three young guys who shadowed Ben, apparently around the clock. At first, Danny thought they were bodyguards for the enigmatic multimillionaire.

But they didn't act or look like bodyguards. They had close-cropped hair, and Danny initially thought they might be skinheads. These young guys wore almost-identical, tight-fitting clothes, and they had pronounced muscles, like they were all bodybuilders or something.

These guys went everywhere Ben did, driving a big, black Suburban — just like the kind of vehicle the Secret Service guys favored.

When Ben wasn't around, they were loud and goofed around and attracted some attention. When Ben was present, though, these guys would stand still and straight, like military academy recruits, and not say a word. One time, Danny watched one of these guys in an extended conversation with Ben. It ended with Ben affectionately patting the young man on his enormous shoulder.

From his seat in the Jeep, Danny could see that the muscle-bound guys put the Secret Service guys on edge. When Earl Turner was meeting with Ben, the

Secret Service would observe Ben's entourage carefully and sometimes speak into the little microphones they had up their sleeves. Most of Ben's guys were armed, Danny suspected.

Earl Turner swung his cowboy boots out of the Jeep and stood on Commercial Street. He turned and smiled at Danny. "When I come out of the Hilton, you and I are going to go celebrate somewhere, Danny. We are about to move this campaign to an entirely different level. We are going to dial up our ad campaign — and we are going to have a few things to say about your former friends, Danny."

Danny O'Heran wanted to ask what this meant, but he didn't. Instead, he just said, "Yes, sir."

Turner swaggered toward the main doors of the Hilton and disappeared.

Ben's three big guys were standing near the big, black Suburban, which was parked near the Hilton's entrance. They watched, too. And then one of them — the one Ben had patted on the shoulder that one time — turned and stared at Danny.

It made Danny uncomfortable, so he looked away, toward Casco Bay.

CHAPTER 29

Okay, class. Time for my little lecture about sex and gender and punk rock, okay? Get comfortable and listen up.

So, as I've said already somewhere else, punk wanted to destroy what rock 'n' roll had become. It wanted to smash it to fucking bits — every self-indulgent drum and guitar solo, every synthesizer, every costume change, every overpriced ticket, every stupid lyric about metaphysical bullshit, every hippie haircut, every honorific bestowed on another overpaid musician, every phony love-and-peace sermon recycled from Woodstock, every pompous Studio 54 rock star millionaire, every fawning focus-grouped profile in *Rolling Stone*, every performance by coked-up assholes standing motionless on a stage that is so far away they resembled ants. All of it. Smash it to fucking bits, and then start over again.

On some of that stuff, punk was successful. Rock 'n' roll songs became shorter again, and a lot of bands went back to a sound that was raw and more real.

Twenty-minute guitar solos became the exception, not the rule. Hair got shorter. Buckingham Palace, briefly, found fewer takers for medals. Bullshit rhapsodies about peace and love got supplanted, at least temporarily, by the gritty reality of hate and war. Gig venues became smaller. Guitars were being heard more, synthesizers less. Musicians wore clothes that real people wore, or at least clothes that didn't cost a real person's annual salary. And bands started writing lyrics about things they knew, taken from the lives they actually lived, and not some distant, surreal, fantasy bullshit world inhabited by druids and hobbits.

Hallelujah, class! Praise the Lord! About fucking time!

But, after all that effort, there was still work to do, especially the socioeconomic kind of stuff. Having learned that pissed-off punks could change rock music, and having learned that punk's DIY spirit could change the way a lot of people approached the future, and having learned that punk could change the way that some people actually lived their day-to-day lives, it was only natural and normal that punks should turn their attention to politics.

Politics was, after all, the subject matter of a lot of songs by a lot of British bands, such as the Clash, Sham 69, Stiff Little Fingers, the Tom Robinson Band, X-Ray Spex — and even unknown local bands like Tit Sweat. (The Hot Nasties, not so much; we rarely wrote songs about politics. We preferred lyrics about *Star Trek* and teenage relationships and going to 7-Eleven.)

For some bands, singing about politics and social change was good. Doing something to bring about actual political and social change, however, was *better*. And punks *have* had a bit of an impact.

Because punk has always been basically leftist in its politics — leftist because punk is anti-authority and the douchebags in charge in the Western world almost always lean to the right — it's usually influenced stuff like women's liberation, anti-racism, anti-capitalism, and voter rights. On those issues, punks *have* changed things, a bit. In my opinion, anyway.

And my opinion is what you came here for, right? *Right*.

Anyway. The fact that rock 'n' roll (and the world) was a toilet bowl swirling with the shit that is sexism and misogyny was so obvious, I shouldn't even have to say it. Men mostly ran politics, and they mostly ran rock 'n' roll, too. Women were the *exception*, not the rule. The whole music "business" was run by guys. The musicians, the writers, the technicians, the engineers, and the producers were all men. Everyone knew that, but not everyone was pissed off enough to try to change it.

At the end of the hippie-era "sexual revolution," some women correctly decided the whole thing had been a big con, a pretext for men to get women to have sex with them. The seventies, in which I was being held as a prisoner wholly against my will, hadn't been much better. Whatever gender idealism had existed in the sixties gave way to no fucking idealism at all.

Bimbo culture was being celebrated on *Charlie's Angels* and lots of other places, like discos. Reproductive rights were still being denied. There was still wage discrimination. Women were still being under-represented in politics, media, certain professions, and whatnot. And surveys even showed that most *educated* men believed a woman's place was in the home.

It was bad, bad, bad, class. Really bad.

Punk did what it could. Punks declared war on the disco era's stupid fashion standards and the total sexualization of women that went with it. It pushed back hard on bigotry and prejudice with movements like Rock Against Racism. Punk *grrrrls* formed all-girl bands, like the Slits and the Punk Rock Virgins and Tit Sweat. And — let me emphasize this next point, class — punk didn't just decide to *sound* and *look* different, it decided to approach *human relationships* differently, too.

"Boy meets girl, boy marries girl, boy and girl have more boys and girls": that whole thing our parents did, that whole "construct," as X calls it, was and is bullshit. It's a lie. Fifty-five percent of marriages end in divorce, anyway, like my parents' did.

The notion that there are "races"? When there's been so much intermingling between people over the centuries, some people still believe there is "racial purity"? Seriously? It's fucking idiotic, just like the notion that there are clear-cut genders or traditional gender roles. To punks, there are no races, there are no genders anymore.

And traditional relationships? Traditional marriage? Traditional roles? Also gone. Blown up by clandestine punk rock terror cells. We are the snipers, picking off your June and Ward Cleavers, with extreme prejudice.

That's what most punks believe, anyway. That's what I believe.

Which leads us back to the little drama that erupted at the Horseshoe in Toronto, between X and Patti Upchuck and Tit Sweat's lead singer, Nagamo.

Patti, you see, was kind of taking a more traditional approach to relationships: she was in one with X, and she expected that to be respected. Monogamy and all that.

Nagamo had a more modern, punk view of things: she was attracted to X, and she wanted to fuck his brains out. Simple.

X, meanwhile? Well, I actually can't tell you what my best friend was thinking. I can't. No one, most of the time, knew what X was thinking about anything.

And, on this occasion, it was getting him in *a lot* of trouble.

CHAPTER 30

Tommy and Pete Schenk finished their burgers, and Theresa Laverty ate as much of her salad as she was going to. They were back in Fanelli's little room behind the curtain. Tourists streamed by the window outside.

It was still the best burger in Lower Manhattan, Pete Schenk declared.

Theresa Laverty agreed.

Schenk then turned the discussion to Billy Klassen. "So, Laverty," he said, "why in the name of Christ can't we get a warrant to search that dry-cleaning front? And, more to the point, why doesn't anyone seem to know where Billy Klassen is, seeing as how we apparently think he killed these three kids?"

Laverty looked at Tommy, slightly annoyed that he'd almost-certainly blabbed to Pete Schenk. Tommy gazed back, saying nothing. He crossed his arms.

"It's complicated," she said.

Schenk was unmoved. "I bet it is. But I'm from Brooklyn, and I'm a little slow. Maybe you can fill me in? Feel free to use small words."

Tommy grinned slightly, a rare occurrence. Laverty knew that the old boxer didn't trust many people, but — when Laverty returned from Burlington and Ottawa — he admitted to her that he'd grown to like Pete Schenk. And he let her know he shared Schenk's frustration with the FBI's hands-off approach to the Church of the Creator's homicidal lunatics.

Laverty grimaced. She trusted Schenk, too, but the Federal Bureau of Investigation generally regarded local police forces as farther down the evolutionary ladder. They were to be tolerated, but seldom trusted.

Her superiors in Fort Myers had been clear. The Church of the Creator investigation — and the possibly related murders of the three counterculture kids — was to be handled with "Q clearance," which was the most restricted. For one thing, Laverty had been told, the COTC had been recognized as a legitimate church by the idiots at the IRS. The bureau did not want a massive lawsuit for violating Bernhardt Klassen's constitutional rights.

And, for another thing, Laverty had been told, the Church of the Creator's founder was not without connections to some powerful people. He'd been a politician himself, in Florida's legislature, and he knew his way around Republican Washington.

Laverty looked at Schenk, pondering how — and whether — to proceed. *Screw it*, she concluded. She'd tell him what she could. "You cannot tell anyone *anything* at the precinct," she said.

"Agreed."

"And you cannot do *anything* with the information I am about to give to you."

"Agreed."

She paused. "All right … Bernhardt Klassen is a very, very powerful man … and he's busily working to try to set off an actual civil war, a race war you might say. And he may just do it."

CHAPTER 31

Click. Ring ring ring.

"Hey."

"Hey, man. How are you?"

"Good. You good?"

"As good as I can be, I guess. It's fucked up."

"It's getting worse?"

"Yeah."

"I've been thinking about *all this* …"

"Don't try and talk me out of it again. It's the only way."

"It's you, brother. I'm worried about you."

"Don't be, man. Don't be. I'm good. I know what I have to do."

―――――

Downside: I was bored.

So, when I got tired of the high school drama still

unfolding at the Horseshoe, I just left and walked back to my room at the Rex. When I got there, I found a baby-blue pamphlet tucked under the door. It was from Narcotics Anonymous.

"Really?" I said out loud, even though no one was around. I glared up and down the Rex's empty hallway and raised my voice. "REALLY? SERIOUSLY? We're going to leave antidrug pamphlets around, LIKE OUR FUCKING PARENTS WOULD?"

I slammed the door, hard.

I crumpled up the pamphlet and threw it on the floor, then tossed my biker jacket at the TV set. I missed. Sitting on the bed, I pulled off my Docs and threw them in the farthest corner of the room. *Narcotics Anonymous? Seriously? What self-respecting punk would actually slide that under the door?*

I fumed a bit. I looked up. I looked down. Then I looked at my arms. On my right bicep, there were two letters tattooed: *JC.* For Jimmy Cleary. Our friend, killed last year. I promised myself that I would get his initials tattooed on my arm, and — just before the tour started — I did. I wanted everyone who came to our shows to see those letters and ask me what they stood for.

Some thought they referred to Jesus Christ, of course. But, if they asked, I'd tell them: "Our friend Jimmy Cleary. *My* friend."

I sniffed a bit. I looked at the tattoo, still fuming. Then I examined my arms. Both of them. I was skinny, a lot skinnier than I'd ever been. I'd lost a lot of weight, as Sister Betty had said to me when we were waiting to cross the border into Quebec, and when I'd had that bag-of-speed-dumped-down-the-toilet episode.

Getting more speed to replace it in Montreal had been really easy. I just quietly mentioned something to one of the bartenders at Foufounes, and I was in receipt of a shiny new baggie full in no time at all. Montreal was awesome!

But, you know: my arms. They *were* skinny. My legs, too. All of me, in fact.

I looked up at the long mirror that was screwed to the back of the door. Same fetching bleached-blond spiky head of hair, same captivating blue eyes. But the rest of me? Well, there was indeed *less* of me than there used to be. I wasn't wasting away or anything like that, but there was decidedly less Kurt Blank walking the earth than there had been, say, a year earlier.

I pondered. I sniffed. I was not an addict. I was not a speed freak. Speed, as I have previously advised y'all, is pretty hard to get addicted to. It doesn't really work on the brain in that way. Dependent on it? Sure. That's possible. Addicted? No way. Fuck you, man.

I looked down at the crumpled NA pamphlet and started to get mad again. "Fuck you, whoever you are," I said. I reached down and picked it up. "Fuck you," I repeated.

I stalked into the puny bathroom, lifted up the toilet tank cover, and reached inside. There, in the most cliché d of hiding places — but a *pretty good* hiding place just the same! — was a fistful of speed, sealed in three baggies, floating on the surface of the toilet water. Dry as a bone and as inviting as home.

I carried the bundle over to the bed like it was a newborn, carefully opened up the three meticulously sealed packages, and extracted a heaping helping of my powdery white friend. Call it what you will — crank, glass, chalk, spoosh, scootie — whatever it is, I expertly dumped it onto the NA pamphlet and got ready for blastoff.

"What better act of defiance than to ingest a ton of speed off your stupid pamphlet, Narcotics Anonymous?" I said to the not-present Narcotics Anonymous folks.

I then commenced snorting away, and — in no time at all — was engaged in what the doctors would later call "a pathological overactivation of the mesolimbic pathway," but that I usually called "getting wired." It happened fast.

Then, just as quickly, I was convulsing on the filthy carpet at the Rex, heading toward a coma, and being handcuffed to a bed in a shared room at Toronto's St. Michael's Hospital.

Upside: Canadians don't ask you to pay for health care!

CHAPTER 32

The Turner campaign had alighted, yet again, in Dover, New Hampshire. Danny O'Heran had been there so many times he could practically maneuver through Dover's quaint streets with his eyes shut. Because it was an early primary state — like Iowa, like Nevada, like South Carolina — Earl Turner and his Republican opponents needed to spend a lot of time there. Momentum in New Hampshire could mean victory later on.

The campaign office, at 83 Main Street, resembled every other campaign office Danny had visited in the past few months: receptionists at the front (to welcome new supporters and answer the phones) and a small army of volunteers at the back (to assemble lawn signs, send off fundraising and thank-you letters, or put together the propaganda that canvassers would hand out door-to-door). In offices like the one in Dover, there usually weren't any campaign bigwigs — just one or two paid full-time or part-time staff to oversee the place.

Nothing super important happened in these Turner campaign offices that were now found, more and more, across white America. No big deals were conducted in regional campaign offices. But they were spreading across the country like a virus.

Earl Turner's arrival in town — *him, personally*, in the flesh — was a pretty big deal, however. For one thing, since he'd last been in town, he had become The Great White Hope. The media called him that, thinking they were insulting him, but Earl Turner wasn't insulted in the least. "Literally — I'm the white man's great hope!" Turner had said in the Jeep one day. Danny said nothing, as usual. But he knew that there was a lot of excitement among Republicans about this outsider who just might possibly become the president of the United States.

There was another reason why Turner's arrival in Dover was a bit of big deal: Dover was a longtime Democratic town. It had a vibrant union movement and a long line of Democratic mayors, and it prided itself on being progressive. But, as Danny pulled the Jeep into the parking lot on Main Street, a crowd of maybe two hundred people were already there, whooping and hollering, hoisting TURNER FOR PRESIDENT signs into the air.

Without a word to Danny, Turner leapt out of the Jeep and into the adoring crowd. He'd barely waited for the Jeep to come to a stop. "See you later, Danny," Daisy Something said, as she clambered out of the back seat, all legs and boobs and hair. Danny knew he wouldn't be needed for a couple of hours, so he decided to go get an early lunch at the Cross Roads.

He waited a bit, watching Turner wade into the crowd of supporters. He then did a U-turn and pointed the Jeep toward Central Avenue. The Cross Roads Diner, he knew, had the best fried seafood around.

Ten minutes later, after a quick pay phone call home, Danny sat on a stool at the counter. He was eyeing the menu when he felt a presence beside him and glanced to his right. There, perched on the nearest stool, was a really odd-looking, overweight guy, sweating and stuffed into a cheap suit. The guy had thick eyeglasses, a thick mane of black curls, and a big smile. He seemed to be delighted that Danny had noticed him.

"Danny?" the guy said loudly, pretending that it was a chance encounter, for the benefit of the few patrons scattered around the Cross Roads, Danny assumed. "Danny O'Heran? I've been looking for you!"

Danny said nothing. He looked for a notepad or a tape recorder. There were neither. If the guy was a reporter — and not a few reporters had approached Danny over the preceding months — he wasn't acting like one. Danny waited, unsure whether he should forget about ordering and bolt.

"You're thinking about what to do," the guy said quietly, nodding vigorously. "I understand that. I support that. Some weird fat guy comes up to you in a diner in the middle of nowhere in New Hampshire and pretends to know you, and starts talking to you. And you don't want to talk to him, because you have a reputation for not talking to anyone. I understand that."

Danny inched a bit off the stool. The smiling guy noticed. He touched Danny's arms with one plump digit. "Hear me out, Danny," the guy said. "Hear me out, and then you can go. You don't have to say a word, okay? Not a word."

Danny watched the guy out of the corner of his eye, waiting. Whatever was about to happen, he figured, wasn't going to be *good*.

The Cross Roads was filling up with the lunchtime crowd, and getting busier and noisier, so the guy leaned a bit closer. "Good, good," the guy said, his fake smile blazing ever brighter. "Thank you. I appreciate you staying on that stool. Good decision." He paused, seemingly savoring the moment. "Now, you can call me Ezra, if you want, but that's not my real name."

Danny grimaced, but said nothing.

"I know who you work for, of course. I don't intend to say his name out loud, however, because I don't want to attract any undue attention, but mainly because I don't want you to feel uncomfortable and get back in your Jeep and rush back to the rally at the campaign office on Main Street, okay?"

Danny watched "Ezra," knowing that he should have left a few minutes ago, but also curious about what was coming. He stayed put, and Ezra smiled even more. He did not take his bright little pig eyes off Danny.

"So, look, Danny, I want to talk to you about something serious, okay? It's something good for your guy, so don't worry," Ezra said. "It's good. And it's in your interest to listen, okay? It is. You have a nice family — all those brothers and sisters, and your mom, Edith and your dad, Bob. A nice family."

Danny stiffened.

Ezra lowered his voice. "Danny, we will kill Edith and Bob, and all of your siblings, if you call the cops or speak to anyone other than Earl Turner, do you understand me? Your family will all be tucked in Bob's nice new Cadillac after eleven o'clock Mass at the Cathedral of the Immaculate Conception, and then they will be blown to fucking bits when your dad turns the ignition, do you understand me, Danny?" Ezra kept smiling, watching Danny. "They will be scraping bits of your little brothers and sisters off the big stained-glass window for a week, do you understand?"

The room started to move. Danny felt faint. He felt like he was going to be sick. Ezra pointed at the glass of water the waitress had left for him at the counter. "Drink it, Danny. You look really pale."

Danny gulped down the water and stared at the bottom of the glass. He waited.

"So, better?"

Danny nodded.

"Good," Ezra said, sounding legitimately pleased. "So, Danny, this is what you are going to tell Earl Turner. You are going to tell him you were approached by a guy who you have never seen before, but who threatened to kill your entire family if you spoke to anyone but him. You are going to tell him you believe the guy. Next, you are going to tell your candidate that this guy knew every fucking thing about him — like, how he really wasn't a war hero in Vietnam, and how he really wasn't much of a farmer when he was in Farmington. And then you are going to tell him that he wasn't a fisherman in Eastport, at all, at all." Ezra smiled, clearly enjoying himself. He watched Danny for his reaction.

"He wasn't a fisherman, Danny, and that's what you will tell him. He was, in fact, really short on money, and he was letting lonely old queers suck his cock in motels outside Eastport to make a bit of extra dough. And you are going to tell him that when he was passed out on a motel room floor one night, one of these old faggots snapped a Polaroid of himself with Earl Turner's cock in his mouth. And that you can clearly see Earl Turner's handsome face and everything. And you are going to tell him that your new acquaintance Ezra has the photo, do you understand?"

At that point, Ezra slowly reached down and unbuttoned his too-small jacket. He extracted a photocopy of a Polaroid. Danny only saw it for an instant, but it was enough. The photo showed a naked and much younger Earl Turner sprawled out on a carpet, eyes closed, with his limp dick in the mouth of some old guy with a mustache. The old guy looked pretty pleased with himself.

Danny also saw something else, very briefly. It was the handle of some kind of a revolver, in a holster attached to Ezra's belt.

Then Ezra buttoned up his jacket, but only just barely. He was sweating. He smiled, a big-bucks smile.

"A half-million bucks, Danny," Ezra said, tapping the counter, preparing to leave. "To start. I will be in touch to tell you when, how, and where. If you tell anyone other than Turner, we will kill your family, got it?"

Danny nodded, feeling short of breath.

Ezra slapped him on the back, like he was an old friend. "Good boy," he said. "See you soon."

CHAPTER 33

What?

"… she has these spectacular tits, Kurt. Just fucking huge tits, and they were all sweaty and bouncing right above me. And she has these long, long legs, and they were on either side of me …"

How?

"… and she was riding me, brother, for like the third or fourth time, I honestly can't remember. This fucking amazing little ass, and we were in my room at the Rex, and she was just totally in control and I was just her sex slave, you know? And her face …"

Why?

"… her face is just, like, wow. Like out of this fucking world. Like a model or something. And I just lay there, all night, knowing that I would never be fucked like this again for the rest of my life. This fuck should have been in the Smithsonian, it was so fucking historic, brother."

Who?

"I know I wasn't her first choice, man. She wanted X. But I was okay with playing second string on this assignment, you know what I mean?"

My eyes started to focus. It was dark. I was in a hospital room somewhere, in a bed. There was another bed, and it was occupied. A screen prevented me from seeing who was in it, but I recognized the voice. It was Eddie Igglesden, our drummer.

But why was he in a hospital bed? Why was I, for that matter?

I grunted. Then I saw Eddie sit up on my bed and look over at me. "Brother? Are you awake?"

I grunted again. Eddie jumped off the bed and clapped his big hands. "I did it! I told you as many pornographic stories as I could to wake you up — and it worked!" Eddie patted me on my arm — which, I noticed for the first time, was handcuffed to the metal bed frame. "Sorry the stories were heterosexual in nature, brother. That's all I've got in my repertoire."

"Who the fuck were you talking about?" I said, my voice like Lazarus after a bender. "Who …?"

Eddie smiled. "Oh, that? The chick who sings for Tit Sweat. Nagamo. Holy fucking hell, brother, she fucked me like I was her last meal." He paused, grinning like a goof. Which he was. "She couldn't have X, so I volunteered!"

Despite myself, I laughed, but it came out like a crow's croak. Eddie busied himself looking for a glass of water. I drank it using my free arm.

"Where am I?" I rasped. I indicated the handcuffs. "And why am I …"

Eddie's goofy smile disappeared. He looked at the door of the room. "I dunno, brother," he said. "Maybe I should get the doctor so they can talk to you …"

"Fuck the doctor." I coughed. "How the fuck did I get here?"

"You snorted a bit too much of the crystal, bud," he said. "Sam and Luke found you convulsing and stuff on the floor of your room. Thank Christ your door was unlocked." He paused. "You need to cool it on that shit, Kurt, man."

No kidding, I thought.

"Where is everyone else?" I said, sounding a bit more human. "What about the show?"

"The show's been rescheduled until you're back on your feet, brother," he said. "Sam, Luke, me, and Leah and Sister Betty did this fuck band thing and called ourselves the Hot Virgin Punks. We were actually not bad." He laughed. "Bembe and Mike even came up and we played some really bad covers of reggae stuff by Desmond Dekker. It was hilarious."

I frowned. "What about Patti?"

Eddie rolled his eyes. "She freaked when Nagamo hit on X. Took off to stay with some feminist punk chick she knows out in Toronto's east end. Lisa or something." Eddie shrugged. "The Nasties couldn't play without you, so we did the fuck band thing with Betty and Leah. The Horseshoe actually liked it. We drove plenty of people to drink." He laughed.

A "fuck band," in case you're wondering, which you probably are, happens when a band (or bands) are short a member or two and they form a band to fuck around and be stupid. My old band with Danny Hate, the Social Blemishes, was basically a two-year-long fuck band.

I surveyed my surroundings, wondering (a) how to get out and (b) what had happened to my baggie full of speed. I then remembered something.

"Wait," I said. "Where's X? You didn't say anything about X."

Eddie scowled and surveyed the floor. "Yeah, well …"

"What?" I asked him.

"X is gone, brother. He took off. Nobody's seen him in a couple days."

CHAPTER 34

Lighthouse Cleaners looked like what it claimed to be.

It even had customers. It was Lower Manhattan, early morning on a weekday, and the customers could be seen going in with bundles of shirts and suits to be cleaned and pressed, and out carrying plastic-covered shirts and suits and dresses.

Theresa Laverty, Pete Schenk, and Tommy were in a fake FedEx van on Lafayette Street, pointed south and just down from the Church of the Creators' New York City hideout. The van had tinted windows, ensuring no one could see in. Looking out, however, Schenk confessed that he didn't see anything all that unusual happening.

"So, are all those customers going in and out Church of the Creator types?" he asked Laverty and Tommy, clearly skeptical. "They look like a bunch of SoHo yuppie types to me."

"Yes," Laverty said, her eyes remaining focused on Lighthouse Cleaners. "And, yes, they're real people. Real customers. Which also partly explains why we haven't charged in there, executing a warrant for Billy Klassen, guns blazing. We're still not sure he's there. And we're not sure some innocent yuppie wouldn't get hurt, either."

"Gotcha," Schenk said. "No perp. No dead yuppies. No shooting up so-called churches." He grunted, wondering again why he'd agreed to do the way-too-early stakeout. It seemed like a big waste of time. "What's the last known location of Billy?"

Tommy spoke. "Ever since he was kicked out of the military, he's been his father's shadow. Runs what they called the COTC Security Legions. A few dozen pumped-up young guys like him, some ex-military, armed to the teeth. They like to blow up ordnance and improvised bombs in remote areas outside their headquarters in Otto."

"But he's in the wind now," Laverty said, sipping at a Dean & Deluca green tea. "No sign of him anywhere. Which maybe lends credence to the notion that he killed those three kids. He knows we're looking for him, I suspect."

"So what's up with the punk band, with their tour?" Schenk asked. "Any more corpses show up?"

Laverty shook her head. "Not yet. They've done shows in Burlington, Montreal, Ottawa, and now they're in Toronto." She paused, looking unhappy. "Their lead singer almost overdosed a few nights ago and is now chained to a bed in a Toronto hospital."

"The glorious rock 'n' roll lifestyle," Schenk said. "What is it with these fucking kids? Do they all want to die at twenty-seven?"

Laverty didn't answer. "The show in Ottawa I saw was practically nonstop violence," she said. "It was ridiculous. These punks don't dance — they slam into each other at the foot of the stage, and it inevitably leads to fistfights and brawls. Call me old-fashioned, but I don't quite see how that can be called entertainment. Or even dancing."

"So, do you have anyone watching them while they're in Canada?" Schenk asked.

There was a long pause.

"We can't, of course. No jurisdiction," Laverty said carefully. "But the RCMP told us they'd keep an eye on things as best they could."

Schenk looked at her. She wasn't telling him something. Again. "But no bodies yet."

"No bodies," she said. "Lots of black eyes and bloodied noses, but no murders. If Billy Klassen killed those three kids, he's laying low now."

The trio continued to watch Lighthouse, saying little. It was getting closer to 9:00 a.m., and the number of customers was slowing down.

Shortly past nine, the place emptied out. There was no one inside apart from the beefy young man at the counter. He, too, was COTC, Laverty said.

A white limousine suddenly appeared, turning onto Kenmare off Center Street. It screeched to a halt at the minipark that faced Lighthouse Cleaners. Two muscular young men in tight black suits jumped out and circled the limo to open a door on the other side from the phony FedEx van.

"What the fuck?" Schenk said.

"What do you know," Laverty said, preparing a battered FBI-issue camera to take a few snaps. "It's him."

They watched as the two bodyguards escorted their charge to the doors of Lighthouse.

"Bernhardt Klassen," Tommy said, "in the flesh."

CHAPTER 35

After a few months of working for Earl Turner, Danny O'Heran had gotten used to the unexpected.

Turner claimed to be a churchgoing family man, but he was regularly fucking his two press secretaries — and possibly others, in other states. *That* Danny had not expected.

Turner had entered the Republican presidential race as a garden-variety populist rural conservative, but he had turned into a racist, gay-hating anti-Semitic demagogue. *That* Danny had not expected. Turner had professed to be the candidate for the little guy, but the only guys he cared about, truly, were the ones who gave him money — for his ad campaigns and to line his pockets. *That* Danny had not expected, either.

And Earl Turner's reaction to the news that a photo existed of him passed out in a hotel room in Eastport, Maine, his dick in some old guy's mouth? He barely reacted at all. In fact, Earl Turner reacted like he had been expecting it.

That Danny O'Heran had definitely not expected.

They were back in Portland, sitting in the campaign Jeep. Danny had parked in an old part of town, a block or two from Gary's, where he had once been known as Danny Hate and where he had once played the drums for the Social Blemishes with his friend Kurt Blank. Danny stared at Turner, who — while not quite blasé — was far from panicked or upset. To Danny, Turner seemed almost serene. It was weird.

"So, you had never seen this Ezra guy before?" he finally asked Danny. "Not at any of your punk rock shows, or something like that?"

"N-n-no, sir." Danny was yellow-pale and looked terrible. He had been up all night. He spent most of it sitting on the floor outside the bedrooms where his younger siblings slept, his dad's Heckler & Koch 9mm at his side.

When Danny picked him up at his west end home, it had been difficult to persuade Earl Turner to go somewhere other than the campaign office. At first, Turner was concerned that Danny planned to quit. It would be inconvenient and give rise to unhelpful news stories.

"It's not that, sir," he said. "I just need to speak with you someplace where we will not be bothered for a bit."

Reluctantly, Turner agreed. Twenty minutes later, Danny was parked on Congress, up the road from Gary's. The Secret Service parked their big, black Suburban a few car lengths back.

Haltingly, Danny told Turner about Ezra, and the photograph, and the gun, and the promise to kill the entire O'Heran family after they left Mass at the Cathedral of the Immaculate Conception. By the time he finished, Danny O'Heran was again a yellowish-pale, and sweating, and shit-scared.

"They're not going to kill your family," Turner eventually said to him, sounding almost irritated. "That was just to ensure you didn't speak to anyone but me." He looked sideways at Danny. "You haven't spoken to anyone else about this, have you?"

"No, sir," Danny said. "No way."

Earl Turner sucked air through his perfect teeth. "Good. And he said a half-million to start, is that correct? That's what he said: 'to start,' right?"

"Yes," Danny said. "He said it was just to start."

Earl Turner shook his head. "They're fucking dreaming if they think I'm going to be someone's lifelong lottery ticket," he said. "That is not going to fucking happen."

Danny was still in shock — by Ezra's blackmail attempt and by how calmly Earl Turner was now reacting to it. "What are you going to do, sir?"

There was an uncomfortable silence. "I'm going to pay it, Danny," Turner said. He looked at him. "And you are going to take him the money when he tells you when and where."

"Me?" Danny said, feeling sick. "Shouldn't we call the police, sir?"

"The police?" Turner snapped, glaring at him. "Are you out of your fucking mind? It'll leak to the press ten minutes after you call them. And the photo will be in one of the supermarket tabloids the very next day." He paused, grimacing. "With parts of it blacked out, of course."

Danny was almost wild-eyed with fear. "Sir, what if the photo is a fake …"

Turner cut him off. "It's not fake," he said, glaring at Danny. "It's real."

"But …"

"Danny, all of us make mistakes," Turner said, impatient. "You made a mistake getting involved with that punk rock shit, and I made a mistake once or twice when I was younger. Had too many drinks, made a couple bad choices, and shit can happen. Shit happened."

Danny stared at him.

"This Ezra guy, or whatever his name is, is like a million other guys out there," Turner said, waving a big hand at the Jeep's windshield and, presumably, the world outside. "He's had this picture for a while, and he's been waiting for the right moment to use it. If I weren't doing well in the primaries, we might have never heard from him. I'm doing well, so he's decided to make a million or two." Turner actually shrugged. "That's how this business is sometimes."

By "business," Danny assumed Turner meant politics. After he'd worked on the Earl Turner campaign for a few months, Danny learned that politics was far dirtier than he ever imagined. But *this*?

"You're going to pay him? Isn't he just going to keep coming back for more?"

Earl Turner looked at Danny O'Heran, his contempt plain. "Of course he is. And of course we're going to pay him," Turner said. "Initially."

"Initially?"

"Yeah, initially," Turner said, looking in the Jeep's side mirror at the Secret Service's vehicle and straightening his tie, already getting ready for his first meeting of the day, with a bunch of antiabortion zealots from Vermont. "We need to get through New Hampshire and Iowa. We need to get through the next couple weeks. And then we're going to erase any sign that he ever existed."

CHAPTER 36

Ring ring ring.

Click.

"Hey."

"Hey! How are you? Are you okay?"

"I'm good."

"How are the others?"

Pause. "They're good. Some more than others."

"He …"

"Yeah."

"Was it bad?"

"It was bad."

"Where is he now?"

"Being watched. He's okay. He'll be okay."

"Good." Pause. "Will it happen again?"

"The way he's going, probably."

"I'm sorry to hear that."

"Yeah. Me, too."

"Where are you now, if you don't mind me asking?"

"In the States … you're not home, right?"

"No. No way. Pay phone. Different one than last time."

"Good."

"You been following what's going on?"

"Hard to miss. Yeah."

"Yeah. It's crazy, man. It's fucking insane. It's …"

"What? Is something wrong?"

"What you said would happen has happened. Couple days ago."

"How did it go down?"

"That's a good question. It was … weird."

"But you're okay?"

"Yeah, I'm okay. Thanks."

There was a long, long pause. Almost a full minute.

"You don't have to do this, you know."

"I know."

"You can quit and come home. I will protect you."

"I know," he said. "But you can't protect me from everything."

I was in the passenger seat at the front of the van, still feeling strung out. I wasn't stoned or anything, but I felt disconnected from planet Earth, sort of. I was this crumpled-up piece of paper, blowing around on the ground, and there was all this garbage around me, and I didn't know how to stop it.

I coughed. I felt like shit.

We were bumping along a road. I looked out the window of the Econoline. The buildings were kind of ramshackle, scattered here and there. Out front, there were dogs running around and lots of dark-haired little kids. They all stopped to watch the van.

"Where the fuck are we?" I asked, not for the first time. "What is this place?"

Mike, who was driving, said nothing. Bembe, who was seated right behind me — to keep me from jumping out of the van and locating the nearest dealer, I suspected — was silent, too. Neither of them had said much to me since we'd left Toronto city limits, about ninety minutes before.

In the back of the Econoline were Sister Betty, Leah Yeomanson, and Sam Shiller. One of the members of Tit Sweat was in the back, too. I'd forgotten her name. She had been calling out directions to Mike once we got off the highway.

"Welcome to Six Nations, Kurt," Leah said. "This is the home of the Six Nations of Grand River."

"I'm where …?" I squinted out the windows as Mike started driving onto a dirt road. "What the fuck?"

"You're a guest," the Tit Sweat chick called up to me. "Fucking act like it."

I wasn't expecting that, to tell you the truth, so I stopped talking. I saw Mike and Bembe exchange a look in the rearview mirror. Bembe smiled. Mike chuckled.

The dirt road got narrower and narrower, and we were bumping all over the place. Fewer houses could be seen. I looked in the side mirror. Behind us, still, was the Punk Rock Virgins' station wagon, being piloted by Eddie Igglesden. Beside him, up front, was Tit Sweat's singer, Nagamo. Beside her was Luke Macdonald. The other members of Tit Sweat seemed to be in the back seat. No sign, still, of Patti or X.

My discharge from St. Mike's Hospital had happened without much fanfare. I had dried out, and they needed the bed. A doctor came and solemnly spoke to me about drug abuse as a couple of residents looked on. Sister Betty and Bembe appeared. They helped me sign out, then Bembe pushed the wheelchair while Sister Betty held my hand.

I tried to make a couple jokes, but they weren't laughing. When we got down to the lobby, the Hot Nasties, Leah, and most of Tit Sweat were there waiting for us. Leah hugged me, Sam squeezed my shoulder, Luke and Eddie kissed the top of my head. I thought Luke was going to cry, but he didn't.

I almost did.

Bembe and Mike helped me get into the van, because I was still feeling a bit unsteady. Everyone else got in, and the others piled into the Virgins' station wagon. Before we'd gotten out of downtown and onto the highway, I fell dead asleep.

When I woke up, I was seriously jonesing for some speed. It felt like my head was going to split open like a great big watermelon. I needed my powdery white friend. Sister Betty reached up to the front and squeezed my hand, but none of them really said anything.

When we turned off the highway and onto a dirt road, we passed a sign that read HAUDENOSAUNEE CONFEDERACY. When we reached the end of the road, Mike stopped the van and turned off the engine. Everyone was looking at me. I could see a path winding off through of the trees, but that was it.

"Where the fuck are we?" I asked. "Are we going back to the States?"

"Not yet, baby," Sister Betty said.

She only called me "baby" when she was worried about me. She had her hand on my shoulder. I was still wearing the Ramones T-shirt I'd put on when I was discharged.

I was turned around in the seat, feeling completely uneasy, when Leah Yeomanson looked right at me. She was more serious than I'd ever seen her. "Kurt, we're going to a sweat lodge ceremony," she said. "Your life isn't in balance. You are going to be purified and reborn, and we're going with you."

"What the fuck?"

Sister Betty smiled at me. "We love you, baby," she said. "But you could've died. This shit is going to stop right fucking now."

CHAPTER 37

Earl Turner looked out at the crowd. Things were getting ugly, and he looked super happy about it. Raging, angry, potentially violent crowds made for great TV. "And if it doesn't happen on TV, it didn't happen," Turner would often tell Danny. He was probably right about that.

Turner was at the podium, behind one of his AMERICA FOR AMERICANS signs. Behind him was his favorite prop: a couple dozen average-looking people, all white. "All normal," as Turner liked to say, when he'd point them out. "All *normal* people, like you and me."

Some fans had been placed here and there so Earl Turner and his "normal" people wouldn't get too sweaty under the klieg lights. But it wasn't really working. The Albany Convention Center was a furnace, with lots of angry people stacked in there like cord wood. Danny could feel the heat throbbing up from Turner's swarm of followers. And what a swarm it was, he observed, as he peered out from behind the curtains on the sidelines. It felt like something terrible was about to happen, in an explosion of blood and sweat.

Some protestors, about three or four hundred of them in all, had somehow gotten into the convention center. Meanwhile, the protestors were surrounded by what seemed like thousands of spit-flecked Earl Turner fanatics, on the left side of the stage, closer to the entrance. A smattering of media and TV cameras were nearby, ignoring Turner and filming all the shoving and the pushing and the brawls that were breaking out.

As a former drummer in a punk rock band, Danny had some experience watching crowds and knowing when things were about to turn ugly. In the old days, he'd sit on his stool behind his drum kit, observing punches being thrown, then chairs, then tables. When it got to that point — or when the cops arrived to beat the shit out of some punks and shut everything down — Danny would tuck his snare under one arm, grab his high-hat with the other, and get the fuck out as quickly as possible.

He couldn't do that now. Watching the Turner supporters start to encircle the protestors, pushing and shoving at them, Danny was reasonably certain someone was going to get badly hurt tonight.

Some big union types were with the protestors, because the labor movement detested everything Turner stood for. A couple of them were black, which made them stand out in this crowd. These big guys looked like they could take any one of the Turner faithful who were present. But not when they were outnumbered by a factor of twenty to one.

The pushing and the shoving got worse. There was lots of cursing and yelling, too. The convention center's security staff looked completely overwhelmed.

The Secret Service detail that had been following Turner everywhere he went, meanwhile, were on or near the stage. They were speaking more and more into the little microphones in their sleeves, which Danny knew was never a good sign.

One of the Secret Service guys, who liked Danny but hated his boss, walked over and spoke into his ear. "Be ready to move, Danny. This is a fucked-up situation."

Long before the big Turner rally had gotten underway, the Secret Service had angrily argued in favor of cancellation — or at least drastically reducing the number of people being allowed in. But Turner would hear none of it.

"I'm not the kind of candidate who hides from the people," he told them as Danny looked on. "I am of, by, and for the people. Deal with it."

So they'd let in this big crowd, maybe fifteen thousand in all. There were plenty of all-American moms and dads, of course, and farmers and truck drivers and fishermen and laborers and all that. And there were several neo-Nazis and Klansmen there, too, carrying signs saying NIGGERS OUT and WHITE IS RIGHT and HEIL TURNER.

Danny had seen them before, at other Turner rallies, but never in such numbers and never acting as bold as they were tonight.

He glanced at Turner, who couldn't have looked any more pleased. The candidate had just finished his usual rant; his big hands were gripping the sides of the podium and he was nodding his head as the crowd chanted: "RIGHT! RIGHT! RIGHT! WHITE! WHITE! WHITE!"

The trouble didn't take long to start. Turner had only been speaking for about five minutes when it happened. The big union guys were pushing back at the neo-Nazis and the Klansmen, and fights were breaking out all over the place. And then — according to the media reports, because Danny couldn't hear anything over the yelling and chanting of the crowd — a shot rang out, then another and another. People started screaming and rushing for the exits. It was bedlam. A fucking madhouse.

As the floor of the convention center started to clear, Danny saw a fat guy in a homemade Nazi-style uniform holding a gun, standing over the body of one of the big union guys. Then half the Secret Service detail had their guns out, too, and they were shooting at the man with the gun. He dropped like a bag of wet cement.

The other half of the detail, meanwhile, had surrounded Turner and were hustling him out of the venue. Turner didn't look happy about it.

One of the agents appeared and grabbed Danny's arm. "Come on, kid," he said. "Time to get the fuck out of here."

CHAPTER 38

Chief John Rarihokwats was a small guy, under five feet tall, I'd say. He looked super old, too: his long hair was pulled back in a single braid that was just about pure white, and his face was hairless and lined. But when he shook my hand, it felt like he could crush it. He was clearly Native — "Indigenous," he told us — but he had these deep blue eyes, hinting at the presence of white man's blood, too.

He was wearing running shoes, jeans, and this amazing leather thing that was sort of a jacket and sort of a shirt. A million tiny, colored beads had been stitched into it, in various designs. He pointed at one of them: "Bear. I'm from the Bear Clan," he said.

I pointed at my Ramones T-shirt. "I'm from the punk rock clan," I said. No one laughed, but Rarihokwats smiled a little.

Rarihokwats was standing in front of the sweat lodge. It was a low-lying hut, basically, with a rounded roof. It had been made out of saplings, it looked like, and then tarps and blankets and one big animal skin had been draped over it. It didn't look like anything special to me, but to the members of Tit Sweat and Leah, I could tell it was a big deal.

When Rarihokwats stepped out to greet us, the Native girls looked at him like we Catholic boys used to look at the cardinal when he'd come to the Cathedral of the Immaculate Conception to pay us a visit: a bit wide-eyed and a bit intimidated.

We were in some sort of a clearing. There were tall trees all around us, birch and maple, and no houses or other people at all. In the distance, I thought I could hear a stream or river. It was already starting to get dark.

Apart from the little sweat lodge and a raging fire pit, there was nothing else and no one else there. Just us and Chief Rarihokwats.

The Chief reminded me of X, sort of mellow but highly intense all at the same time. After the introductions, his blue eyes lingered on me. He barely acknowledged the existence of any of the others. It made me uncomfortable.

He pointed at some big birch stumps that had been placed around the fire pit, in which an impressive fire had been burning. "Sit," he said, and we all did. Rarihokwats looked at me for an uncomfortably long time before he spoke. His voice was deep and it resonated, like an acoustic bass guitar.

"Do you know what a sweat lodge is?" he asked.

I shook my head.

"The sweat lodge is a place for teaching, for healing, for cleansing oneself," he said slowly. "It is a very sacred place to us."

The fire crackled and spit.

"Inside the sweat lodge, as you will see, it is pitch black. In the old days, they would put animal skins like that buffalo skin on the roof, to keep out the light," he said, then chuckled a bit. "Now we use tarps, too."

He continued: "The sweat lodge has been cleaned out. There is grass for you and your friends to sit on and be comfortable. In the center, you will see a mound of earth covered by blankets."

I looked over and saw what he was talking about. The mound went to the door of the sweat lodge and disappeared inside it, like the back of a whale in the water.

On top of the blankets was the skull of some animal and a bunch of necklaces and other stuff.

"That is the altar. It points to the east, where the sun rises," Chief Rarihokwats said. He gestured to the east, which was getting decidedly darker. "The altar ends at a pit inside the sweat lodge. In the pit, we place the rocks we are heating in this fire." He pointed at the fire pit, where I guess the rocks were getting heated. "These rocks are sacred, too. I call them grandfathers. This is our path to the Creator and the universe. This brings us closer to the Creator. This will open up closed doors in your mind, Kurt."

It was the first time he had said my name, and it startled me. It was as if he'd touched me.

After another long silence, and being the reigning small-talk champ, I asked about the trinkets on the blanket-covered altar.

"Those are things that are important to the people who participate in the sweat lodge ceremony," he said. "When they leave, they take those things with them and it connects them back to the energy of the ceremony." He paused. "Do you have a possession like that?"

I didn't; I'd just come from a hospital and all I had with me were the clothes on my back. I basically didn't have anything, in fact, besides my wallet and the keys to my mom's house. But before I could say anything, Sister Betty spoke up. "Kurt didn't know this ceremony was going to happen, Chief, so he had no time to prepare," she said, reaching into the folds of her army surplus jacket. She pulled out a small jewelry box. "His best friend X could not be here but he knows about it. He wanted to give this gift to Kurt to use in the ceremony."

Betty opened the box. It was a silver chain with a shiny silver metal thing hanging from it. My eyes widened. Nobody else knew what it was, with the possible exception of Betty, but I sure did. It was the top of one of the machine heads from Jimmy Cleary's guitar, the one he'd been playing the night he was killed. Jimmy's mother had given X her son's guitar after his funeral as she was cleaning out Jimmy's room for the last time.

Sister Betty and Chief Rarihokwats and everyone else were looking right at me. I really didn't want to get emotional at that point, but my vision was getting a bit blurry.

Sister Betty handed the box to me, hugged me, then sat down again.

Rarihokwats looked satisfied. I think he had concluded that I was now taking the sweat lodge stuff more seriously, and I certainly fucking was. It felt like something really important was about to happen. There was another long silence, and then the chief told us that his name, Rarihokwats, meant "he writes."

"I understand you are a writer, too, Kurt," he said.

I nodded.

"What happens inside the sweat lodge is very important to us," he intoned. "It is sacred. I would ask that you do not write about it and publish it so others can see it."

I nodded again, turning over X's gift in my hands, trying not to cry.

Chief Rarihokwats then started to explain what would happen. There would be smudging outside the sweat lodge, using some sage. Then there would be the passing of the pipe inside it. We were expected to wear "sweat clothes," he said, which apparently meant wearing as little as possible.

There would be drums and rattles and then things he would say, and then the Native people he had chosen — Leah and a couple members of Tit Sweat, apparently — would very carefully carry the sacred rocks, the grandfathers, to the pit in the sweat lodge, using a couple of metal shovels. The Chief would pour water on the rocks, and it would get very hot in there. If I felt sick at any point, he said, I needed to tell him. The same went for the others.

The Creator would be thanked, as well as Mother Earth and the "totem powers," he told us. The "spirit guides" would then be called.

"Kurt," Rarihokwats said, looking at me. "Kurt, what is the question you want carried to the Creator? What is the prayer you wish to make?"

I looked at him, and then at everyone else, their faces reflecting the fire. I was conscious for the first time of my breathing, which felt kind of painful. My face felt wet.

"I want to get better," I finally said, and then I started crying in earnest.

CHAPTER 39

The execution of union leader Tom Edwards — because that's what it was, really, an execution in cold blood, and in front a national TV audience, no less — complicated the lives of Theresa Laverty and, to a lesser extent, Pete Schenk. It also became an occasion for "police bureaucracy clusterfuck," Schenk said to Laverty and Tommy, who both agreed.

That was because the neo-Nazi who killed Edwards was not just a standard-issue Holocaust-denying, minority-hating supporter of Earl Turner. No, the killer (a sweaty, porcine loser named James S. Schipper) was also a card-carrying member of the Church of the Creator.

By the time Laverty got the call from her boss in Fort Myers, James S. Schipper had been dead for three hours, a half-dozen Secret Service .357-magnum rounds embedded in his chest and neck. The blood-stained COTC membership card in his wallet, signed by Bernhardt Klassen personally, sent the Secret

Service in search of the only known Church of the Creator expert working for law enforcement in the United States: Theresa Laverty.

Tommy, of course, knew as much about the COTC as Laverty did, if not more. But Tommy wasn't "official," Laverty's boss told her by phone. "Tommy is *our* resource. He is not to be shared with those overpaid, arrogant bastards in the Secret Service, got it?"

"Got it," Laverty said, then hung up the phone. They were in their meeting space at the back of Fanelli's again. She looked at Tommy. "They don't want you helping out the Secret Service," she said.

Tommy grunted. He didn't seem surprised.

"Why not?" Schenk asked, genuinely bewildered. "A presidential candidate could've been shot, and the Secret Service needs help seeing if *this* Schipper guy acted alone or if there was some sort of COTC conspiracy. Why can't Tommy help?"

"At the bureau, we don't like to share resources," Laverty said. She paused, then half laughed. "And if this presidential candidate had actually been shot ..."

"It would have been a waste of a bullet," Tommy said, arms crossed.

"As a registered Republican, I'll pretend I didn't hear any of that," Schenk said, only sort of joking. "Can one of you explain to me why the Secret Service is interested in learning about the Church of the Creator all of a sudden? The maniac who killed the guy at the rally is dead as a doornail. What more do they want to know?"

Tommy pointed at Fanelli's window, in the direction of Mercer Street. "In a few hours, you'll know."

Laverty nodded solemnly.

"Sorry, folks, I don't speak in FBI code," Schenk said, frowning. "Can someone tell me what exactly is going to happen in a few hours?"

Laverty looked at him and shrugged. "Rioting. People throwing rocks at cop cars. Cops shooting at rioters. That sort of thing. The usual thing that happens in America when a black man is killed without cause by a white racist."

"Has any of that happened yet?"

"The bureau says there's already trouble in and around Albany, as word is spreading," Laverty said. "The media are obviously leading every broadcast with the story — it happened right in from of them, on live television — so we figure there'll be lots of trouble to-night. The black community sees this as an execution, one aided and abetted by Earl Turner."

"More will die," Tommy said matter-of-factly. "Tonight, tomorrow."

Schenk was getting agitated. "Well, that's just great," he said. "Terrific. So what are we supposed to do, sit here with our dicks in our hands, waiting?"

"The Secret Service wants me to come in to their field office in Brooklyn," Laverty said. "They want to know everything there is to know about the Church of the Creator and Klassen, apparently."

"Is that a good use of our time?" Schenk asked.

"No," Laverty said, pulling on her Yves Saint Laurent jacket and heading toward the door. "A better use of our time is to head over to Lighthouse Cleaners first. They'll know what this means for them."

She walked out of Fanelli's, heading east on foot. Tommy and Schenk weren't far behind.

Detective Schenk and FBI special agent Laverty, the New York media later reported, were the first from law enforcement to arrive at Lighthouse Cleaners. The *Times* said they were there to "assist in the investigation into the shootings at the campaign rally for Republican presidential candidate Earl Turner."

"No, we weren't," an exhausted Laverty said, disgusted, surveying the papers in the early hours of the morning after. "We were there to see if the Church of the Creator was going to try to cover its tracks after one of its members killed a man on national television."

She read aloud from the *Daily News* for the benefit of Schenk: "'Upon arriving at the dry cleaner, which serves as one of the business arms of the Creative Church' — they got the name wrong! — 'the officers witnessed suspicious activity. The Church is a registered charity and is not under investigation, police sources stressed.'"

Laverty shook her head, angrier than Schenk had ever seen her. "It isn't a fucking church. It's a fucking

NEW DARK AGES   263

hate group, for Christ's sake. And it *is* under investigation. Or at least it should be."

She continued, from another report in *Newsday*:
"'The officers spotted workers carrying boxes of documents and materials out of the dry-cleaning business.
They approached the workers to make inquiries about
the shootings at the Albany Convention Center.'"

Laverty frowned again and swore. "They weren't
workers. They were armed members of the COTC
Security Legions, trying to load hockey bags full of
weapons into a truck. And the documents were records
of their money laundering and payoffs to politicians
in Washington. And the only person who approached
them, because we didn't want to start a gunfight in the
middle of SoHo, was Tommy."

"'Witnesses on the scene are unclear what happened
next'" — this from the *New York Herald* — "'Some heard
shouting, and others heard sounds like firecrackers. All
said that bystanders were diving for cover behind cars
parked along Lafayette Street.'"

Laverty inhaled, once, twice. She rubbed her eyes,
the mascara now long gone. "They weren't firecrackers,
you idiots. They were heavy tactical rounds from fucking assault rifles." She paused, as Schenk watched her.
"And there was no shouting. They just started shooting."

Next, she read the *Post*'s description of what they
thought happened next. "'Some of the Church's security
officers started to shoot, and a bystander was critically
hit. Two officers on the scene — one a Fifth Precinct

detective, the other an FBI special agent — returned fire and fatally wounded two of the Church's security team. A police source who was not authorized to comment said that one of the dead, Bill Klassen, was the son of the founder of the Church of the Creator. Klassen, a former marine who had been discharged dishonorably, was known to police.'"

Theresa Laverty sat in the Lower Manhattan Hospital's emergency room, the crumpled newspapers on a chair beside her. She was weeping. Pete Schenk reached up and squeezed her hand, but said nothing. "He was 'known to police' because he was the one who killed those three punk rock kids," she said, sobbing. "And the critically wounded bystander wasn't a bystander. It was Tommy. And those bastards killed him."

CHAPTER 40

So, we played the makeup gig at the Horseshoe.

Stiff Records hadn't been happy when I crashed-and-burned, naturally. Neither was the Horseshoe's management. Nor our tour manager Bembe Smith or our driver/security dude, Mike. The scheduled gig was canceled.

But we made up for the missed gig, and then some. Patti returned from Toronto, bringing her feminist punk chick friend Lisa with her for emotional support or whatever. Lisa was tall and subdued — kind of like Patti.

The rest of us, meanwhile, returned from Six Nations feeling totally different. I had promised Chief Rarihokwats I wouldn't write about what happened in the sweat lodge ritual, and I won't. But I can say that after about four hours in there, in the middle of the night — a completely saturnalian experience — we all jumped in this little stream that was nearby. The Chief told us we actually should. It was dark and cold as fuck, but it was the most amazing thing, too. I'd felt as if I was washing away a ton of grime and sweat and accumulated shit. I was new again. I got out of the stream and was towelling myself off when the Chief came up and asked me how I was feeling.

"It sounds corny, but I feel like I'm brand new," I said. "I feel like I crawled out of the womb. Is that weird?"

He laughed. "It is not weird. Many people say that afterward."

"I don't want to say *reborn*, because those phony born-again evangelical people say that. But it isn't that. It feels … real."

"It is."

And it was. Everything was in focus. There were sharp edges to everything. Colors were brighter, even.

It was fucking weird. But it was awesome.

I was also shagged and bagged, my brothers. I was spent. I passed out in the Econoline five minutes into the drive. And — once back in Toronto and in my room at the Rex — I crawled into the bed and slept for ten hours straight, in my clothes. When I got up the next day, I saw that someone had cleaned the place up. My other clothes had all been washed and folded, my Docs and brothel creepers and Converse were all in a neat row, my jackets were hanging in the closet, and there was no sign of the baggies of speed. Or even the offending Narcotics Anonymous pamphlet.

That night, we had the sold-out makeup gig and it was one for the history books. The Toronto crowd was stoked, and so were we.

All of us were a punk rock force to be reckoned with. Tit Sweat were just as intense as before, but the Punk Rock Virgins (and especially Leah and Sister Betty) were leaping around the stage, manic, wild, like solar flares. They played better than I'd ever seen them: intense, focused, note-perfect. And the Nasties (all of us) went at our hour-long set with a heads-down vengeance — and ended up playing a half-hour encore that only ended because Sam and me broke most of the strings on our guitars, and Eddie put a big hole in the middle of the skin of his snare.

At the end, I invited all of the sellout crowd up onstage with us. Dozens of punks clambered up onto the Horseshoe's hallowed stage, on which everyone from the Strolling Bones to the Ramones had played. The tavern's security guys didn't look too happy about that, but it was the way we always finished epic shows — and this one was particularly epic.

The crowd did the "oh yeah" chant as we played our fave closing tune, "The Invasion of the Tribbles." I screamed myself hoarse and hugged just about everyone who was up there with us.

The only downer was that X wasn't there. I wanted to run up to him and tell him that I was clean as a whistle and fit as a fiddle, and that I was back among the living. I wanted to hug him and get X's absolution. But he was still AWOL. Nobody seemed to know where he was, either.

So, the next day, we packed up at the Rex and headed back home. We were all exhausted, but we were feeling exhilarated, too. Toronto had been a turning point for us, and for me. So we sped back to the United States of America, which — as it turned out — was no longer the country we'd left just two weeks before.

The first indication that the country had gone mad came at the border crossing at Niagara Falls. All of the border cops regarded us with open contempt. We were punks, and we were used to getting hassled by uniformed douchebags — for our hair, for our clothes, for our existence. It went with the territory.

But these guys weren't interested in us, so much; their focus was *Bembe*.

They ordered us to pull over the Econoline and the station wagon. One of them, some creep who looked sort of like Mussolini, barked that we needed to have "secondary inspection." We stepped out as a bunch of these uniformed creeps stared at us.

Mussolini ordered us all to go stand on the sidewalk, away from our vehicles. Bembe, however, was told to stay right where he was, beside the van. Mussolini glared at him, his little pig eyes lingering on Bembe's dreads and black skin. After about a minute of that, Mussolini signaled a couple pimply faced border guards over. "Take Mr. *Macaca* inside," he said.

The rest of us sat or stood on the sidewalk for the next two hours, watching as a half-dozen border Schutzstaffel took our vehicles apart. They'd open our bags and then toss the contents and our gear onto the parking lot. When they were done, I asked one of them if they were putting our things back where they found them.

"Do it yourself, punk," he sneered.

"What about our friend? When will you let him go?" I asked, raging inside. "Has he been stopped for DWB?"

"What's DWB?" the Sneer said, his pinched features darkening.

"Driving while black," I said.

Behind me, I could hear Sam Shiller and Mike laughing. A few tense moments passed, and the Sneer looked like he wanted to slug me. But a couple other cars had been pulled aside for "secondary inspection," too, and the occupants were all watching. There'd be no punch today. Abruptly, the Sneer swore and stalked away, one hand on his service revolver. One of his underlings told us we could repack our vehicles.

Bembe stormed out of the border station a few minutes later. He looked pissed off but obviously ready to leave. Mussolini stepped out behind him, and he was looking at Bembe differently.

"Let's go," Bembe said. So we did. No one said anything.

Back on the Interstate, and back in the U.S., I asked Bembe if he was okay.

"I'm okay," he said, his Jamaican passport still clutched in his big hands. "I'm fine."

"What did they do?" Sam asked. "Why did they have you in there for so long?"

Bembe shrugged his big shoulders. "Oh, you know," he said. "I look suspicious. They said I look like some-one on a wanted list." He paused. "We all look alike to them."

"I'm sorry, Bembe," I said. "I'm really sorry you had to go through that shit." I paused. "They called you something … Mack?"

"It's Macaca," Bembe said. "It means nigger, basically."

And, at precisely that moment, we came up to a farm where someone had painted TURNER: AMERICA FOR AMERICANS on the side of the barn.

We all watched it go by, and nobody said anything.

For the rest of our journey Stateside, we did Earl Turner sightings.

It made us fucking miserable, but we did it anyway. Whenever we'd see a Turner bumper sticker, or bill-board, or T-shirt, we'd point it out to each other. "There's another one," we'd say. Then we'd lapse back into silence.

All along Highway 90, we were reminded that we weren't in Canada anymore. But it didn't feel like the United States we'd grown up in, either. Strangers in a strange land didn't quite capture it. It was like we were astronauts and we'd landed on a planet where everyone had gone fucking insane, except they sort of looked like they did before. Until they opened their mouths, that is.

When we were in Canada, it had been safe to call Earl Turner a fucking racist and gay-hating anti-Semite out loud, because he was all of those things, and because Canadians generally aren't politically fucked in the head. But back in the States, I felt this little tug inside of me, urging me to shut up. I sort of became aware that there was possibly a risk associated with saying those things out loud at home. First Amendment or no First Amendment.

And, let's be clear: most Americans never talked about politics, anyway. They didn't *care* — which was why so few of them voted, and why pieces of shit like Earl Turner were frequently getting elected: apathy was the best friend of the Far Right.

Middle America's moms and pops would always rather talk about the Super Bowl or what megachurch they go to or the PTA or whatever. Not politics.

But the X Gang was political, even if our songs weren't so much. Every punk is political, or should be.

"As the only Jew in the X Gang, I'd like to thank everyone for not reporting me to the border Gestapo," Sam said as we passed yet another TURNER AMERICA bumper sticker. Bembe, up front, gave a dark sort of laugh. Being the X Gang's resident gay guy — and being still in the closet to all but a few — I knew what Sam meant. It now felt different to be in his skin, or Bembe's, or mine. It felt like trouble waited around every corner, now.

Luke, who was albino and therefore the whitest guy we knew — and who was arguably therefore safe — spoke up. "I keep trying to spot someone who I think couldn't possibly be a Turner supporter," he said, "but I keep getting it wrong. When we get closer, I see that they have an Earl Turner bumper sticker or whatever. It sucks."

Everyone nodded, silent.

At one rest stop, not far from Albany, Sam picked up a discarded copy of *USA Today*. "Look at this," he said. The headline, above the fold, was "Turner Rally Shootings Set off Turmoil Nationwide."

The first couple paragraphs read:

> The United States today entered the fifth straight day of racially charged lootings, riots, and shootings, with deaths reported in Dallas, Chicago, and Los Angeles, police said. In Washington, most Democratic leaders and some Republican senators lay the blame at the feet of GOP presidential candidate Earl Turner, saying that Turner has needlessly provoked racial tensions nationwide with a divisive and negative campaign, and a deadly rally in Albany, NY.
>
> Turner, however, rejected those criticisms, telling a press conference at his Portland, ME, headquarters that he was not to blame. "White Americans aren't the ones breaking windows and looting and shooting our heroes in uniform. It's being done by illegal aliens, brought here by wealthy foreign interests to divide and destroy us."

Below the headline were four photos grouped together: a guy in Philly, wearing a bandana, getting ready to toss a Molotov cocktail at a barricade of National Guardsmen; a young black girl in Chicago, crying and clutching at her bleeding head and surrounded by a bunch of angry-looking white cops; a cop car on fire in L.A.'s South Central; and a picture of Turner outside his headquarters in Portland, arms up in triumph, a big crowd cheering him on. Some of those in the crowd were making what looked like Nazi salutes.

"Jesus Christ," Patti said, "what the fuck is happening?"

We kept driving. As we slid deeper into America's dark heart, nobody wanted to talk about politics or Earl Turner or anything like that anymore. It was too depressing. It was too awful. So, we just stopped talking about it.

After a while, everything was silent, except for the growl of the Econoline. It was getting a bit dark. Mike was driving; everyone else except me was asleep.

Reluctantly, I picked up the copy of *USA Today*. On the inside pages, there was a long AP story about a Gallup Poll that studied Earl Turner's supporters. The byline on the story was our old journalist source-*cum*-nemesis from our hometown rag, the *Portland Press Herald*, Ron McLeod. I read it, even though I knew it would depress the shit out of me.

Turner's core vote is comprised of older, whiter men. But Gallup says some assumptions previously

made about the core Turner vote were misguided.
Until recently, most political pundits believed that
Turner's vote was rooted in economic insecurity
and resentments. They believed that Turner
was attracting the support of older white men
in the primaries who believed they lost their
manufacturing jobs in America's Rust Belt. But
that view is mistaken, Gallup says.

Gallup makes clear that the number-one
preoccupation of Turner's supporters isn't the
economy: it is race. Concluded the pollster:
"Turner's supporters tend to be less educated
and more likely to work in blue collar occupations.
But some also earn relatively high household
incomes and live in areas more exposed to higher
levels of international trade. There is compelling
evidence that racial isolation and less strictly
economic measures of social status, namely
health and intergenerational mobility, reflect
more favorably toward Turner, and these factors
predict support for him but not other Republican
presidential candidates," Gallup said.

Racism. That was why Earl Turner was winning.
America was racist at its core, and Turner knew it.
McLeod's story went on from there, but that was the gist
of it. I couldn't read any more.

It *was* racism, and it wasn't an accident. It was *deliberate*, and all of the experts agreed it was paying

dividends, too. It explained why Turner had done the exact opposite of what the so-called experts had said he should do, and why he started viciously attacking blacks and Asians and gays and just about every other minority. And it was why he was getting close to capturing his party's presidential nomination, McLeod wrote. Some candidates were even thinking about dropping out of the race and endorsing him.

As we moved east along the turnpike, it occurred to me that Earl Turner had awoken a beast, and that the beast was now snaking through the countryside, infecting people and killing everything that was good and decent. I looked again at the photos on the cover of the *USA Today*.

"I fucking hate you," I said out loud.

Mike, startled, glanced up at the van's rearview mirror and at me. "What did I do?"

"Not you, Mike," I said. "Earl Turner. And Danny. I fucking hate them."

CHAPTER 41

Click. Ring, ring.

"Hey."

"Hey, man. Thanks for calling."

"You okay?"

"Yeah. I guess."

"How can I help?"

Laugh. "This situation cannot be helped."

"I've been thinking. I'm really wondering if this is the right move."

"It is. I have no fucking doubt in my mind."

"Are you sure?"

"I've never been more sure about anything in my life." Pause. "I'm done, anyway."

"When?"

"Soon."

Danny O'Heran's eyes widened. His heart started to race.

It was early morning. He was clutching a copy of the *Union Leader*, the newspaper published statewide in New Hampshire. On one of the inside pages, in a column marked "Police Blotter," there was a brief story headlined "Dover Police Seek Info on Murder Victim."

The story read:

> DOVER — Police are seeking information to assist them in identifying a man found dead off Highway 4, north of Durham, NH.
>
> The man was described by police as being of medium height, somewhat overweight, with wavy dark hair. Police say that the man's wallet contained identification belonging to "Ezra Faber," but they believe that is a false name. Police are appealing for anyone with information about this man to come forward.
>
> A police source, who did not wish to be identified, stated that the man was bound and had been shot "execution style." A leaflet was found stuffed into his pants pocket, the police source said, from the Otto, NC, Church of the Creative.

Danny blinked, then blinked again. He looked up and around the parking lot at the Earl Turner campaign office in Dover, on Main Street. Turner was still inside, beaming as he posed for photos with staff, volunteers, and local luminaries. The plan for the day was to do meet-and-greet type events across New Hampshire, Maine, rural Massachusetts, and southern Vermont. At the moment, therefore, nobody was paying any attention to Turner's personal assistant, who was sitting in the campaign Jeep, freaking out.

Danny wanted to make a call, *that call*, but didn't. Instead, he jumped out of the Jeep and slid a dime in the pay phone located at the far side of the parking lot. The phone rang a couple of times before Danny's mother picked up. "Hello, Mom?" Danny said. "Is everything okay? Is everyone there okay?"

He listened to his mother's questions. She was telling him that everything and everyone was fine, but now she was worried about Danny. She asked him what was going on.

"Nothing," he said. "It's okay, Mom." He paused, unsure, then coughed a couple times. "I may be going away for a bit. Some campaign stuff. But everything is fine?"

His mother wasn't reassured, but Danny O'Heran said he had to go collect Turner. He told her he'd call her later. And that he loved her, which he knew was something he didn't say often enough. His guts felt aflame. His hands were shaking.

Danny looked in the direction of the campaign headquarters, where Turner was smiling away, cheerfully signing autographs and posing for pictures with his fans.

He was winning. And now, Danny knew, almost nothing stood between Earl Turner and the nomination. *Nothing.*

CHAPTER 42

Theresa Laverty slammed down the receiver and swore. Pete Schenk, sitting at his battered little desk in the Fifth Precinct, watched her. She'd been in a pretty bad way since Tommy was killed, and she looked like she hadn't slept at all. Her always-fashionable outfits looked like they needed a dry cleaning.

"More Secret Service questions?" he asked.

"No," she said, shaking her head and rubbing her eyes. "A different group of law enforcement idiots, this time."

"Who?"

"The FBI field office in Portsmouth, New Hampshire," she said. "The entire bureau is on the lookout for anything and everything to do with the Church of the Creator in the wake of Albany and Tommy. As you know. But these guys in Portsmouth didn't bother to tell anyone about finding something that is very significant."

"What?"

"Some grifter using the fake name of Ezra Faber was found killed, execution-style, off a highway in rural New Hampshire a couple of days ago," Laverty said. "Bound, gagged, shot twice in the back of the head. They found a COTC leaflet stuffed in his pocket, one about Jews being the enemies of mankind. It was left behind like it was a calling card. Just like all of the punk rock victims."

"Well, if his name is something like Ezra Faber, I'm assuming he's Jewish. And I'm assuming that's the main reason why some COTC nut killed him," Schenk said. "Or am I missing something?"

"No," Laverty said. "That would make sense, except for one thing."

"What?"

"I impressed on the field office the need to dig deeper. So a couple of agents finally went back to this guy's hotel room after the local P.D. had cleared out," she said. "There was nothing unusual, with the exception of a bunch of copies of Earl Turner's public campaign schedules, and an address book, and what was in it."

"So, he was an Earl Turner fan," Schenk said. "So what? Everyone else is these days. Anything important in the address book?"

"Yes," Laverty said. "It had the unlisted home address and numbers of Danny O'Heran and his family. He's the kid who used to be part of that punk rock gang in Portland. And he's now Earl Turner's main personal assistant. And that is significant."

CHAPTER 43

Where the fuck did X go? I kept thinking all the way home. *Did he screw around on Patti with that Nagamo chick? Why does he have to be so fucking mysterious all the time?*

All good questions. All unlikely ever to be answered. This was X, after all, and if you're the kind of person who's unenthusiastic about big information gaps in your daily routine, I would recommend against becoming one of X's close friends.

But there he stood, at my mom's door, the day after we got back.

When we got back to Portland, I spent a bit of time with my mom, and I saw my dad at his apartment out near the naval base at Kittery. Sister Betty had called to tell them I'd been in the hospital, but she didn't tell them what for. I told them it was because I got a bad case of the flu. I could tell my dad didn't believe a word of it. He didn't grill me about it, though.

Patti had told me X was back in Portland, too. I decided not to ask her if they were still the Portland Punk Rock Super Couple, but I certainly wondered if they were. She didn't sound like a happy unit and quickly signed off, saying she was going to be spending some time with her family in Boston until the next leg of the tour.

So, I was doing laundry — when you go on tour, you have a small mountain of it — when the bell rang. And there X stood, holding a guitar. And not just any guitar. It was *Jimmy Cleary's* guitar. I could see it had been all fixed up, too: new pickups, new machine heads, new strings, all buffed and shined.

We just looked at each other, neither of us saying a word for the longest time.

"So," I finally said. "Is that Jimmy's?"

"It is. I got it fixed up." He held it out. "He'd want you to have it. He'd be proud of you. I am, too."

For that, I got a bit emotional, and I grabbed the guitar and one-arm hugged him. Being X, he naturally stood there stiff as a board. "I missed you, brother," I said, pulling back to look at him. "I thought you were gone for good. Or that you were done with me for good."

He arched one eyebrow and almost grinned. "Well, I admit I was getting a bit fed up with some of the drama," he said, his head down. Then he looked right at me: "But you're my best friend. You're my brother. And I'll never give up on you."

That made me want to cry again, but I didn't. He cocked an eyebrow at me. "Can I come in?" he asked.

"There's something I need to talk to you about. It's important."

"Of course, man," I said, ushering him in. "My mom's out, so we can use the living room."

I sat on the couch, Jimmy's guitar across my lap, and waited. X sat on my dad's old La-Z-Boy. He actually looked a bit anxious, which wasn't something I'd seen very often. X got up and started pacing around. His brows were furrowed.

Eventually, he sat back down and started to tell me the story. The one call to London, months ago, the two things no one knew, the three dead punk kids. All of it. It was a life-changing story, you might say. It was, he said, "the new dark ages."

At the end, I yelled, I shouted, I pleaded with him. I begged him. I tried to talk him out of it, of course, but it was way too late.

So, in the end, I went along with it. He's X, and he's my best friend, after all.

CHAPTER 44

Theresa Laverty and Pete Schenk sat in the cramped waiting area at the Earl Turner campaign office in Portland. The place was busy. There were a half-dozen receptionists answering the constantly ringing phones and receiving deliveries. Dozens of people wearing volunteer badges ran in and out. It had the feel of a campaign that was well financed and well organized. It had the feel of a campaign that was winning.

Laverty's return to Portland had been easy to arrange. She had the mandate to travel wherever the Church of the Creator made its presence known. Pete Schenk, however, was wholly outside his jurisdiction. His request to his bosses for permission to accompany Laverty should have been denied. But after the killing of Tom Edwards at the Albany rally and Tommy's death afterward, permission had been quickly granted.

Laverty and Schenk had called ahead to meet with Danny O'Heran and were told he was unavailable. They called again and were told he was out with the candidate. The third time, after being put on hold for ten minutes, they decided to pay Danny a visit in person.

So there they stood, clearly unimpressed. After speaking worriedly to someone on the phone, the receptionist had told them that Danny O'Heran was unavailable. She looked scared. A couple of the other receptionists were watching them nervously.

Laverty was in no mood for further delay. "I'm a special agent with the FBI," she said loudly. "My colleague here is from the NYPD, and he's investigating multiple murders. If you do not bring Danny O'Heran out now, we will be coming back with a warrant."

Schenk piped in, smiling: "And the press will probably find out we're here, and they'll want to know why the police are executing a warrant at the campaign headquarters of Earl Turner."

The receptionist was wide-eyed as she picked up the phone. She spoke to someone briefly, then hung up. "Mr. Hailey is coming out to speak to you. He is the most senior person here at the moment."

A man arrived a minute later, looking like a balding praying mantis and extending a hand that resembled a tobacco-stained spider. "Miss Laverty, Mr. Schenk," he said. "I'm Derwin Hailey, a senior advisor to Mr. Turner. The candidate is out of the office at the moment, and Danny O'Heran is with him. They should be back soon, however. Would you like to wait? Can I get you a coffee or a water?"

"No, thank you," Laverty said icily. "When will they be back?"

"Very soon," Hailey said, all fake smiles and solicitude. He lowered his voice. "May I ask if Danny is in some sort of trouble?" He sounded hopeful.

Laverty glared at him. "Danny O'Heran is in no trouble. We do need to speak to him, however."

"I see," Hailey said. "Is there anything I could assist you with?"

"Not unless you know something about the Church of the Creator," Schenk said, then immediately regretted it. Laverty gave him a hard look.

Derwin Hailey's phony smile dropped for a moment, then quickly returned. "I'm not familiar with it," he said.

Laverty knew he was lying and glared at him. "Given that one of its members killed a protestor at your rally in Albany a few days ago, Mr. Hailey, I rather doubt that," she said. She paused for dramatic effect, but it wasn't necessary. Derwin Hailey looked as if he had stopped breathing. "You know it is an offence to lie to a federal agent, don't you?" she added.

Hailey gulped, his Adam's apple moving like a snake. "Yes, yes," he said, plainly terrified. "Of course, yes, I should have remembered that the shooter was involved in that church. Of course."

"So, let's try again," Laverty said, now actually glad that Schenk had said what he said. "Are you familiar with the Church of the Creator?"

"Not beyond what I have read in the papers," Hailey stammered. "I'm not familiar with that organization."

All of the receptionists were watching the unfolding drama now. Some of the volunteers had stepped out to watch, too.

"What about Bernhardt Klassen?" Laverty demanded. "Have you ever heard of him, Mr. Hailey?"

Before Hailey could answer, there was a sudden commotion at the doors behind them.

Earl Turner and Danny O'Heran had returned.

CHAPTER 45

Gary's. Home.

Gary's was the grimy, gritty bar that was the center of the Portland punk scene. Where it all started.

It was opening time on a Thursday, so few people were in the bar. The Hot Nasties, the Punk Rock Virgins, and the rest of the X Gang had decided to convene a summit of sorts: Earl Turner was planning a rally at the State Theatre, a few blocks away, and some of us wanted to do something about that. X and I suggested holding a show to protest Turner and possibly a march on the State Theatre with as many punks as we could assemble.

Bembe Smith shook his head and tapped the top of one of Gary's tiny round tables. "This is a very, very bad idea," he said. "It is a crazy idea. When this Earl Turner held his last rally, in Albany, two people were shot to death! Please don't do this."

Sister Betty was sitting beside Bembe and nodding a bit. "Maybe Bembe is right. Maybe this is a bad idea, Kurt."

I crossed my arms and shook my head. "There are two reasons why we need to do this. One is general, and one is specific."

Eddie was standing behind Betty. He frowned. "Specific? What?"

I held up two fingers. "One, this racist piece of shit is from Portland, and we need to show *everyone* that not everyone from Portland is a minority-hating, woman-hating, Jew-hating, everyone-hating motherfucker," I said.

"And two … Danny." I looked around the table at all of the Nasties, Virgins, Mike, and X. "Danny was one of us, and now he is working for that racist prick." I spat out his name. "Danny! Lots of people think that we're okay with that, or that we don't care. We need to show them that we're *not* okay with it, and that we *do* care. We need to say we condemn what Danny is doing."

Patti looked at me. "Those are actually good reasons, Mr. Kurt."

Nobody said anything as they thought about what I'd said. Sam Shiller, resident worrier, spoke first. "Guys, I don't know," he said. "This feels like we're just looking for trouble. I agree with Bembe. If we do just a show here, fine. But the minute we step outside, and go near that bastard's rally, someone is going to get hurt. And nobody'll be upset if it's one of us."

"I agree with Sam," Betty said, reluctantly. "Enough people have been hurt — or worse. Can't we just stay here and avoid looking for a fight, for once?"

Bembe again started tapping the orange terry cloth cover on the table. "Guys, this is Gary's, on Brown Street," he said, then indicated another spot on the table, a couple inches away. "And this is where the Earl Turner rally is taking place, at the State Theatre on Congress Street. That theater is going to be surrounded by an army of police and Secret Service, especially after what happened in Albany. You are never going to get near it!"

Sister Betty nodded. "And if we do, it'll end in a huge stupid fight, and I'm sick of all the violence."

Eddie spoke up, sounding uncharacteristically political. "I like the idea of showing everyone that Portland isn't all racist. I want to do it."

"We still have a few days until the tour starts again in Boston, right?" Luke said. "I wouldn't mind doing a free show for Nasties fans in Portland. And I think it's a good idea to show them that what Danny did was wrong. I'm in."

Mike, who'd been silent up till then, was wearing his FUCK THE WORLD T-shirt and an indifferent expression. "Bembe and me will make sure everyone is safe when they're at Gary's. And if they go to that bastard's rally?" He shrugged. "Everyone is allowed to exercise their constitutional rights, right?"

Eddie, Luke, and I laughed at Mike's invocation of the U.S. Constitution. We all then looked at X.

He spoke quietly, so we had to lean in to hear. "Portland is our town. It isn't Earl Turner's," he said. He paused and looked straight at Bembe. "And I agree with Bembe — the police are useless. But Danny O'Heran is a fucking traitor. And we need to make sure everyone knows that."

There was silence for a moment, because almost everyone was surprised — not because X favored the gig and a protest, but because he had spoken so harshly about Danny.

I wasn't surprised.

I watched X and Bembe exchange a look, and kind of wondered who knew what. After a bit of that, I spoke, clapping my hands. "All right then! We do the free show. And afterward, if anyone wants to head over to the State Theatre with us to protest, they can … and then Bembe can bail us all out of jail or collect our remains at the morgue."

Bembe shook his head. "You guys are crazy."

CHAPTER 46

Derwin Hailey, having briefly been a bottom-feeding personal injury attorney before he became a bottom-feeding pollster, insisted on sitting in on the meeting with Laverty, Schenk, and Danny. Like most people in politics, Hailey liked to pretend that he was Someone Important, even though he really wasn't.

What was surprising was that Earl Turner insisted on being there as well. "Danny's my friend, and he is very important to my campaign," Turner said, smiling his big homecoming smile and slapping Danny on a knee. "Besides, I was a lawyer not too long ago. I want to be here if he needs any help."

But Danny knew the real reason Turner wanted to sit in on the meeting. He wanted to know if the two investigators knew anything about "Ezra."

Turner led them all to the campaign headquarters boardroom. When they'd all taken a seat, Laverty looked at Turner, expressionless. "It's not necessary for you to be here, Mr. Turner," she said. "Danny isn't in any trouble. Far from it."

"Then what is this about?" Hailey said, scrawny arms crossed, frowning.

Laverty ignored him, looking only at Danny and Turner. "A few days ago, a man was found murdered on a stretch of road near Durham, New Hampshire," she said, watching for any reaction. "He had been bound and shot execution-style. Two bullets in the back of his head."

Despite his best efforts, Danny blanched. His eyes had a yellowish tinge. He grabbed at his middle, which was throbbing.

"What does that have to do with this campaign, Special Agent?" Hailey asked, likely wondering where the campaign's real lawyer was.

Laverty kept her focus on Danny O'Heran and Earl Turner. "This man, who used a false name but was a fraud artist with past convictions for extortion and racketeering, had two things in his hotel room that are of interest to the FBI and the NYPD," she said. Danny was sweating. "He had a number of your public schedules, Mr. Turner, and he had an address book with details about Danny and his family in it."

Before Danny or Turner could say anything, Derwin Hailey spoke. "Anyone can walk in off the street and get one of our public schedules," he said. "Some newspapers even print those schedules in their campaign coverage. It is not unusual."

Laverty and Schenk kept watching Turner and Danny. "The fact that this man had the unlisted address and phone number of the O'Heran family is unusual, wouldn't you say, Danny?" Laverty said, more as a statement than a question. "Did you know this Ezra person?"

Danny shook his head, but did not speak. He had gone even more pale.

Pete Schenk spoke up. "Had you ever met him, Danny?"

"No," Danny croaked, looking profoundly uncomfortable.

Laverty immediately knew Danny was lying; he was a lousy liar. Earl Turner could probably see this, too. He smiled, waving his big football hands around as he spoke. "Pete, Theresa! There could be any number of explanations for that, right?"

"And what would those be, Mr. Turner?" Laverty snapped, her dislike for the Republican presidential candidate obvious. "We are drawing a blank on how your personal assistant's private information could be known to a man who had been executed and dumped on the side of a road in another state. What would your explanation be for that?"

Turner smiled again, unfazed. "The O'Herans are very active Christians and very active in their church. I would imagine many people know them, Special Agent Laverty. What do you think it means?"

Laverty was deadpan as she responded. "We think it means someone was targeting you, Mr. Turner. Possibly with blackmail, possibly with threats. But we do not think it is a coincidence."

The boardroom was silent for a full half-minute.

"Are you familiar with the Church of the Creator, Danny?" Laverty abruptly asked.

Danny O'Heran's face was a blank. Derwin Hailey looked surprised. And the big smile on Earl Turner's face completely disappeared.

"Wait a second, wait a second," Hailey said, raising his voice. "We have spoken to the Secret Service about Albany, and we don't have to speak to you about it …"

There was suddenly a loud knock, and the door to the boardroom flew open. The campaign lawyer had arrived, out of breath and stuffed into what looked like a ten-piece pinstriped suit. He made a big show of slapping his briefcase down on the table. "This interview is over, officers. My clients have nothing more to say!" he said, wheezing.

Seconds later, a smiling Daisy Something stepped into the room and handed Derwin Hailey a pink message slip.

As he read the message, Hailey smiled, too. "Mr. Turner," he said, clearly overjoyed. "You have just been endorsed by two former vice-presidents and the widow of a former president."

CHAPTER 47

Patti Upchuck was crying.

We were sitting on the steps leading to the basement at Sound Swap. The Punk Rock Virgins had finished practicing for the Gary's protest gig, and Sister Betty and Leah had left to pick up spray paint and cardboard to make anti-Turner signs.

The rest of the Hot Nasties wouldn't be arriving for a half-hour or so, so Patti and I had the place to ourselves.

"I don't know why he just took off when we were all in Toronto," she said, her mascara streaked down her cheeks. "Where the fuck did he go, Kurt? Did I piss him off?"

I squeezed her hand. I knew things that I just couldn't tell her. But I wanted to make her feel better.

"You didn't piss him off, babe," I said. "Not a chance." I paused. "I think I know the answer already, but I assume you tried to talk to him, and he didn't tell you anything?"

"Of course," she said "Why the fuck would he communicate anything to me? I mean, it's not like we're intimate or anything!"

She sobbed a bit. I waited a bit.

Then she looked at me, right at me. "Kurt, don't you fucking lie to me," she said. "Don't lie to me. Did he fuck that chick?"

I shook my head a million times. "No way. No way, not a chance, no fucking way," I said. "Never. *Never* would he do that."

"Then where did he go? Why did he just leave? Why won't he tell me anything?" she said, sobbing again.

I wanted to tell her something. But I couldn't.

"Babe, all I know is that he came back here early," I said, then lied. "I'm not sure why. Maybe something to do with his family."

"That's fucking bullshit and you know it, Kurt," she said, slapping my arm. "He's got the most perfect and well-adjusted family there is. It had nothing to do with his family."

"Okay, fine. I don't know for sure. But he didn't step out on you. Not X. Not ever."

She looked at me and evidently decided I was telling the truth. "All right, then," she said. "So he didn't fuck that chick?"

I shook my head. "No. Eddie did."

"Eddie did?" She started to laugh, and I burst out laughing, too. "Well, that makes sense. Eddie is a fucking slut."

"Yes, he is. And he told me all about it when I was in the hospital." I pretended to shudder. "Breeder sex. Gross."

She laughed more. At least she seemed to be feeling a bit better.

"One more question," she said. "And no bullshit, okay?"

"Okay."

"I overheard him and Mike talking at Gary's. I thought he was saying something about Mike needing to look after me, because he might be going away again for a while. Is that true? Could he be going away again?"

"No," I said, but that was a lie.

CHAPTER 48

Earl Turner was smiling.

The FBI agent and the New York City homicide detective had only been gone for a few minutes, but the Republican presidential candidate had already forgotten about them. His trusted and wealthy friend Ben had said he would take care of "Ezra," and that he would direct attention away from Earl Turner, and he had certainly done that. The COTC pamphlet had been left behind to attract attention to the Creators, and that had worked, too.

The Turner campaign schedules and the address book had been a sloppy oversight, but Earl Turner wasn't worried. Even though he hadn't practiced law for very long before his first congressional run, Turner knew that Laverty and Schenk simply did not have enough evidence to implicate him or his campaign. Suspicions were not evidence. Besides, he and Danny had been Ezra's *victims*, not his partners in crime.

In his discussion with his millionaire pal, Earl Turner had been careful not to mention why he was so concerned about "Ezra," of course. Most of Turner's supporters were big fans of his anti-black, anti-brown, anti-yellow, anti-punk, anti-Jew, and anti-gay campaign. An old photograph of Earl Turner's dick in some old queer's mouth wouldn't have gone over very well at all, so he'd kept quiet about that.

Instead, he'd simply told his rich pal that "Ezra" had threatened violence against people close to him. Which, in a way, he had: one of the Jews had threatened to kill Danny O'Heran's family.

Turner knew, however, that Danny had also seen the infamous photo and that he would not soon forget it. He might even suspect, as Turner assuredly did, that the original photo was in a safety deposit box at a bank somewhere.

When they spoke, Ben told Turner that nothing was found on "Ezra." Turner was pleased to hear that. He wondered if the photo was in a vault at a place like the Bank of Credit and Commerce in New York City — where Turner himself maintained a couple of secret bank accounts, to hide some money he'd made from various bribes and illegal donations. The Bank of Credit and Commerce was the favored financial institution of terror groups and despots around the globe, too.

Danny wouldn't have known about any of that, of course, but he might one day have too much to drink, and he might mention the photograph to someone. It would invariably set off all kinds of questions and maybe even a press inquiry. And Earl Turner couldn't have that.

So, Danny O'Heran would need to be eliminated. He knew too much — about "Ezra," about the donations from guys like Ben, about the dirty tricks, about the extracurricular excursions with Daisy and Stacey. After he had secured the nomination, the Republican Party's experienced staff in Washington would become part of Earl Turner's campaign organization, and he wouldn't need a small-town rube like Danny anymore. So Danny, a potential liability, would be erased as "Ezra" had been.

At the moment, however, Turner didn't need to trouble himself with any of that. With these endorsements — two former Republican vice-presidents and the widow of a former Republican president — the nomination was now his. He knew this, but he wanted to hear Hailey say it.

"The numbers are incredible, Mr. Turner," Hailey said, relishing the moment, too. "Barring any unforeseen disaster, the nomination is yours. Your opponents are running out of money, or running out of support, or both. And you now lead in every national poll of Republicans. The America for Americans campaign was always a risk, but that risk paid off."

Turner clapped Hailey on the back, then Danny. He was happier than they had ever seen him.

Danny O'Heran, for his part, was still rattled by the visit by Laverty and Schenk. They seemed to know more than they were letting on — and they hadn't looked like they'd been persuaded by his attempt to lie, either. But if Turner wasn't worried, then why should he be worried? "Ezra" was dead, which meant the threat to his family was gone for good. As Turner patted his back, Danny managed a small smile.

"Danny, Derwin, I owe this all to guys like you," Turner said. "We need to turn our rally at the State Theatre into a victory party!" He paused, anticipating what Derwin Hailey would say. "Not a *formal* victory party, of course. We don't have the nomination yet. We can't look cocky, I know, I know. But an almost-victory party!"

Hailey laughed and Danny smiled. Turner then put up his finger, remembering something. He reached into the pocket of his button-down shirt and handed Danny a business card, which was silky to the touch. "Can you call Ben and tell him I want him at the rally? He knows you from my meetings with him at the Hilton." Turner said. "I don't have time — I've got some vice-presidents to talk to!"

"Yes, sir," Danny said, and then he looked down at the card. His heart felt like it stopped, then started again. In addition to the phone number, the card stated.

BERNHARDT (BEN) KLASSEN
Pontifex Maximus, COTC
P.O. Box 100, Otto, SC 28763

CHAPTER 49

By the time we got there, the cops had formed a blue wall around the State Theatre. Wearing helmets and wielding billy clubs, they had set up a more or less continuous line on Congress, along High Street and down Deering.

The cops looked nervous, and it was easy to see why. Hundreds of students, union activists, and visible minority protestors had descended on the area. They'd come from Boston, New York, and as far away as Philly, too — by bus, train, and car. Not every American supported Earl Turner, apparently.

It was fucking awesome.

The cops, accordingly, were jumpy as a box full of crickets. They'd already cracked a couple skulls, and that had pissed off the crowd. The TV cameras were there, of course, and some drunken jerks were performing for them. There was a lot of pushing and shoving going on, a lot of shouted curses and threats. The air pulsed with menace and sweat and the promise of lots of violence.

Most of the Earl Turner supporters had arrived earlier, to avoid the protestors. But some arrived late, and they seemed to be a lot more interested in picking fights and getting seen on TV. Almost all them were guys, and not a few of them were bikers, skinheads, and what even looked like straight edge types.

The Hot Nasties gig at Gary's had gone off without a hitch. Because it'd been free, the bar was packed to the grimy walls with our Portland fans, and they sang along to every song. They knew all the words, which made us feel ten feet tall. Between songs, whenever I encouraged them to oppose Earl Turner and his racism, they cheered and raised their fists.

After the show, we got ready for the short walk to the State Theatre, with X and me at the head of the crowd. I was feeling pumped up and ready to fight, but not everyone in the X Gang was happy. The Upchucks had begged us not to go. They, along with Sam Shiller and Bembe Smith, had decided to stay back at Gary's. But Luke, Eddie, Leah, and Mike all came with us — along with maybe two dozen punk rockers in various stages of inebriation. "Lots of aggro," Eddie said, in a fake British accent, approving.

As we were heading out of Gary's and onto Brown Street, Bembe stopped me and X, holding out a big hand. "Wait, please," he said, and he leaned toward us. He sounded different. "I am urging you guys not to do this. Someone is going to get hurt."

We just looked at him.

Getting no response, Bembe said, "I need to talk to the two of you tomorrow, please. There's something you need to know."

X's face was blank. "We already know it," he said. "We called London."

Bembe's eyes widened; he looked shocked. He stared at X. "Then you know why I'm asking you to reconsider and stay here," he said. "Please."

"Sorry," I said. "This is our fucking town, not his. We're going to protest."

Bembe stood back. "All right," he said, clearly very unhappy. "I'll see you tomorrow. I hope." He watched us go.

We stepped onto Brown Street and started jogging west. Gary's was four blocks or so from the State Theatre, but we didn't get that far. The crowd of protestors was too big, and there were too many cops. It was mayhem: pushing, yelling, and whistles blowing, some union guys yelling chants into megaphones.

X turned to the rest of us and raised his voice to be heard: "The cops are all along Congress, Deering, and High Street. Let's go behind the theater — there's a small road there, off High Street and behind the United Church." And off we went, cheering and chanting, running through Congress Square Park, at the corner of Congress and High Streets. We ran north on the sidewalk along High Street, past the State Theatre, and then we dashed across the street and onto a small street — an alley, really — behind the Williston-Immanuel United Church.

There weren't any cops there, but others were: skinheads, guys with military-style haircuts, big guys looking for trouble. A couple of them were beside a car with the trunk open, and they were pulling on what appeared to be homemade Klansmen's robes.

Seeing that, X didn't wait for me or anyone else. He ran straight toward the two Klansmen, arms up, like he was a football tackle. He barreled them over, then started swinging. The skinheads and the other fascists jumped onto him, but our small army of punks was on them two seconds later. Like any fight, when you're in the middle of it, it's hard to know who's winning. But it felt like we were kicking ass. I stood back-to-back with X and hammered at every fascist who came close.

A minute or so into the brawl, we were surrounded by flashing lights and sirens. A cop car pulled up, then another, and another. The passenger door to an unmarked car flew open, and we saw Theresa Laverty jump out, glaring at us. "You two!" she yelled. "Get in this fucking car, right now!"

At that point, the fight had more or less stopped and the fascists were scattering like cockroaches. X and I looked at each other, shrugged, then got into the back seat of Laverty's vehicle.

She slammed the door. "Are you two out of your fucking minds?" she yelled. "What the hell did you hope to accomplish with a street fight?"

X rubbed his bloody hand on his Clash T-shirt. "We were exercising our constitutional right to protest, Special Agent," he said. "Are you going to arrest us?"

"We might!" she yelled, and then she remembered who was beside her in the driver's seat. She collected herself. "This is Detective Pete Schenk, from the NYPD, by the way. We're working together."

"How did you know where we'd be?" I asked, impressed — despite myself — that she'd gotten to us so quickly.

X answered for her. "She knew where we were because her undercover FBI partner told her," he said, deadpan. "FBI agent Bembe Smith."

It was the last day. It was all over.

X and I sat in a windowless interview room at the Portland Police Department's boxlike headquarters on Middle Street. We were exhausted. But at least we weren't under arrest.

Yet.

We were sitting at a long table with two microphones in front of us that had been plugged into a cassette tape recorder. It wasn't on, however. Across the table from us were Theresa Laverty, Pete Schenk, and FBI special agent Bembe Smith. We looked at Bembe.

"How did you find out, guys?" Bembe asked us, looking very different in a collared shirt and tweed jacket.

He still had his dreads, but his whole manner was different. Formal. Businesslike. Quiet.

X shrugged. "Early on, I had a hunch. Called Stiff Records on the pretext of asking about the tour," he said. "And they said they had never heard of you."

"Right," Bembe said, grimacing. "Good detective work. Well done." He paused. "I would hope you would give the FBI some credit for preventing any further loss of life. Special Agent Laverty and I feel that, by being with you on your tour, we helped to ensure there would be no more victims. Don't you agree?"

X said nothing. I shrugged.

"So, boys," Laverty said, sounding weary, and not so much our special super-duper cop friend anymore. "Danny O'Heran. What can you tell us?"

"Not much," I said. "A friend and then he stopped being our friend."

"Were you angry at him?" Schenk asked.

X looked at him like he was mentally defective.

"No, we thought it was fucking awesome that he joined the campaign of a racist," I said, as sarcastic as I could muster. I paused. "What do you think, Detective? Of course we were unhappy. It was a huge fucking disappointment."

"Did you communicate with him after he joined Earl Turner's campaign?" Bembe asked, looking right at X.

X glared right back. "No," he said. "Fuck him."

"Ever?"

"Never."

"Boys, I am concerned you know more than you've told us. I'm concerned that you knew what was going to happen," Laverty said.

X had been waiting for this. "What could we have done, Special Agent, with your partner with us for every moment for the past few weeks? And, by the way, it certainly wouldn't look good if the media found out that the FBI was right in the thick of it, would it?"

Bembe and Laverty stared at him, astonished by his arrogance.

X waited, then asked, "Are we under arrest?"

"You know you're not," Laverty said, almost whispering.

"Are we facing any charges?"

"No," Laverty said. "But we still have some questions."

"Here's one," Schenk said, clearly unimpressed that X and I weren't in manacles and leg irons. "When you went to the State Theatre, did you go with the intent to harm Earl Turner?"

"No. Hate and violence is Turner's thing," I said.

"When you two were apprehended at the State Theatre, when we caught you, were you planning to do any harm to Earl Turner?" Schenk asked again.

"Even if we wanted to, which we didn't, how would we get anywhere near that Nazi rally? You guys had a million cops surrounding the place. We couldn't have gotten near Turner if we tried. Which we didn't."

Schenk was trying to intimidate us, but it wasn't working. I didn't feel intimidated in the slightest. In fact, I was now even feeling bit cocky. So, I asked *them* a question. "So, what happens to this crazy racist church, the Creators or whatever they're called? Are you holding *them* somewhere, questioning *them* like you're questioning us?"

Laverty and Schenk exchanged a look. "Ben Klassen is under arrest for giving illegal political donations. He will likely face other charges," Laverty said. "And most of the surviving so-called ministers in his Security Legions have been arrested for a string of assaults, weapons offences, and murder."

X smiled. "And the government gave them charitable tax status. Good work, feds."

They didn't like that, of course, because they knew X was right. How the fuck could a bunch of racist, homicidal maniacs ever get certified as a "church" by the government? It was insane.

Schenk was red in the face as he swore under his breath. Laverty and Bembe remained silent, knowing now they couldn't touch us.

When Laverty finally spoke, her question was directed at X. "So, when you left the tour, you came back to Portland?"

X nodded.

"Why?"

He shrugged. "To see my family. To do some laundry."

Laverty looked completely miserable. She'd been outplayed. "You know, we plan to check everyone's phone records. We will investigate where everyone has been,"

she said, sounding like she was trying to convince herself. "Will we find anything you want to tell us about
now?"

"Check all you want, Special Agent," X said. "Knock
yourself out."

It was over. Everyone knew it.

"Whatever happened is on you," X said. "Not us. And
now, unless you plan to arrest us, we're leaving."

EPILOGUE

Hello, you bastard.

Hello, hello.

It was the day before our little talk with Laverty, Schenk, and Bembe. It was before all that. It was still that night in fact — the night of our gig, the night of Earl Turner's rally.

And it was hard to believe, actually. It was like a bad fucking movie. But it was happening, right there, right then, right in front of our eyes. And my eyes hurt.

It was *that* night. The night before the last day.

I looked over at X, and his eyes — one pupil dilated, one not, as always — were kind of squinting. He looked seriously, seriously unhappy. Like he was going to punch the screen or something. I glanced down. He was clenching his fists. There was still blood on them from the fight outside the rally.

The TV cast a bluish glow over our non-family's family room. My mother had heard us come in, when we'd been dropped off by Theresa Laverty and Pete Schenk.

My mother was standing behind us in the doorway to the kitchen, and she was watching the TV, too. She had her arms crossed, but she seemed to be nodding about some of the things being said. By *him*.

I looked back at the TV, and Earl Turner was still behind the podium downtown. There was an American flag stuck to the front of the podium, and below that, in big block letters, was the word RIGHT. *His* slogan. *His* word.

As usual, Earl Turner was wearing a white, button-down shirt, sleeves rolled up. As usual, his regimental tie was loose at the neck. Even though he had a jacket on, you could see he worked out. Behind him, an enthusiastic crowd of supporters were assembled. They were clapping and nodding their heads.

X and me didn't really watch Earl Turner. We mainly watched Danny O'Heran, just behind him. Danny was clapping and nodding his head, just like the rest of them.

I could not fucking believe it. I hated it.

And *hate* was what Earl Turner's speech was all about, pretty much. It always was. Hate for refugees and immigrants and welfare moms and anyone, basically, who didn't look like Earl Turner and his friends. Hate, dressed up in fine-sounding words about patriotism and family and country and all that bullshit. *Hate* was Earl Turner's thing, and it had brought him to this, his big moment. The confetti and the balloons — all red, white, and blue — were ready to be dropped from above.

Turner was coming to the big wind-up in the speech. He always ended it the same way.

"America," he said, his booming, macho voice a bit tiny on my mother's old RCA television. "America is for Americans! America is for the righteous. America is for the bold. America is for those who believe in God, those who love God, those who fear God. America isn't for everyone. America is for normal people, like us!" He paused, a big fist hovering above the podium. We couldn't see them, but the crowd had started to chant: "RIGHT! RIGHT! RIGHT! RIGHT! RIGHT!"

Midway through — and this had happened before — "RIGHT" changed, and they started to chant a different word: *white*.

"WHITE! WHITE! WHITE! WHITE! WHITE!"

Earl Turner smiled, that big square-jawed quarterback all-American douchebag smile of his, and waved for the crowd to settle down. "Right," he said, then he paused. "Right is …"

The crowd screamed as one, like a beast. "WHITE!"

Earl Turner leaned into the gaggle of network microphones. He smiled. This was his moment. This was it. This was when he had won, and we all knew it. He knew it. Everyone knew it.

He started to speak, the part of the speech about how God "created" America. At that point, Danny O'Heran stepped forward a bit. He was also wearing a dark jacket and white shirt and tie, just like Earl Turner. We could see his broad, still-freckled face clearly. At that moment,

Turner saw him, too, and clapped a big hand on Danny's shoulder. I held my breath.

Watching him, I still could not believe it was my friend Danny. When he was drumming in my band, his stage name had been Danny Hate. He looked really different now.

But I knew the truth, too. What was on his liver, ticking like a bomb.

Danny and Earl Turner looked at each other and smiled, like a father and son, like some fucking Norman Rockwell painting. Behind me and X, my mother spoke, just one word: "Danny!"

The crowd kept on cheering, calling out RIGHT and WHITE. They were screaming it.

"Enough," X said, as if Danny was there with us. "Do it."

And Danny did. It was like he had heard X, you know? It was like they were talking again, on their pay phones on the fringes of parking lots: planning and getting ready for this moment.

Danny reached into his jacket and extracted his dad's Heckler & Koch VP70. It was made of polymers, X had told me — plastic, basically — and was therefore pretty easy to get past the old metal detectors at the Earl Turner victory rally at the State Theatre.

Danny still had one of those triangular Secret Service pins on the lapel of his jacket, too, and that meant he usually wasn't even searched before getting onstage with his candidate. When he reached under his jacket, the little lapel pin flashed under the klieg lights. A little bright star.

Earl Turner didn't see it coming, but those of us watching on TV did. Danny quickly reached up and put the 9mm about six inches away from Earl Turner's temple and pulled the trigger. There was an explosion of blood and brain matter, a cloud of gore, and Earl Turner dropped to the floor of the State Theatre. He dropped like the sack of shit that he was.

There was a huge commotion, then, with people running, screaming. Lightning-fast, Danny pointed the gun down and fired two more shots into the prone Turner. At that point, the Secret Service guys started firing at him. He jerked around like a marionette and then disappeared too.

The cameraman remembered why he was there, I guess, and he pointed the TV camera down and focused on the two bodies lying on the stage. At that point, you could see Danny's face. He didn't look like he was gone. He looked like he was sleeping. You could even make out some of his freckles. He didn't look like he was sick or sad anymore. He looked peaceful.

Earl Turner, meanwhile, had a section of his head blown away and his face was twisted into a grimace. He was as ugly in death as he had been in life. Earl Turner was dead.

Goodbye, you bastard.

ACKNOWLEDGEMENTS

Thanks to Ras Pierre; Rockin' Al; Bjorn von Flapjack II; Snipe Yeomanson; the Hot Nasties; Shit From Hell; Davey "Shiller" Snot; Simon Harvey and Ugly Pop; Darryl Fine and the Bovine; Amrazment; Cherry Cola; the Linsmore; Jay Bentley of Bad Religion; John Tory; Kendra Martin and Allison Hirst and everyone at Dundurn; my students at the University of Calgary's Faculty of Law; Laura Jane Grace of Against Me!; Ed Tomwards; Scott Sellers; Jim Lindberg of Pennywise; Heather Barlow, Rob Gilmour, Arti Panday, Faaiz Bilal, Brittany Allison, Ashley Ramjohn and my film agent Andrew Tumilty and all the Daisy gang, past and present; Evan Solomon; Charles Adler; Lorna, my punk rock mom; our kids and their myriad partners — Emma, Ben, Sam, Jacob, Cheyenne, Ray, Jake and Lexi; and our punk rock grandson, Harry.

And, naturally, thanks forever to Lisa, my best friend, my punk rock wife, and the carrier of my tiny black heart.

W.K., TeeDot, 2018

BOOK CREDITS

Developmental Editor: Allison Hirst
Project Editor: Jenny McWha
Copy Editor: Catherine Dorton
Proofreader: Jessica Rose

Cover Designer: Laura Boyle
Interior Designer: Lorena Gonzalez Guillen
E-Book Designer: Carmen Giraudy

Publicists: Kendra Martin, Michelle Melski

DUNDURN

Publisher: J. Kirk Howard
Vice-President: Carl A. Brand
Editorial Director: Kathryn Lane
Artistic Director: Laura Boyle
Production Manager: Rudi Garcia
Director of Sales and Marketing: Synora Van Drine
Publicity Manager: Michelle Melski
Manager, Accounting and Technical Services: Livio Copetti

Editorial: Allison Hirst, Dominic Farrell, Jenny McWha, Rachel Spence,
Elena Radic, Melissa Kawaguchi
Marketing and Publicity: Kendra Martin, Kathryn Bassett, Elham Ali,
Tabassum Siddiqui, Heather McLeod
Production and Design: Sophie Paas-Lang

dundurn.com   dundurnpress
@dundurnpress   dundurnpress
dundurnpress   info@dundurn.com

FIND US ON NETGALLEY & GOODREADS TOO!

DUNDURN